A Gentlewoman Scholar

A Gentlewoman Scholar

Sarah M. Eden
Michele Paige Holmes
Nancy Campbell Allen

Mirror Press

Copyright © 2021 Mirror Press
Print edition
All rights reserved

No part of this book may be reproduced in any form whatsoever without prior written permission of the publisher, except in the case of brief passages embodied in critical reviews and articles. These novels are works of fiction. The characters, names, incidents, places, and dialog are products of the authors' imaginations and are not to be construed as real.

Interior Design by Cora Johnson
Edited by Joanne Lui, Lorie Humpherys, Cassidy Sorenson, and Lisa Shepherd
Cover design by Rachael Anderson
Cover Photo Credit: Arcangel. Photographer: Malgorzata Maj

Published by Mirror Press, LLC

A Gentlewoman Scholar is part of the Timeless Romance Anthology® brand which is a registered trademark of Mirror Press, LLC

ISBN: 978-1-952611-11-7

Table of Contents

Blessing in Disguise
By Sarah M. Eden _____ 1

An Unexpected Education
By Michele Paige Holmes _____ 85

Good Heir Hunting
By Nancy Campbell Allen _____ 197

Timeless Victorian Collections

Summer Holiday
A Grand Tour
The Orient Express
The Queen's Ball
A Note of Change
A Gentlewoman Scholar

Timeless Regency Collections

Autumn Masquerade
A Midwinter Ball
Spring in Hyde Park
Summer House Party
A Country Christmas
A Season in London
Falling for a Duke
A Night in Grosvenor Square
Road to Gretna Green
Wedding Wagers
An Evening at Almack's
A Week in Brighton
To Love a Governess
Widows of Somerset
A Christmas Promise
A Seaside Summer
The Inns of Devonshire

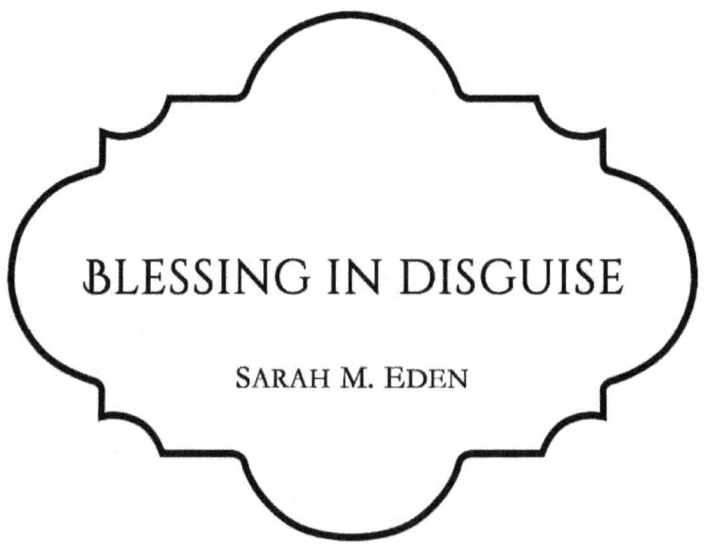

BLESSING IN DISGUISE

SARAH M. EDEN

Chapter One

1858, Dublin

Liam Rafferty's time at Trinity College was nearly over. He'd arrived at Ireland's most prestigious university four years earlier, thanks to an unforeseen windfall from a distant relative, followed by a hard-won scholarship. Liam hadn't wasted a single moment or a single guinea. With a mind for numbers and problem-solving, and a logical view of life, he'd found himself well-suited to the study of engineering. He'd worked hard and applied himself and harbored great hopes for his life after university.

He was not, however, one of the more noteworthy students who easily caught the attention of the dons and fellows. Unfortunately for him, he *needed* one of them to take note. Membership in the Institution of Civil Engineers of Ireland would help him obtain an apprenticeship after he completed his studies, which would significantly improve his chances of securing a prestigious job. A recommendation from one of the professors would increase his chances of being accepted. Therefore, when he received a summons to call at Provost House, he did not hesitate. To be known personally to the provost of Trinity College would be quite a boon.

Liam donned his best suit, took great care with his razor, and invested extra effort in combing his hair. He arrived precisely at noon, as instructed, clanked the knocker, and held his breath.

Rev. MacDonnell's housekeeper showed him inside and announced him in the library, where the provost and one other man were seated. Likely in the neighborhood of fifty years old, with a head of gray hair and eyes that seemed to always be searching, the second man was, more likely than not, a Trinity don, but in a school other than engineering.

"You must be Mr. Rafferty," Rev. MacDonnell said.

Liam dipped his head. "I am."

"Please, be seated."

He was directed to a nearby chair, in which he sat without hesitation.

"It has come to my attention, Mr. Rafferty," the provost said, "that you have something of a reputation amongst your fellow students, as well as the professors and dons."

"Do I?" He looked to the as-yet-unnamed man for some explanation, but none was forthcoming.

"You, it seems," Rev. MacDonnell continued, "have quite a mind for mysteries."

"I do enjoy solving what seems unsolvable." He had, in fact, founded a student society at Trinity—the Conundrums Club—dedicated to riddles and the discussion of detective literature. They had even, on occasion, worked to sort out mysteries off the page.

"We have just such an 'unsolvable' enigma we wish to put to you." Rev. MacDonnell motioned to the other man present. "This is Dr. Poole from the school of medicine. He has recently joined the faculty at Trinity."

Quick pleasantries were exchanged before Rev. MacDonnell retook the conversation.

"Whispers have begun circulating that medical schools across the kingdom will soon be coming under increased scrutiny from the government," he said. "Understandably, the board wishes our medical program to be viewed quite favorably by those who might wish to make the running of it more difficult."

Liam wasn't certain what any of this had to do with his ability to solve a mystery.

Rev. MacDonnell motioned for Dr. Poole to continue the explanation.

"To make certain all is as it should be," the gray-haired doctor said, "I have reviewed our medical school curriculum, as well as those students who will soon be completing their course of study. While nearly all is at it should be, there is one student about whom I find myself uneasy."

"In what way?" Liam asked.

"That is what makes this mystery so perplexing. I cannot put into words quite why this particular student raises my suspicions. Or even what those suspicions are. But there is something about him which strikes a person as not quite as it should be."

"And what is it you wish for me to do?" he asked them both.

"It is imperative that we be found to be above criticism," Rev. MacDonnell said, "not because we wish to deceive, of course, but because we have worked so tirelessly to create a remarkable school of medicine. We want its noteworthiness to be recognized, even in the coming months of heightened scrutiny. To graduate a student who later proves to not have warranted graduation would be a mark on our record."

"And this student is my only point of concern," Dr. Poole said. "Something about him strikes me as . . . odd. Inconsistent. It may prove to be nothing at all, but I need to be certain."

"And you wish me to investigate this medical student?" Liam asked.

"We wish you to *meet* him," Rev. MacDonnell said. "Chat with him a spell. See if you find yourself with the same impression as Dr. Poole. If not, then we can breathe more easily, knowing it is likely nothing more than a bit of awkwardness on Mr. Fitzsimmons's part. If, however, you are also struck with a sense of something being not what it seems, we would appreciate your keen eye on the matter."

Liam was still a little uncertain what he was meant to be looking for. "Can you give me any idea what, precisely, I am meant to be evaluating in him?"

Dr. Poole shook his head. "He is an odd duck."

"Being odd is no reason for a person to be prevented from graduating from a course that person completed." Liam didn't mean to hound some poor man simply because he was awkward in company.

"There is something more to it than mere oddity." Dr. Poole seemed legitimately flummoxed. "If you spend some time with him and feel he really is nothing more than strange, so much the better. But if you, too, find that there is something a little suspicious about him, I am hopeful you can sort out the mystery of what that unusualness is."

Liam did enjoy a perplexing riddle, but he had never before been asked to spy on a person. "I may not be the right man for this assignment."

Both men looked surprised.

Rev. MacDonnell spoke on their behalf. "It was our understanding that you are the founding member of the Conundrums Club on campus. Were we misinformed?"

"No, sir. You were not."

"You seem very intelligent and thorough," the provost added. "And, as one pursuing engineering, you are, I would hope, quite logical and observant."

"I would like to think I will be a fine engineer," Liam said.

Indeed, he would benefit greatly if Rev. MacDonnell thought so as well. A prestigious internship seemed within his grasp, if only he could make a good impression here.

"Would you help us with this?" Dr. Poole asked. "The future of our medical school may depend upon it."

The oddity of this Mr. Fitzsimmons must have been enormous if it threatened to destroy a school. Either that, or the changes Rev. MacDonnell and Dr. Poole anticipated being made in the governance of medical educations were significant.

"I suppose I can at least meet the man," Liam said.

"Excellent." Rev. MacDonnell rose and extended his hand.

Liam did the same. He received a firm handshake from both men, along with what sounded like sincere words of gratitude. It was an unexpected way to obtain a recommendation into a professional society, but solving mysteries was a talent of his. He only hoped it served him well this time around.

The village of Kinnelow in County Wicklow was not what it had once been. The Hunger had claimed members of every family. Short years later, the young men of the village, desperate to alleviate their want and poverty, left en masse to join the cause of the Crimean War.

The remaining population was quite old and quite young, with few in between. It was also mostly female. Over the last fifteen years, Kinnelow had lost its vicar, blacksmith, and physician. They had managed to fill two of the three vacancies.

Kinnelow needed a man of medicine, but the village had very few men.

A village meeting had been called early in the year of 1854, at which a desperate plan was devised. One of the orphans in the village—a young woman of nineteen with a sharp intellect, a sense of daring, and a somewhat flat build—would be sent to Dublin to study medicine. But as Trinity College, like most institutions of higher learning—certainly any that taught medicine with any degree of reliability—did not accept female students, she would attend in disguise.

For four years, Winnifred Fitzsimmons had, whilst on the campus of Trinity College Dublin, pretended to be her own brother. She wore a flattening corset, one which had little to accomplish, and men's clothing just loose enough to hide any curves not pressed into submission. She had chosen to live in a flat just distant enough from campus to give her some degree of anonymity, and she had kept a significant distance from all of her fellow students. Her disguise was a well-devised one, but she dared not test it too severely.

She had managed the ruse for nearly the entirety of her studies. She was within mere weeks of finishing her education and returning to Kinnelow with the knowledge to serve and save her village.

Winnifred sat beneath a tree in Library Square, bent over a book, studying in preparation for the last examinations she would endure before completing her degree. Her loose-fitting jacket bunched up around her, hunched over as she was. She knew she always looked a sight, her clothes wrinkled and ill-fitting. But they hid her figure perfectly. And the oddity of her clothing made the oddity of her smooth jaw and soft features less obvious. She was labeled a misfit, which served her purposes quite well.

The other students whispered about her; she'd overheard them often enough to know that for a fact. She was disliked and ridiculed and left out of every social gathering and event. 'Twas necessary. But she was desperately lonely.

She was also almost finished.

"Do you mind sharing the shade?"

She looked up at the unfamiliar voice and directly into a pair of beautiful mahogany eyes and a pleasant face framed by night-black hair. The past four years had taught her to expertly hide her reaction to crossing paths with men she found handsome, but it did not stop the butterflies that always took wing in her stomach when such a man talked to her.

"I don't mind," she mumbled, using the lowered and raspy voice she'd chosen four years ago for "Fred." That her natural voice was a bit lower than most women's had proven an advantage.

The man sat on the ground, near enough to still see her but far enough apart that she didn't feel endangered at all.

"You don't happen to be studying engineering, do you?" the man asked.

She shook her head. "Medicine."

"Shame. There're a few bits of my studies I'm struggling to sort out."

"Don't know a thing," Winnifred muttered, keeping her head down, her voice quiet, and her posture slumped. He would label her an "odd duck" like everyone else had and move along.

"You must be a first-year student." The dark-haired stranger didn't, it seemed, mean to leave her be.

"Final year." Short answers offered fewer opportunities for giving herself away.

"You seem too young."

How much prying did the man mean to do? "I'm older than I look."

"Apparently."

She flipped a page, keeping her eyes firmly on the book, hoping he would get the message she was attempting to send.

"You sound a bit country."

Good heavens. "I am."

"Whereabouts?"

"In the corner of Ireland where we keep to ourselves," she mumbled.

"Has my friendliness offended you?" he asked.

"I've exams soon. I'm needin' to study."

Someone else spoke next. "Fred wouldn't talk to you even if exams were months off."

She didn't have to look up to identify that speaker. Gerard Hopkins was another student in the medical school. He would be completing his studies this term as well. He, like all the others who knew "Fred," treated her like a calf with two faces. He, however, didn't bother whispering as most others did.

"Don't waste your breath," Gerard said to the talkative stranger. "He thinks the lot of us are beneath him. Best leave him on his pedestal."

A chorus of laughter followed. She was seldom mocked without an audience.

"I don't know why they have to be so cruel," she muttered to herself.

"Perhaps," the stranger said, his tone a touch dry, "they're not from the corner of Ireland where they keep to themselves."

Winnifred supposed she deserved that, but it hurt just the same. How seldom she allowed herself to speak out loud the fact that the cruelty of her fellow students injured her. That she had done so now and had been repaid with her own words tossed coldly back at her proved painful. It hurt enough that she couldn't keep her eyes on her book any longer. She looked up and over at him. He was laughing at her; there was no mistaking that.

Only a few more weeks, and she could leave behind the ridicule. She could go back home and stop being Fred, the target of every joke. She would be permitted to live as herself. At last.

She stood, making certain she kept her movements the awkward bumbling sort she always used when in this persona.

"Have a nice day," she said quietly, and left with all possible haste.

Chapter Two

Winnifred enjoyed her studies—the academic aspects of it, at least—but she took great delight in Saturday and Sunday, when she could be at her flat, as herself. Fred could be forgotten for a time. She wore a regular corset and a dress that, while plain, was at least more flattering than the oversized jackets and trousers she wore at school. And she styled her hair with an upward sweep, pinning in place a hairpiece her home village had created for her before she left for Dublin, one that mimicked the look of a bun. It allowed her to appear as though she hadn't cut her hair off in preparation for the ruse she had been undertaking for nearly four years.

She didn't even mind that her Saturdays were spent going to the market and cleaning the flat—mundane but necessary chores she hadn't time to undertake during her on-campus days. She would walk along Cornmarket, past Christ Church Cathedral, feeling at ease in a way she didn't outside of those two days of freedom. She wasn't hiding, and she wasn't afraid.

Until a knock sounded at the door of her flat on a Saturday afternoon.

No one ever visited. She hadn't a single friend in the entire city. Fred certainly didn't. More likely than not, 'twas the landlord looking in. He did now and then, but not so often as to make her worry about her secret being discovered. He must've known Fred's time at Trinity was nearly over. Likely, the man wanted to know how long after the term ended the two siblings meant to continue living here.

Winnifred opened the door, fully expecting to see the older man there. Only with great effort did she keep her mouth from falling agape. Standing on the threshold was the black-haired stranger from the tree at Trinity. The one who had seemed friendly enough—perhaps a touch *too* friendly—but had, in the end, tossed her vulnerability back at her.

"May I help you?" That he was supposed to be entirely unknown to her would, she hoped, explain away the slight quiver in her voice when she spoke.

"Forgive me, miss," he said. "I was told Fred Fitzsimmons lives here."

Good heavens. "He does, ya."

"Could I speak with him?"

Worse and worse.

"He's not here just now. He's near to finishing his studies at Trinity, he is, and spends a great deal of time with his studies and books."

"But he does live here?" the man pressed.

"He does, he does. I'm his sister."

The man nodded in a way that indicated she'd solved a mystery for him. "You bear a resemblance to him."

"I've been told that before, I have." She even allowed a little smile. "I never know if *he* ought to be flattered or *I* ought to be insulted."

His eyes danced with amusement. How long had it been since she'd shared a bit of amusement with someone? Years, really.

"Do you know how long your brother will be away?" he asked.

She shook her head. "When he's engrossed in his studies, there's not a thing that can distract him."

"I got that impression, yes."

With that, the stranger had presented Winnifred with an intriguing and risky opportunity. True to her curious character, she embraced it.

"Have you met Fred?" she asked.

He leaned a shoulder against the door frame, his posture both casual and friendly. "I have. On campus yesterday, in fact. I fear I inadvertently insulted him. I thought I was being clever, but I am not nearly so funny as I often imagine myself to be." He looked genuinely embarrassed. "I'd hoped to apologize to him."

It was an unexpected bit of kindness. No one ever showed Fred the least consideration. 'Twas as much her fault as anyone else's. She had to keep people at a distance; she could hardly blame them for not treating her with warmth.

"I don't know when he'll be back," she said.

The man's brow pulled a bit, as if sorting a question. "Would you allow me to leave him a note? I do wish to offer my apologies."

Winnifred hesitated a moment, allowing her intuition to make an assessment. In the end, she didn't feel the least in danger. "On one condition," she said.

"And what is that?" He seemed to sense the hint of humor in her tone and matched it.

"You tell me your name."

His smile fully bloomed. "I suppose I haven't told you that yet, have I?"

"You've not."

He dipped his head in greeting. "Liam Rafferty, at your service."

She returned a small curtsey. "Winnie Fitzsimmons."

She'd found it best, on the rare occasion when she gave her name, to shorten it so as not to put in anyone's mind the presence of "Fred" in her name. An overabundance of caution was far better than discovering too late that she'd not been cautious enough. "We've writing implements here in the parlor."

He was soon situated at the roll-top desk, paper at the ready, along with ink and pen and blotter. She continued her housework as he drafted his note.

How odd it was that, after four years of not having a single visitor in the flat, she didn't find herself the least uncomfortable with Liam here, and he a stranger. Was she simply lonely? Or was there something about him, in particular, that was calming and comfortable?

"Are you also a medical student?" she asked, though she knew the answer, having conversed with him as Fred.

"No." He spoke as he wrote. "I am studying engineering, though I am also finishing my time at university this term."

Winnifred took up her dust rag and set herself to the task of wiping down the shelves. "What is it you wish to do once you're done at Trinity?"

"I've hopes of being accepted into the Institution of Civil Engineers of Ireland. With their backing, I should be able to obtain an apprenticeship and, eventually, work designing bridges."

"Bridges?"

He looked up from his letter and met her eye. "Do you disapprove of bridge designers?"

"Not at all. I've simply never met one."

"We are a rowdy bunch, I should warn you." Mischief danced in every inch of Liam's expression.

"Are you?" She popped a hand on her hip and assumed a look of doubt.

"Mathematics does things to people, Miss Winnie. Makes a person want to rebel, to shake off the conventions and—" He shook his head and sighed dramatically. "I cannot continue this ruse. We are a boring lot, every one of us."

She laughed lightly, appreciating the bit of absurdity. "And what of medical students? Do you believe they are a rowdy bunch, forever turning their noses up at convention?"

He hooked his arm over the back of the desk chair and turned enough to continue conversation with her. "From my experience, they are a varied bunch. Some are quiet and withdrawn. Some are surly and unfriendly. Some are arrogant."

Again, Winnifred found herself asking a question that did not necessarily have an answer flattering to herself. "In which of those 'somes' do you place m' brother?"

A flash of wariness passed through Liam's eyes, quick but lingering enough for her to see it. He did not wish to answer entirely truthfully, it seemed. "He is quiet."

"He is." She turned back to her dusting, wishing she hadn't pulled that thread.

Fred had to be dour and withdrawn. 'Twasn't safe otherwise. But hearing she'd been quite successful at it did not precisely buoy her spirits. She ought not to have asked. Having a visitor, one she enjoyed talking with, was spoiling her for company. She was allowing herself to imagine having a friend in this bustling city.

Mere weeks, she reminded herself. In mere weeks, she could return to Kinnelow.

The parlor also served as a dining room. Some flats and homes in Dublin were finer than that, with dedicated spaces for the various functions of a home. She hadn't the income for such luxury. She was, indeed, unspeakably grateful that the people of Kinnelow had scraped together enough to see her not living in a hovel or a dangerous corner of the city.

Having dusted the shelf on which she kept her dishes, she took a plate from the stack on the table where she'd placed them and moved to place it in the hutch alongside the others.

"I hadn't meant to upset you."

Liam's voice, directly behind her without the least warning, startled her to the point she dropped the plate. A horrendous bouncing echo of shattering porcelain spread as pain through her chest. She was trying so very hard to keep her expenses as low as possible. To return to Kinnelow with a bit of money left over would help her replenish the doctoring supplies needed there.

"Oh, Miss Winnie. I am so sorry." Liam immediately bent and began picking up the broken pieces.

"There'll be too many tiny bits," she said. "I'll fetch the broom."

The flat was small, and her errand was quickly accomplished. He'd not moved from the spot by the time she returned. To her surprise, Liam insisted on being permitted to sweep up the mess. She chose not to argue.

"I truly am sorry," he said as he worked. "I hadn't meant to startle you."

"Have you always moved so stealthily?"

He flashed her a smile. "My father always used to say I must've spent too much time with the dock cats."

"And do cats also like designing bridges?"

His low, rumbling laugh trickled through her like warm water. Heavens, a person could very easily grow accustomed to hearing that sound fill the walls of her home.

He'd finished sweeping and held the dustpan in his hand. "I'm not certain where your bin is."

She held her hands out. "I'll take it."

He gave her back the broom and dustpan, but his eyes held her there when she ought to have simply seen to the mess.

"You are quite different from your brother, Miss Winnie," he said softly.

"Am I?" Something in his tone brought a hint of heat to her cheeks, something she could usually prevent.

"I could not ignore that he decidedly preferred that no one talk with him. Here, however, I have felt entirely welcome. You must hail from a very friendly corner of Ireland."

"From a *tiny* corner: a village called Kinnelow."

"I'm not familiar with Kinnelow," he said.

"Few people are." And thank goodness they weren't. The anonymity of the place was part of the reason she could manage her current role. "'Tis in County Wicklow. The largest town in the county is Bray, and it is hardly the bustling metropolis Dublin is."

"But maybe that's why you're so welcoming," Liam said. "Dublin hasn't made you cynical."

As far as compliments went, it was a good one. "I *have* enjoyed our visit. We live a very quiet life here in this little flat, and it has been nice to have company."

His smile was soft and empathetic. "Perhaps I might call on you again."

Winnifred shook her head. "M' brother would not be best pleased if I had callers."

"He denies you the companionship of friends?" A thin layer of alarm had entered his words.

She had best tread lightly, lest she find herself with a rescuing knight attempting to save her from *herself*. "No, he is simply so very uncomfortable with people that having this house bustling and busy would be a misery to him."

"But not to you?" Liam pressed.

"I am here to support him as he finishes his schooling. I can endure loneliness a bit longer."

He seemed as if he meant to argue further. The topic was too fraught with pitfalls.

Winnifred offered a quick dip of her head, then turned to leave and empty the dustpan into the bin and put the broom away. Doing so would afford her time enough to regain her footing and her resolve not to risk everything she'd accomplished the past four years. Indeed, she remained in the kitchen longer than necessary, reminding herself of all that was at stake and how very careful she needed to be.

I have mere weeks remaining. I cannot risk everything now.

When she returned to the parlor, Liam had left. On the writing desk was a piece of parchment containing a brief note addressed to "Mr. Fitzsimmons."

Winnifred picked up the letter and moved to the armchair in the corner where she sat most days. As nervous as she was curious, she read it.

Mr. Fitzsimmons,

I called at your flat today to offer my apologies for my ill-executed attempt at humor when I sat near you under a tree in Library Square. My jest caused you pain, and for that, I am truly sorry. I hope that, should our paths cross in the future, you will permit me to offer you a greeting. I, in return, will solemnly vow to do my utmost not to be a muttonhead.

Yours, etc.
Liam Rafferty

Chapter Three

Liam stepped from his final lecture of the day onto the Trinity grounds and, unexpectedly, directly into the path of Dr. Poole.

"Mr. Rafferty," the man greeted. "Have you made progress on the matter Rev. MacDonnell and I put to you?"

"I have, yes."

"And what is your impression?"

They walked as they spoke.

"Mr. Fitzsimmons is quiet and not overly personable. He does not seem to have friends among his fellow students."

Dr. Poole nodded as Liam spoke. This, apparently, was not new information.

"I did not find anything truly suspicious about him," Liam said.

His conversational companion's silver brows pulled low. "Nothing at all? He hasn't a single friend in all the school. And none of the dons or fellows seem overly fond of him. He is given a wide berth by literally everyone. That does not seem unusual to you?"

"If lawmakers intend to pull down medical schools because one of their students isn't friendly or social, there won't be any left."

Dr. Poole seemed neither amused nor convinced. "I am

not concerned that Mr. Fitzsimmons is unpersonable, though that will make his professional life more difficult. There is something else not quite right about him. I cannot shake that impression."

"He struck me as odd," Liam admitted, "but not sinister."

"How much time did you spend with him?" Dr. Poole asked, his eyes narrowing.

How had things moved from "look into this suspicious student" to "*you* are now the subject of my suspicions"? Good heavens.

"I admit, I didn't spend a terribly large amount of time with him," Liam said. "But I did have a nice gab with his sister, and she did not give the impression that the family is hiding anything."

"I asked him about his family once," Dr. Poole said. "He flatly refused to speak on the matter."

"That confirms my evaluation that he is shy."

Dr. Poole shook his head. "There was anger in his refusal. Firmness, or even annoyance, I could understand. But anger was too unfounded a reaction not to catch my attention."

That *was* unusual. Oh, heavens. What if there truly was something about Fred Fitzsimmons that needed investigating? Liam found the mystery of it intriguing. But the lingering memory of Winnie's expressive eyes, her cleverness and friendliness, and her soft, lovely smile gave him hesitation. He didn't want to cause her any grief.

As luck would have it, Fred himself came within view, crossing the green with his arms full of books and his head dipped downward as always. He wore a hat as ill-fitting as his clothes. His jacket was horribly wrinkled. His trousers hung large on his slight frame. The students he passed eyed him before looking almost immediately away. Sometimes, they rolled their eyes. Sometimes, they laughed. Most looked disapproving and dismissive.

"Perhaps I could simply ask the students who know him what they think of Mr. Fitzsimmons," Dr. Poole mused aloud.

That couldn't possibly end well. Fred was already looked down on. He'd be endlessly ridiculed if he were known to be the subject of an investigation. At least Liam would be kind to him, spare his feelings and, hopefully, prevent some jesting at his expense. There was no guarantee that Dr. Poole's approach would offer the man any such consideration.

"I'll chat with him some more," Liam said. "I'll let you know if I discover anything."

"And I will let Rev. MacDonnell know you are not one to give up overly quickly." That was too pointed a remark to be ignored. It seemed Dr. Poole knew the provost's approval would be quite beneficial to Liam.

With a quick word of parting, Liam slipped off to catch up with Fred. How had he gotten himself mixed up in this? He'd assumed, when he'd taken on the puzzle, that it would prove to either be a great deal of ado about nothing and Dr. Poole would accept that, or Fred would prove a truly dastardly person he could feel good about tossing to the dogs. That neither was the case complicated things significantly.

"Fred!" he called out as he hurried toward the man.

Hunched over, his face hidden beneath his hat, Fred twisted enough to look back at him.

Liam caught up to him at last. "Good afternoon. You likely don't remember me."

"The tree," Fred said, gruff and muttered as always.

Liam nodded. "I didn't catch you at your flat, but still wanted to apologize in person."

"I got your note." Fred began walking once more.

There was nothing for it but to walk alongside him. He'd far rather let the man have the privacy he clearly preferred, but if he didn't make a show of investigating Fred, Dr. Poole would simply begin interrogating everyone else, and likely with far less consideration to the impact doing so would have on him.

"I fear I owe your sister an apology for the broken plate," Liam said. "She was very kind about it, but I still feel awful."

"She wasn't upset." Fred kept his books tight against himself, his gaze on the ground ahead of him.

The same student who'd sneered at Fred that day under the tree passed by in the very next moment. With a laugh, the student said to Liam, "I don't know what wager you're trying to win, but cut your losses, mate."

Fred didn't look at either of them. He didn't respond, but his jaw tightened. The insult wasn't lost on him.

Perhaps Dr. Poole's real problem in the medical school wasn't the quiet, grumpy students, but the ones who took delight in tormenting them.

"Seems to me I'm winning my wager," Liam said to the tormentor. "The subject was whether you'd come along and be an utter saucebox."

He swore he saw a hint of a smile on Fred's face. The man's hat and insistence on keeping his eyes on the ground made it almost impossible to say for certain, but Liam took the change as a good thing.

Mr. Saucebox flared his nostrils but didn't say anything else. He moved along without another jab at Fred.

"Thank you," Fred muttered, still walking with unshaking focus. Indeed, the two of them hadn't even slowed their forward progress during the back-and-forth with Fred's insulter.

"He seems like a bonehead."

"He is." A loud exhale followed. "But thank you."

Fred spoke in spurts—quick bursts of words kept quiet and muttered. 'Twas little wonder so many found him a bit off-putting. He gave the impression of being exasperated. Perhaps he was. But he was also mistreated and looked on with suspicion. That would render anyone a bit exhausted by company.

Which meant Liam's mystery was, rather than sorting out Fred, determining whether Fred's tendency to be withdrawn and disdainful was pushing people away and making him seem questionable, or if people pushing him away and treating him questionably made him withdrawn and disdainful.

And he needed to sort a way of doing it that didn't put Fred in an even more unenviable position. He suspected the man suffered enough as it was.

Chapter Four

Dame Street midday on a Saturday rivaled any spot in Dublin for sheer number of people. It was, in fact, the reason Winnifred chose this time and place each week to go to market and run her various errands. There was anonymity in a crowd.

She enjoyed some aspects of living in a large city. Dublin had an energy and a pulse one didn't find in the country. Merchants of every kind filled the web of endless streets and alleyways. Nothing a person could possibly want couldn't be found somewhere in the city.

But it wasn't home.

She longed for the market cross in Kinnelow. She missed the familiar faces and the feeling of being amongst family even having no family left. She had been orphaned by the Famine, but the village had taken her in. They had raised her and cared for her, and they were giving her this chance at a future, however risky it was.

In only a few short weeks, she could go back and begin to live her life.

"Miss Winnie?"

She spun around, shocked to hear someone call her by name. She recognized the man immediately. "Liam—er, Mr. Rafferty."

He smiled warmly. "You are welcome to call me Liam. I truly don't mind."

She ought to have refused—it was a very familiar way to address him—but it made him seem more like a friend, and she needed one. "It's a pleasure to see you, Liam."

"Even though, last time I saw you, I wreaked destruction on your parlor?"

With a dramatic sigh, she said, "I have recovered. Though, I do intend to hide the dishes should you call again."

Oh, that soft, rumbling laugh of his.

"Would you mind if I walked with you?" he asked. "I've a few errands to run, myself." He motioned with his head toward her basket.

She ought to say no. 'Twould be far safer if she did. And yet, she heard herself answering, "I would like that very much." Why was it she so easily threw caution to the wind where he was concerned?

Actual relief entered his eyes, and her heart flipped about in her chest. He wanted to spend time with her and would've been disappointed if she had refused his request. She could not remember the last time that had happened.

She shouldn't have been surprised, though. He had shown Fred kindness, and no one ever did that. She had spent the days since his very artful dismissal of Gerard Hopkins thinking back on that moment with delight. Liam had defended Fred, even though Fred had given him no reason to.

Winnifred did her utmost to make certain the people at Trinity kept their distance from her. But she hadn't anticipated how unkind so many of them would be because Fred was so withdrawn. Over the years, that unkindness had rendered her persona all the more gruff and grumpy. It had become more than a strategy for preventing people from looking too closely at her; she was truly unhappy there.

"I don't know which shops you need to visit," she said, hesitantly. "If I am impeding your ability to see to your own needs today, please tell me."

"None of my needs are so pressing that I would abandon the opportunity to spend a little time with you in order to pursue them."

While that response could quite easily have been little more than an empty bit of flirting, there was nothing but sincerity in his voice. She wasn't certain what to make of that. Winnifred had kept so many walls up since arriving in Dublin. Her secret was too dangerous to take lightly. It was always for the best to assume people couldn't be trusted, and far too often, they proved that to be true.

But Liam, this chance-met stranger, was overturning all that. She had to proceed warily, but, heaven help her, she could feel herself plunging into these unknown waters.

Shrugging a single shoulder, she said, "Suppose one of my stops today is to the corset maker? What do you mean to do then?"

With a smile too mischievous to be anything but teasing, he answered, "I shall simply have to be fitted for one myself."

Winnifred laughed; she couldn't help herself. She so seldom laughed any longer. As Fred, she didn't dare. As herself, she was always alone.

They made a meandering walk along the streets and alleys of Dublin. As needed, one or both of them would drop into a shop to make a purchase. A few times, they wandered inside places in which they didn't mean to do anything but browse.

The bookseller's proved particularly enticing to both of them. They quickly discovered they had similar tastes in books. Their visit was filled with casual and easy discussion of titles they'd read, some of which overlapped. Though Liam repeatedly poked fun at himself about the sedate and boring nature of those who studied engineering, his taste in books indicated he was anything but monotonous. He'd read quite a variety, on many different topics. He read fiction as well as nonfiction. When she spoke of things that interested her, being quite careful to avoid the topic of medicine, he showed an interest in that as well.

They made their way to the green grocer's. Whilst there, anything she needed, he fetched for her and placed in her basket. He gathered his own purchases as well. They worked together as naturally as if they had been doing so all their lives.

How very easily she could grow accustomed to this.

They had spent nearly two hours together when, passing by a pie seller's cart, Liam bought two, then invited her to join him for lunch. They found an obliging bench in St. Stephen's Green, and settled in.

It was a lovely, cool day. Spring in Ireland could be a bit unpredictable, but this day was fine. They talked as they ate and found more and more things in common.

"I must admit," Liam said between bites of pie, "I'm a little disappointed in our afternoon."

Winnifred's heart seized at the declaration. "You are?"

"Yes. We never did stop by the corset maker."

They both laughed. What a perfect afternoon it was proving to be. He was friendly and personable and seemed to genuinely enjoy her company.

But like most perfect things, it ended. Gerard Hopkins passed by. With effort, Winnifred prevented any sort of reaction from showing in her face. It was Fred who knew Gerard. Winnifred wasn't meant to be acquainted with him at all. And yet, there he was. She knew what to expect, but had to leave herself open to what was coming.

"A much better wager this time around," Gerard said, motioning subtly with his head toward Winnifred.

"I don't understand." Liam said.

"Your company has improved."

Liam kept his expression one of confusion. "I don't understand."

Gerard was clearly unsure why he was receiving that response. "I was referring to our conversation at Trinity."

"I don't understand."

With what looked like a barely prevented eyeroll, Gerard began walking away, but not fast enough for his muttered, "Imbecile," to not be overheard.

Far from offended, Liam grinned at Gerard's retreating back. "That was tremendously fun."

"Do you know him?" How she disliked having to be less than honest with her newfound friend.

"Unfortunately. And, more unfortunately still, your brother knows him."

"Ah. He and m' brother don't get on."

Liam shook his head. "And while your brother doesn't seem to particularly enjoy company, the animosity between him and that man cannot be laid on Fred's shoulders. That muttonhead," he motioned toward the man Winnifred had long considered her tormentor, "seems to take delight in being cruel to your brother."

"You are kind to Fred. Few people seem to care what happens to him."

Liam set his hand gently on hers. "But you do."

"I worry about him."

He kept his hand in hers. She accepted the comfort he offered while it was available.

"Do you think your brother worries about you?"

It was very difficult not to let the irony of that question show in her face. "You wonder if he does because he shows so little regard for people, ya?"

"I'd rather not speak ill of your family member."

She ought to have been pleased to hear that her disguise as Fred was working so well. But she wasn't. "Fred is not unkind nor unfeeling. He's simply . . ." She wasn't certain how to end that thought.

Liam made a suggestion. "Shy, perhaps. Or perhaps he simply struggles to interact with people. I've known others like that, people for whom even the most basic social interactions present a tremendous struggle."

"I do think he is more comfortable when he's left alone." Heavens, she was trying very hard to be truthful, but all the while knowing she was intentionally deceiving him. What a horrible turn to play on someone who was showing her such kindness.

They continued on their way, having finished their meat pies. She enjoyed his company as always. They wandered a bit longer before he walked her back to her flat.

He stopped at the doorway. "I'll not ask to be invited in. If Fred is home, my being here would likely make him uncomfortable. I don't wish to cause him distress. But please offer him my greetings."

"I will."

Liam took her hand once more and, raising it to his lips, pressed a sweet and friendly kiss there. She watched as he walked away, chastising herself for having let things go this far. She could feel herself growing more and more attached to him, more and more fond. How very unwise she would be to let this continue.

And yet, the heart seldom listened to the pleadings of the mind.

Chapter Five

Liam spent most of his Sunday afternoons sitting on a bench under a shady tree overlooking the River Liffey. He would listen to the gulls and terns giving their shrill calls, and his mind would travel back to Howth, the seaside town where he'd grown up. He liked Dublin, but at times, he felt homesick. Sunday afternoons at the water eased that longing.

He found, however, sitting in his usual spot the afternoon following his very pleasant day with Winnie, that his thoughts were on her more than on home. Had she enjoyed their exploits as much as he had? Did she think of him? What would she think if she knew the real reason he'd made her brother's acquaintance or why he had taken the extra effort to seek out Fred's flat?

Rev. MacDonnell had sent a note just that morning thanking him for helping with the matter of Fred Fitzsimmons, especially in light of Liam's upcoming examinations and his, no doubt, already burdened mind and schedule. Assisting with the investigation was gaining him precisely the sort of approving notice that would do him worlds of good as he embarked on his post-Trinity life.

Yet, he felt more than a little guilty about the whole thing. Was it simply that he'd come to like Winnie? Perhaps that he felt a little sorry for Fred? He didn't know the answer to *his own* puzzle, let alone the one handed to him by the provost and medical professor.

A seagull shuffled closer to him, no doubt hoping to be tossed a bit of bread or a crumb of some kind. Even the birds in Dublin were citified.

"Liam?"

So far afield were his thoughts that, for a fraction of a moment, his mind refused to let go of the idea that the bird was speaking. Fortunately, he came quickly to his senses and looked, rather than at the bird, at the newly arrived woman standing beside his bench.

"Winnie." He was both pleased and shocked to see her there. For four years, he'd sat on this bench under this tree watching this river and had never once seen her. Then again, until very recently, he'd not known her. She might have passed by him here for years with neither of them the wiser.

"I debated stopping to give you a good day," she said, "but it didn't appear I'd be interrupting anything."

"Nothing at all." He scooted over to free up the side of the bench nearest her. "I'd be honored if you joined me."

She sat and set a small basket on her lap, not the same one she'd carried the day before. "If I attempt to eat m' lunch, do you suppose the birds will allow me to do so in peace?"

"They'll likely squawk your ear off, but if we keep an eye on them, I'd wager you'll manage to finish your meal."

"Have you eaten?" she asked him. "I've an extra vegetable pie. I made them m' own self this morning."

"I'll not say no."

She smiled at him. Nothing in the expression was any different from any other smile, yet it settled in his chest like warm sunlight on a cold winter's day. He'd known her mere days, and yet he found himself more pleased with her company than nearly anyone else he knew.

"How are your studies coming along?" she asked as she unfolded the cloth tucked in her basket. "You are closing in on your final examinations."

"I'm near drowning in studies at the moment," he said. "Which makes an afternoon at the river all the more needed."

She looked over at him. "And I'm interrupting."

He shook his head. "Your company is more than welcome."

"Is that because I brought you food?" She raised an eyebrow.

He shrugged. "Doesn't hurt."

Winnie laughed. Just as her smile had a moment earlier, her laugh warmed him through and through. How was it possible that someone he'd only recently met could have such an impact on him?

He was soon in possession of a beautifully golden hand pie. She had one of her own. And they sat there on the banks of the river, talking as easily as they had the day before. They laughed at the antics of the birds and enjoyed watching the people walking up and down the river or poking their heads from windows on either side. Her company was so natural and easy. He couldn't remember the last person he'd been instantly at ease with.

"Do you have a river in Kinnelow?" he asked her.

Her eyes pulled wide with pleased surprise. "You remembered the name of my home village."

"It is in County Wicklow," he recounted, "and is smaller than Bray, which is the largest town in your county."

He'd discovered she didn't blush easily, but color touched her cheeks in that moment.

"I suppose I am not accustomed to people giving much heed to what I say."

"Does your brother not listen to you?" He worried a little

about her brother's treatment of her. He'd not been able to ascertain if Fred was neglectful or dictatorial or simply a grump. But he suspected living with him would not have been Winnie's first choice.

"Fred keeps very much to himself," she said. "And he, like you, is very near his final examinations. That has him even more distracted than usual."

"But he's not unkind to you?" Liam pressed.

"He's not."

That was, at least, a relief. He took another bite of his vegetable pie, enjoying the food nearly as much as the company.

"We have a small river," she said. "Not nearly so impressive as the Liffey."

"I'm not certain I could live anywhere that didn't have at least some water," he said. "I'm so accustomed to it that I'd likely feel utterly lost without water nearby."

"Did you grow up near water?"

He nodded. "In a seaside town called Howth. 'Tisn't terribly far from Dublin but is a far sight smaller."

"Then you are country, no matter that you don't sound like it," she said.

"Has Dublin invaded my words?"

Winnie wiped a crumb from the corner of her mouth. "I assumed you were from here. You don't have country heavy in your words like I do."

"Your brother does as well," he said.

"I'm surprised he's said enough words to you for you to hear anything in his voice."

"Other than annoyance?" Liam asked dryly.

Her expression, rather than amused, looked a little apologetic. "He is uncomfortable in company."

He reached over and set a hand on hers. "I hadn't meant

to insult him, I swear to it. I can tell he'd rather be left alone, and I can't say I fault him. Not everyone's company is worth keeping."

"Is mine?" she asked quietly.

"Exceptionally."

She kept her hand in his. They continued watching the birds and people, chatting effortlessly and comfortably.

How easily he could imagine himself sitting with her like this every Sunday afternoon, and walking around Dublin every Saturday. He stopped himself before allowing a mental picture to form of evenings spent at their flat, speaking of their days, and feeling peaceful and at home.

A man of sense and logic, which he considered himself to be, didn't jump to such things after so short an acquaintance. He simply didn't. And yet, his mind and heart found the possibility almost unbearably appealing.

He needed, for the sake of his own sanity and conscience, to sort out the matter of Fred and the puzzle he'd been given. He needed to untangle himself from that particular web before allowing even another moment of daydreaming.

If only his logical side was the loudest in this matter. But it wasn't. Not at all.

Chapter Six

Liam had told himself the last four years that once his time at Trinity was over, he could begin searching for and eventually court a woman he could spend the rest of his life with. He assumed romance would find him when he was ready for it. When he had a profession, and an income sufficient to support a family. When he had time for things like romance and courtship. Winnie Fitzsimmons had arrived in his life and upended those plans. She was an utter delight. He enjoyed talking with her, enjoyed hearing about her thoughts and her interests. They had so many things in common.

But he couldn't help thinking she was holding something back. Every once in a while, she would seem to remember that she was talking with him and pull back into herself. Why was that? He had a suspicion it had something to do with Fred. Perhaps she didn't think anyone would be willing to overlook his often grumpy and gruff behavior. Perhaps Fred would disapprove of her having a gentleman caller. That would make things difficult for her.

Liam didn't know the answer, but he wanted to. Far more than the investigation Rev. MacDonnell and Dr. Poole had sent him on, he wanted to solve *this* mystery.

He was in the library at Trinity a few days after his

Saturday and Sunday with Winnie when he spotted Fred seated at a table, bent over what appeared to be a letter. He knew from Winnie's explanation that Fred preferred to be alone. Saints, he knew as much from his own interactions with the man. And, yet, how could he solve the mystery of Winnie's reluctance if he didn't solve the mystery of Fred?

He sat at Fred's table, but at the far end. If he showed any inclination to allow conversation, Liam would take it up. If not, he would simply have to try again another day. If only he'd met Winnie a year or two earlier, then he would have plenty of time for earning the trust of her brother. As it was, both of them were set to complete their time at Trinity in only a couple of weeks. It wasn't nearly enough time.

He did his utmost to watch Fred without being too obvious about it. The last thing he wanted was to make the man immediately uncomfortable.

When one was really looking, the resemblance between the siblings was remarkable. Shocking, even. He'd known a family like that in Howth, one in which all six of the siblings looked as though they could be identical twins, despite the differences in their ages and genders. Some families were like that.

Fred and Winnie had the same nose, and the same chin, which was a little unfortunate for Fred, as it was very soft and rounded—the sort most often associated with women. Perhaps if Fred grew his whiskers out, his appearance would lend itself more toward what was considered masculine. But he appeared to be quite regimented in his shaving routine. Liam had never seen him with even the tiniest bit of stubble. Fred allowed his hair to hang a little bit long, certainly longer than was fashionable. That, combined with his choice of clothing, indicated a person who didn't care much what he looked like and certainly paid no heed to what was fashionable. That had likely made him the recipient of ridicule from the very beginning at Trinity. Poor man.

He had his hat off, being indoors, which made it easier to see his expression. Something in the letter he was reading had upset him.

"Is something the matter?" Liam asked.

Fred looked up at him. The resemblance to Winnie was remarkable in that moment. He'd seen uncertainty in her eyes before, and it looked precisely like what he saw in Fred's now.

"I'm not meaning to pry," Liam said. "You simply seem upset."

"I won't bother you with it." A gruff few words as usual.

"You needn't think I'm a stranger prying out of curiosity. I'm a friend of your sister's."

That added a hint of curiosity to Fred's uncertainty. And with that came a softening.

Liam moved to the chair directly across from Fred, allowing the conversation to be kept quiet, removing the possibility of being overheard. "Sometimes, it helps to talk about things that are difficult."

Fred shrugged.

"There is nothing the matter with Winnie, is there?" Liam asked, that worrying possibility suddenly occurring to him.

Fred shook his head no. "'Tis a letter from home."

"Containing bad news, it would seem." Perhaps they had lost a family member. Having lost his own mother only three years earlier, while he was a student here, Liam could appreciate the weight of such news.

But, again, Fred shook his head. "'Tis *confusing* news, not mournful."

"I have a good head for mysteries. I founded the Conundrums Club, which is dedicated to the solving of riddles and mysteries. Working out puzzles is a specialty of mine."

"'Tis a personal one, this," Fred said.

"I understand," Liam said. "I wouldn't speak of it to anyone."

Fred dropped his gaze to the letter once more. In a quiet voice, he said, "Someone from Trinity has been sending letters to the people of m' village, asking a great many questions about me. Questions that cast shadows on m' character. Questions that indicate someone here thinks I'm guilty of something."

It was the largest number of words Liam had ever heard Fred say at one time. Hearing him speak more, he got a better sense of the man. He would wager Fred was not naturally grumpy or dismissive. Being on campus and amongst others made him uncomfortable. Winnie had indicated as much.

That, however, was the least of his realizations in that moment. He had continued with Rev. MacDonnell and Dr. Poole's investigation because he'd thought he was protecting the Fitzsimmons siblings from scrutiny and misery. That was proving to not be the case. They were taking the investigation further than they had indicated.

"Surely, the people of your village know you are beyond reproach," Liam said.

Fred nodded but did not seem the least reassured by this logic. "Someone's asking so many questions. Why?"

Heaven help him, Liam knew the answer to that. But explaining it would require admitting his role in the scheme. While he didn't imagine he had much of Fred's good opinion, he felt he had gained a good amount of Winnie's. To lose that would be a crushing blow.

"The answer to that mystery can likely be found in what type of questions are being asked," Liam said.

Fred's eyes scanned the letter again. "They suspect me of something. Can't say what."

The questions they were asking likely meandered a lot, since neither MacDonnell nor Poole knew what they suspected Fred of.

"They have to stop," Fred said. "They have to."

"I'm certain it is uncomfortable," Liam said, "but you will soon be done with your time here at Trinity, and I doubt anything suspicious will be said of you by your village."

Fred shook his head over and over again, almost driven by panic, it would seem. "They have to stop."

His level of worry increased Liam's. He had assumed from shortly after meeting Fred that the provost and the professor's suspicions were unfounded. Fred's panicked response to these questions indicated otherwise.

"Are you in some kind of trouble, Fred?" Liam asked.

With that, Fred abruptly got to his feet. He popped his hat on his head, then gathered up all of his books and papers. He clutched them to himself the way he always did when trudging around campus. Without another word or backward glance, Fred left.

No matter that the man hadn't answered the question—Liam knew the answer. Fred Fitzsimmons was hiding something, after all. Something he was afraid would be uncovered.

Chapter Seven

Winnifred's mind was heavy. Who was asking so many questions of the people in Kinnelow? And why? Mrs. Devon, who had taken her in after the Hunger had left her without a family, had written to Winnie with great concern. "They are asking very prying questions about Fred." She'd listed a few, everything from who were his parents to who was his schoolteacher? These questions were being posed to people throughout the village. While Winnifred had little concern that the people of Kinnelow would intentionally betray her, the more people who were pulled into this deception, the more likely it was to be accidentally revealed.

What had brought on this interrogation? Had someone seen through her disguise? Suspected something odd about Fred?

She sat at her dressing table Sunday morning, too weary and tired to make her way to church. She had put on her proper corset and a dress, but she hadn't yet pulled her hair up nor pinned in her false hairpiece.

At the moment, she had the strange look of Winnie and Fred melted together. It was fitting. She had been Fred for so long now that she sometimes wondered how much of him had become a legitimate part of herself. She'd always been social and outgoing, but she found herself increasingly more comfortable being alone. She often longed for the quiet of her flat when she had once found such a degree of isolation to be suffocating. And yet, she didn't like being so lonely. It felt almost as though she didn't know who she was anymore.

A knock sounded at the door below. Who would be calling on her on a Sunday morning? She was ill prepared to have any visitors. With her hair hanging loose, exactly the way Fred wore it and not at all as she usually did, and without the hairpiece to make it seem as though it were quite long, she might very well give away the game. But there wasn't time for securing it.

For a moment, she scrambled to think of a solution. In the end, she reached for her cotton cap, and pinned it on her head, tucking her hair back into it as best she could. It was not the way she would prefer to receive a visitor, but it was the best she could do with so little warning.

Somewhat put together, she made her way down the stairs and to the door. As she opened it, she discovered Liam standing on the other side.

"Forgive the disruption," he said. "I am suddenly realizing how early I am calling. I'd hoped to speak with your brother."

Botheration. "He has gone to church." Good heavens, now she was even lying about church.

"Again, I realize it is early, but with your brother gone, may I speak with you instead? It is of utmost importance that I share some critical information with the two of you."

Worry began to tiptoe through her. She pulled the door open and motioned him in. He went directly to the parlor, apparently remembering where it was from his last visit. Utilizing the manners she had found were innate with him, he waited for her to be seated before sitting himself.

"I will confess, Liam, you are worrying me a little."

"I wish there were a means of conveying this to you without causing you worry, but I suspect there is not."

Merciful heavens, more bad news. It was the last thing she needed. But not hearing it wouldn't make it go away. So, she motioned for Liam to tell her what he'd come to say.

"Did your brother tell you about the letter he received?"

"I have read it," she said. It was a more accurate answer than simply saying yes.

"He seemed very upset about it," Liam said. "And he seemed particularly worried about the reasons for the questions that are being asked in your home village."

Winnifred nodded, unsure what Liam could have to say that touched on this topic.

"I believe I know who is asking the questions," Liam continued. "Or at least, who is having the questions asked."

"You do?" That seemed unlikely.

"Dr. Poole is, as I understand, a newer member of the faculty of the medical school."

"He is." Winnifred, as Fred, had attended a number of his lectures. He had spoken to her a few times as well.

"Word has reached Rev. MacDonnell, the provost of Trinity, that changes are likely soon to be made regarding the governance of medical schools in the United Kingdom. There's a great deal of concern about the scrutiny that might be brought down on Trinity as these changes are considered and enacted. In what is likely an overabundance of caution, the two of them are looking into anything and everything that might be at all unusual or wrong in the medical school."

"At risk of seeming to quote to you from our lunch at St. Stephen's, I don't understand."

Liam stood and paced away. Apparently, whatever he meant to tell her he found uncomfortable, or difficult. "Dr. Poole has questions about your brother."

A weight settled in the pit of her stomach. "About Fred?"

Liam nodded slowly, with emphasis and palpable tension. "I wish I could tell you precisely what it was he found concerning about Fred, but even he doesn't know. He simply feels there's something unusual about him. His worry about the school coming under scrutiny has made him almost ridiculously vigilant about any and every inconsistency."

Winnifred tucked a loose chunk of hair back up in her cap, thinking, trying not to worry. "And this is why he's been interrogating the people of our village? Attempting to find something about Fred that is . . . wrong?"

"It would seem that way." Liam paced past her chair once more. The lines of his face were made sharp with concern. She didn't think he felt this close to Fred. Perhaps his concern was for *her*.

"Fred is an unusual person," she said. "Dr. Poole will likely find that is the impression our village has of him as well." How she hoped that was what the professor was told of her brother.

"There is a tenacity to Dr. Poole's investigation that tells me he will not stop at that explanation."

A question began creeping into her mind that she could not readily dismiss. She stood, slowly, and stepped into the path of the circuit Liam was making. She met his eye. "How is it that you know so much about this?"

His Adam's apple bobbed, and his posture grew ever-more uncomfortable.

She tucked back another chunk of hair that refused to stay up in the cap. "Liam?" She didn't like that he hadn't answered. It did not bode well.

"They told me about their concerns," he said. There was worry in his expression still. He was not telling her everything.

"Why did they tell you of it?" she pressed.

He pushed out a breath, tense and weary. "I have a mind for mysteries."

"Yes, I know. The founding member of the Conundrums Club."

He took a large step back, allowing him to continue his pacing around her. "There is a mystery to your brother, which they couldn't solve. They needed someone with a knack for puzzles."

In a flash, the horrible truth became clear. "You are part of their investigation."

Liam turned to face her and held his hands up in a gesture of supplication. "They only asked me to talk with Fred and see if I thought there was anything unusual or worrisome about him. I told them I didn't think there was."

She turned away, rubbing at her forehead. "And is that what you were doing when you called here the first time? Investigating?"

"In part." He spoke with the tone of one who had been caught out at something he would rather not admit to having been doing.

He hadn't, then, come for strictly friendly reasons.

"Your apology was a ruse."

"No," he said, plaintively. "I truly did have an apology to make to Fred. That it afforded me an opportunity to come visit him here was a benefit but not the reason."

"A benefit to your investigation. To your efforts to determine what was 'wrong' with my brother."

He turned to her with an expression of absolute pleading. "I first made your acquaintance and Fred's as a result of this assignment, but it is not why I have continued these connections."

"I do not think it matters why you have continued," Winnifred said. "It has to stop. It must stop now. My brother is in more danger than you know, and you are contributing to it." She rose and moved swiftly to the door, pulling it open. "You need to leave, Mr. Rafferty. You need to leave now."

"Winnie, please—"

"Go," she said. "If you have any drop of human kindness in you, please. You are making a difficult situation far worse."

It seemed for just a moment that he meant to argue further, but then thought better of it. Head hung low, he left. She closed the door behind him and rested her head against it.

Liam had been investigating Fred. Her first friend in four years. The first man since she'd come to Dublin to touch her heart in any way.

And it had been a lie.

She knew she was not innocent of being deceitful. But that only made the situation worse. She had let herself imagine something tender and sincere between them. But what connection could there truly be between two people when neither of them had been telling the truth?

Chapter Eight

Liam had the most ridiculous suspicion.

It had begun while visiting Winnie. Bits of her hair continually escaped the cap she wore but did not fall over her shoulder as would be expected, considering she usually wore her hair pulled up in a bun. It hung, instead, at the precise chin length that Fred wore his. It even held the same tiny hint of a wave. Ended in the same blunt cut. And was exactly the same color.

And when he had told her that he solved mysteries, she acknowledged his role in the formation of the Conundrums Club. But they had never discussed that. It was, of course, possible Fred had told her, but he was beginning to dismiss that explanation.

Fred and Winnie looked enough alike to be twins.

Fred was never seen with even the slightest hint of whiskers, no matter the time of day.

Winnie was tall for a woman—the precise height, in fact, of her brother.

Fred's clothing hid everything about his build. Even those who saw him every day would be hard-pressed to know if he was thin as a rail or built like a pugilist.

And, more odd yet, the two siblings were never seen

together. Not once. Liam had visited their flat on more than one occasion, and Fred was always away. Always.

'Twas a maddening prospect, what his mind was concocting, but he was beginning to firmly believe it.

Dr. Poole suspected something was deceptive about Fred Fitzsimmons. Liam was nearly certain he had discovered what that something was. And it was enormous.

The matter weighed so heavily on him that he struggled to focus on his studies with exams looming large. Joined to that mental burden was the all-too-acute memory of Winnie tossing him out. He could hardly blame her—he'd been less than forthright with her—but if his suspicions were correct, she had been far from honest with him.

He intercepted Fred stepping through Trinity's Front Gate and out toward Grafton Street. Liam hooked his arm through Fred's and tucked him up firmly against himself.

"Let's take a walk," he said quietly.

"I need to get home," Fred muttered.

"I know the way. We can talk as we walk."

But their excursion began in silence. Fred's hair peeked out from beneath his hat, landing precisely as Winnie's had from under her cap the day before. *Precisely.*

The profile was the same. The baggy clothing could easily hide a slim woman's frame.

"Oh, Winnie," he whispered on a frustrated sigh.

That brought "Fred's" eyes to his, wide and wary.

"Did you think I wouldn't sort this out?" Liam asked.

"Sort what?"

"I would gladly say it out loud, but I suspect you'd rather not risk being overheard." Liam motioned to the many people coming and going on the busy street. "I know the connection between you, 'Fred,'" he gave her a knowing look, "and Winnie, who I'm realizing is actually 'Winni*fred*.' Clever."

She had grown quite stiff beside him. Seeing the fear in her expression softened some of his frustration.

"If I release your arm, do you promise not to run off?" he asked.

"I suppose I'd best discover what you know and what you mean to do about it." She used her "Fred" voice, no doubt owing to the number of people nearby.

"Wise." He released her arm, and they walked on. "Do you actually have a brother Fred, or was he entirely invented?"

"I have no siblings, and my parents are both dead."

So a complete invention. "And what inspired you to undertake this ruse?"

"Rules forbidding me from obtaining an education unless I did."

Women weren't permitted to study at Trinity. Or, as far as he knew, any other medical school, for that matter.

"And you desperately wanted to become a doctor?"

She shook her head. "Desperately *needed* to."

"I don't understand."

"You and I say that a lot, you know."

Under other circumstances, he might have found that observation amusing. "Why did you need to become a doctor so badly that you would undertake all this?"

"My village doesn't have a doctor," she said. "The nearest one is in Bray. Most of the time, when people need one, they die before getting help."

"So, Fred will be returning to Kinnelow without Winnie?"

"No. T' other way around."

That didn't make any sense. "How can Winnie be a doctor in the village? The people won't—" But then another piece of the puzzle fell into place. "The village knows about this."

She nodded. "'Twas the village's idea."

"Why would they take such a risk? Why would you?"

She breathed slowly. "We've lost all our other options. What the Famine didn't take, the Crimean War did."

"You have no young men left?"

"Two have returned in the last year, but there were none when I began here four years ago."

Which drove home to Liam the fact that she had managed this deception for four years without being found out. That took both determination and cleverness, and a lot of half-truths.

"If the governing board sorts this out, you won't be granted your degree."

"The least of my worries," she whispered.

"How do you mean?"

"If this is sorted out, I will go to jail."

Mercy. "You will?"

She tugged her hat ever lower, hiding her face from view. "It is fraud, Liam. Significant, at that."

He hadn't thought of that. Merciful heavens.

They'd reached the door of Winnie's flat. She stood on the stoop, likely looking at him from under the hat. "What do you mean to do?" she asked.

"What do *you* mean to do?"

She held up her hands in a show of helplessness. "I don't know."

"Neither do I," he admitted.

"I made certain no one was injured by this," she said. "I intentionally did not take the scholars exam, leaving those to be awarded to men. I did not take any space in student boarding houses. The village has paid my tuition, none of it subsidized. I need only a few days more, is all."

What an utter mess. "MacDonnell and Poole will be expecting me to tell them what I have discovered."

"And do you mean to tell them?"

He hadn't a ready answer for her.

She gave the tiniest of nods, then turned and, unlocking the door, slipped inside and out of sight.

What was he going to do?

Chapter Nine

Liam grew up in the seaside village of Howth. His father was a fisherman. And while Liam enjoyed watching the sea and the boats floating out on their daily catches, he'd never had a love of fishing the way his father did. Until he'd been given the unexpected opportunity to go to school, he had assumed he'd have no choice but to pursue the family line. He had jumped at the chance to pursue a profession he found far more appealing, leaving Howth behind four years earlier and making the relatively short trip to Dublin.

He had been back a few times over the years of his study, but not as often as he likely should have been. He was mere days from his final examinations, and yet here he was, in Howth once more, walking the docks to his father's boat.

His mind was swimming, confused by the conflicting voices that were there. He had been given a task by someone with the ability to deeply influence his future, and he didn't want to let him down and, as a result, let himself down. And yet, fulfilling that task would hurt Winnie, and he didn't want to do that, either. She'd claimed a place in his heart, but even that didn't make sense. He'd been less than honest with her; she'd been quite dishonest with him. How could he still have tender feelings for someone he wasn't even sure he knew?

In addition to the conflicting demands of these two

individuals, he was fighting the uncertainty of his own conscience. Protecting Winnie meant joining in her lie. Could he bear more lies on his conscience? And what if she was found out? The consequences would be quite dire.

No matter what he chose, he would be in the wrong. He could protect Winnie, but he would have to lie to do it. He could tell the truth, but that would hurt Winnie.

Liam's father was the wisest man he knew. Four years spent amongst academics and scholars had not convinced him that wisdom resided only in the learned.

As it was late in the day, he was quite certain he would find his father's boat back in the dock. And he was correct.

He shouted out a "halloo!"

Da's head popped into view from behind the mast. His face lit when he saw Liam there. Seeing an excited welcome in his father's eyes was unspeakably comforting. "Liam, my boy. Wasn't expecting you."

Liam carefully stepped onboard and crossed to his father. He was embraced quickly and firmly, as always. No one hugged him tighter than his father did.

"What brings you home to Howth?" his father asked. "Did you finally grow tired of the city?"

"I like Dublin," he said.

Da shook his head. "Can't understand that. All the bustle and the noise."

Liam felt compelled to be honest. He'd done enough bending of the truth lately. "I do like Dublin, but I miss the peace of the country at times."

"The country is in your blood, Liam. No amount of city living is going to change that." There was no criticism in his voice or tone. He didn't begrudge Liam the education he'd received. And, Liam felt certain, his father wouldn't hold against him his decision to make a permanent residence in

Dublin. But he knew, as Liam did when he was being honest with himself, that there was a part of him that would always be the countrified son of a fisherman. And Liam was not ashamed of that.

"Don't just stand there being an academic. Help me repair this net." Most of the heartfelt talks Liam had had with his father over the years occurred while repairing nets or fishing equipment or tending to the boat. While he wasn't pursuing fishing as a profession, he certainly knew how to do the work. He took up the net and began mending.

"I know you aren't meant to be done at Trinity for another week or so," Da said. "Which means you've come here with a problem."

Liam nodded. "I have a dilemma, one I'm not certain how to resolve."

"Spit it out, then."

Liam spoke as he worked, relating to his father the difficulties he was under, but doing so in vague enough terms that he wasn't betraying any secrets. He told him he was stuck between a duty to report to someone quite important at Trinity the truth of a situation there, and hurting someone who didn't deserve to be hurt by telling the truth.

"I'm not certain what to do. I don't particularly like to lie, but neither do I care to see people injured for circumstances that are complicated."

"I notice you say this person you'd be hurting isn't innocent," Da said.

"No, but there's a remarkably good reason for the guilt."

Da looked up from his work and directly into Liam's face. "You always were one for black-and-white thinking, lad. I suppose that's why you're so good at designing your bridges and solving issues of crossing ravines and gaps. But, Liam, spanning gaps in life isn't so cut and dry. With people, you're not always trying to *cross* the ravine; sometimes, you're looking for a way around it."

Liam thought on that for a moment. "You're saying there's likely to be an answer somewhere between telling the full truth and telling a complete lie."

"What I'm saying is you're needing to find a new answer. Find one different than what it is you think you're limited to." Da looked out over the sea, calm and serene at the moment. "Imagine how it would be if, when I headed down to the water, I never allowed m'self to change course. If I went to the spot where I'd expected to find a catch, and no fish were there. Do you suppose I'd drop anchor, shrug, and curse fate? No. I'd find a new spot to fish. A new answer."

"I do rather feel like I'm sailing in terribly choppy waters at the moment."

"Ah." Da took up his work again. "Then there's a woman involved."

Liam laughed. "Spoken like a man who was tossed about more than once by a woman."

"Your ma was a lovely and loving colleen, but she could rage like a hurricane at times." Too much fun lay in his father's tone for the reminiscence to be anything but entirely pleasant.

"I can't say my troublesome lass rages, necessarily. But she's fearsome in her own way. And she's probably the bravest and most determined person I've ever met."

"And I'd wager she is the one who'd be hurt by you being bluntly truthful."

Liam nodded. "One of two."

"Then if you don't return to Dublin first thing in the morning and find that elusive new answer, I'll lose all faith in this fancy education you've been getting. Because, my boy, hurting a woman who's captured any bit of your heart would be inarguably stupid."

"Return *in the morning*?"

"You'll not come all this way and refuse to take supper with me," Father said. "I've not seen you in ages, and once you get your fancy Dublin apprenticeship you've talked about, you're likely to come back even less."

"Oh, I doubt that. As you said, the country is in my blood."

Da arched an eyebrow at him. "But it's hardly in your voice anymore. You're sounding more and more Dublin every time I see you."

"This troublesome woman we spoke of said the same thing. I could tell she was country, and I mentioned it. And she said I sounded Dublin. I guess I didn't realize until then how citified my voice had become."

"'Tisn't a bad thing," his father said. "Life changes us. Circumstances demand things of us we didn't expect. As long as you continue to be a good person, and never grow ashamed of where you're from, I'll not begrudge you where you live or how you talk."

"I could never be ashamed of Howth, of fishing, or of you and Ma. Not ever."

"And she'd be blessed proud of you, Liam," Da said.

Liam allowed a smile. "And what about you? Are you proud as well?"

Father jerked his chin upward. "Depends."

"On what?"

"Whether or not you're smart enough to win back the woman you've fallen in love with."

Liam didn't know if it was possible. He didn't know the entirety of his own feelings. He didn't know if the deception they'd built their connection on could be overcome. But he wouldn't give up hope. That was something he always found in the country: hope.

Chapter Ten

Winnifred waited on campus, ready to sit for her final examination. She was, of course, dressed as Fred. She hoped it was the final time she would need to be. Thus far, appearing on campus this way hadn't resulted in the catastrophe she'd feared. She hoped the fact that no one had said anything or come to accuse her was a good indication that four years of effort, hiding, and worry were going to pay off.

And yet, she'd not seen Liam since their discussion walking to the flat. He knew everything, and she hadn't the first idea what that meant. She wanted to believe that, whether or not he approved of her deception, he wouldn't place her in danger. But, even if he decided that telling her secret was the right thing to do, she couldn't deny that her own choices had placed her here.

Kinnelow needed a doctor, and they had placed on her shoulders the responsibility for becoming their "man" of medicine. She likely could've left Trinity without taking her exams, knowing the village simply wanted her to have the knowledge to help, not necessarily all of the official credentials. After all, once she returned home, she would be living as herself, not as Fred. There would be no diploma bearing her actual name. She wouldn't be able to rightly acknowledge her accomplishments. It was the knowledge that was important, not the degree.

But she'd never been one to quit a race early. She meant to see her risky education to its conclusion. So there she was, donning her "brother's" clothes, and praying she could manage this ruse one last time.

The other medical students were milling about, all waiting on this moment of truth. They had studied and learned and were now waiting for the chance to show themselves worthy of the title of doctor. She, alone, would never get to used it.

The other students wished each other well, laughed over their shared experiences. Winnifred could see they were all a little nervous, but they were comforted by their camaraderie and togetherness. She wished that could've been part of her time here. Perhaps someday, women would be permitted to attend university as themselves and have a full experience like this. But for now, she would simply be grateful to have managed to learn all she had.

Into the throng of students came a familiar, silver-haired man. Many of those waiting to sit their exams greeted him as he passed. Echoes of "Good morning, Dr. Poole" bounced off the walls and landed as dart after dart in her chest. According to Liam, Dr. Poole was one of the people investigating her. And there he was, approaching her on the final day of her disguise.

She tried to tell herself it was a mere coincidence, that he was not, in fact, seeking her out. But he passed by all of the others and stopped directly in front of her.

"Mr. Fitzsimmons," he said. "May I have a word?"

She didn't know if he was calling her "Mr." on account of the other students nearby or because he had not, in fact, learned her secret. She dipped her head in acknowledgment and stepped to the corner of the room with him.

"Some information has come to my attention," Dr. Poole said, "and I need to speak with you about it."

Merciful heavens.

"I have learned through another student a little bit more about your situation," he continued.

Winnifred did her best to breathe calmly.

"I had harbored some concerns about you," Dr Poole said. "I could not, however, ascertain what it was that made you stand out in my evaluation. I will admit to some doubts about your honesty and your worthiness to be here."

That did not bode well.

"And for that, I must apologize." Dr. Poole could've knocked her over with a feather in that moment.

He meant to apologize? To her?

"I did not realize your state of mourning," he said.

Mourning? What did he mean by that?

"Concern over the welfare of a parent could render anyone unusually quiet and withdrawn. But grieving the loss of both—that would most certainly weigh a person down."

She wasn't certain where this was coming from. But, it was true. She *had* lost both her parents. And while ten years had passed since they'd left this mortal clime, she did still mourn them. Her grief was, perhaps, not as sharp as it had been, but it certainly had not gone away.

"Being orphaned is a terrible thing," she said in her "Fred" voice.

"It is, indeed. And my actions, I fear, have not made it easier. I do not doubt you have learned from your home village of the inquiries I sent there. I am embarrassed to say that many were sent addressed to your parents, I not being aware of their passing."

She nodded, choosing to avoid the extra risk of speaking.

"Perhaps," Dr. Poole said, "when the sting of their loss has grown less sharp, you will be able to look back on your time here as a positive experience, no matter that it was wrapped so closely in your grief."

That answered one of the questions she had. Dr. Poole did, indeed, think her parents' passing was very recent. He had been led to equate Fred's oddity of behavior as the natural result of deep mourning. It was as good an excuse as she was likely to ever be given.

"I hope so as well."

He offered a dip of his head. She returned it. In her mind, she silently pled with him to move along, to leave their interaction to this, and allow her to undertake her exams with a lighter heart and fewer worries.

Amongst the crowd, however, came her tormentor. Gerard Hopkins always seemed to arrive at the worst possible time. He was always there, either in her lowest moments, or what had the potential to be her highest. This time was no exception.

"It's a pleasure to see you here among us, Dr. Poole," Gerard said. "Are you offering Fitzsimmons here a spot of good fortune?" He made the observation with enough jest to render it somehow insulting to Winnifred.

"I am, in fact," the doctor said. "Mr. Fitzsimmons has worked very hard. I hope that his effort is reflected in his results today."

"We all hope that, I am certain." Gerard seemed to suspect he was on thin ice. His tone became far more conciliatory.

"For yourself, or for one another?" Dr. Poole asked.

Gerard's eyes darted about a bit, apparently searching for the right answer. "Both?"

Dr. Poole nodded, but the gesture was more than a bit vague. Whether he approved of Gerard's answer, Winnifred couldn't say.

To her, Dr. Poole said, "I wish you luck today, Mr. Fitzsimmons."

"Thank you."

And he walked away. That was to be all. No revelation of her true identity. No stripping her of her status as a student. No police. No prison.

She walked into the exam in something of a daze. She'd lived in such fear of being unmasked, and now that threat seemed to have been eliminated by a "fellow student." Only Liam knew of her orphaned state and her need for an excuse regarding Fred's difficult behavior. She hadn't a doubt *he* had given Dr. Poole and Rev. MacDonnell the excuse that was now saving her.

Liam.

Who hadn't come to visit.

Who hadn't told her of his intentions.

Liam.

Who still held a surprising degree of her heart.

Chapter Eleven

It took surprisingly little time to pack up the flat Winnifred had called home for four years. She'd accumulated very few things and had left very little mark on the city. She had come to get an education, and she had done it. Most everything she had was contained in two trunks. Rather than pack away Fred's clothes, she had given them to a vendor on the street who specialized in reselling used clothing. That poor woman could make a little money off of them, and Winnifred would never have to see them again. Being Fred had been a trying experience. Having to pretend to be someone was a misery she would not wish on anyone.

She would be leaving Dublin in the morning, returning to Kinnelow as a doctor. She wasn't certain how the village would refer to her, if they would call her "Dr. Fitzsimmons" or simply "Winnifred who knows a great many things about medicine." Amongst themselves, they would all know she was as educated as any man of medicine—more so than some—but amongst anyone not one of them, the explanation would be too fraught with falsehoods and confusion.

The rest of the medical students would be remaining at Trinity for a short time, to have their letters conferred and participate in the celebrations and the honors. Some part of her would regret losing those moments of recognition, but she had not come here in order to be flattered. She had come to save her village, and now she needed to return there to do just that.

Someone knocked at the door. That would be her landlord. The quiet but kind-hearted man had looked in on her a couple of times as she'd been preparing to leave. His building had proven the perfect place for her to live, as he was one who kept to himself and asked very few questions. He had sometimes crossed her path as Winnifred, sometimes as Fred. He had never questioned that. When she had dropped in on him to say she was leaving, she'd done so as herself and told him Fred had returned home to their village already, wishing to get a start on his new practice. He had expressed concern for her, having been left behind to see to all of this on her own. She thanked him for his concern but assured him she was capable of completing the work here.

When she opened the door, Liam stood on the stoop. This kept happening. His smile was uncertain and tremulous. Hers was likely even more so.

"Good afternoon," he said, his tone cautious.

"And to you."

She had not seen him since the day he'd sorted out her secret, and she hadn't had a chance to talk to him since Dr. Poole related the explanation Liam had offered. She owed him more than one word of gratitude, but there was so much awkwardness between them in this moment that she wasn't sure how she would manage it.

"I heard from Dr. Poole that you were not remaining behind for any of the ceremonies," Liam said. "That is, *Fred* was not."

"Fred has left," she said. "And I am leaving in the morning."

For just a moment, she thought she saw regret in his eyes.

But it was gone quickly, tucked behind the friendliness interwoven with a very real discomfort that comes when two people have had a difficult interaction.

"This is likely an impertinence on my part," he said, "but I would be grateful to you if you would consent to taking a little stroll with me. Just a little walk through this part of Dublin."

"Would you really like to?" She couldn't imagine he wanted much to do with her.

"I really would," he said.

Refusing would allow for a clean break, a chance for both of them to go their separate ways and leave this brief but unsettling chapter of their lives behind them without the awkwardness of discussing it. But Winnifred hadn't the strength to deny herself one final afternoon with the one friend she had made in Dublin.

She put on her bonnet and wrapped a light shawl about her shoulders. They left behind the flat and her trunks and walked slowly along the always bustling city streets. They didn't speak as they walked. She couldn't tell if he didn't actually want to or simply couldn't think of what to say. For her part, she wanted to know what he thought, what he was feeling, if he would miss her. But she couldn't bear to ask. The courageous and unshakable Winnifred had disappeared. She had been brave before Fred; surely, she could be brave without him.

They reached the lovely green beside St. Patrick's Cathedral and turned in. Liam broke the silence between them.

"I do not believe Rev. MacDonnell and Dr. Poole intend to pry any further into Fred."

"It seems you did a very good job of convincing them Fred's awkwardness and oddity were the result of mourning."

He looked at her with worry. "It was all I could think of that was both honest and sufficient. I did have to make it seem as though your parents' passing was very recent."

"Dr. Poole did give the impression of believing that," she said. "He even went so far as to apologize for having added to my grief by being suspicious of me—of Fred, that is."

"I discovered he could be very single-minded, but he's not an entirely unfair person."

"One might say the same for you," she said.

A hint of a smile touched Liam's lips. "My father made a similar observation. He told me connections with people are not like bridges; they cannot be defined in black-and-white or mathematical terms."

"Do you often confuse people with bridges?"

His expression lightened. "He wasn't being literal. He was trying to help me see that there is often more than one answer to a question."

"You talked to him about this?" Nervousness fluttered in Winnifred's heart.

"Only in the vaguest of terms. I was at a loss. I didn't particularly want to lie to the two men who asked me to do them this favor, but neither was I willing to see you tossed from Trinity, disgraced, and perhaps even prosecuted. Your reasons for doing what you did are good and honorable. I could not repay that with dastardliness."

"Seems you were in quite a dilemma."

"I was, and my father is the wisest person I know. I was certain he would help me sort it out."

Unsure where the impulse came from, Winnifred hooked her arm through Liam's. "And does your da design bridges as well?" she asked.

"He's a fisherman. Lives a simple but upright life. Wise as the sea." His tone was filled with love and admiration.

"Every time I visit home, my father gives me a difficult time, teasing me that I sound city when he knows very well that I am not."

"Being in Dublin can change a person," she said on a sigh.

He set his hand atop hers where it rested on his arm. "Has it changed you?"

"I believe it has. I came from Kinnelow a very trusting and naïve girl. I am leaving not merely more educated, but more wary. I don't know if that is a positive change in me or not."

"I fear I contributed to that change." He seemed to regret his role.

"But you also helped me realize that being cynical is not always the best way to view the world or the people in it. The wariness I'd learned here convinced me that once you had discovered my secret, you would betray me. But you didn't. You sorted a way to keep me safe and safeguard your own integrity as well. That took a degree of effort I hadn't expected anyone to expend on me. For that, I am grateful. Not merely because you saved me from punishment, but because you showed me there are still people in this world I can trust as well."

"I believe that's more credit than I deserve, but I'll accept it." He grinned at her, that same look of amused bedevilment she had seen in his face during their previous days together. They'd not spent a great deal of time with each other, but in that time, he'd shown her that he was precisely the sort of man she could fall top-over-tail in love with. If only there'd been more time. If only there'd not been so many half-truths between them.

"You have finished your studies now as well," she said. "What comes next for you?"

"Rev. MacDonnell is recommending me for membership

in the Institution of Civil Engineers of Ireland. I was hoping that he would. Membership there will help me find a prestigious internship, setting me on the path to claiming an important place in the profession."

"Here in Dublin?"

"Likely."

"And how does your da feel about you staying in the city? You'll lose more and more of your countrification the longer you're here."

Liam chuckled low. "He'll likely tease me mercilessly, but he'll support whatever path life takes me on."

With more boldness than Winnifred realized she still possessed where he was concerned, she said, "'Tis a shame that path won't take you near Kinnelow."

"Would you like for it to?" He asked the question in little more than a whisper.

"Would it make a difference if I did?" she asked, equally as quietly.

"It's difficult to say, isn't it? Fate saw fit to introduce us when there was so little time and so much to prevent us from coming to know each other truly well."

'Twas accurate, but it wasn't the comfort she had wished for. Her dreamer's heart had not entirely stopped beating during her years in this hard and often cold city. She had wanted him to say that he wished for nothing more than to find a means of being near her. She wanted him to say that if only he could find a way of living near her, there was reason to hope for something more between them. She wanted him to say that he cared.

Instead, he had said, in essence, their time together had come to an end, with no reason to hope for anything else.

They wandered back in the direction of her flat, speaking of inconsequential nothings, and commenting on the day. It was a pleasant conversation, but a strange one. They knew this was a farewell, and farewells were often sad. If not for him, she would not have had any heavy goodbyes to make in this place. But watching him walk away after leaving her at the door of the flat that would only be hers for a few more hours, her heart sat in her chest like lead.

She would miss him, would mourn the tenderness that might've grown between them if only circumstances had been different.

Chapter Twelve

Liam had planned out his time at Trinity and what he'd expected to happen shortly thereafter. Thus far, everything had gone according to plan. He'd graduated, been accepted into the Institution of Civil Engineers of Ireland, and even had two different internship opportunities presented to him. Both were located in Dublin, which wasn't surprising, it being one of the principal cities of Ireland. He likely could've had offers in Belfast if he'd made any inquiries there. Everything he'd hoped for was happening. But he felt discouraged, unfulfilled. And he couldn't sort out why.

He wandered about Dublin for a few days, mulling the opportunities before him, attempting to shake the heaviness from his mind. In the end, he knew there was nothing for it but to go get the advice he needed. And thus, he found himself once more in Howth.

He arrived much later in the day than he had on his previous visit. Rather than going to the docks to find his father, he went directly to the humble seaside cottage where he had grown up. His father answered his knock, and Liam was immediately pulled inside by one of his bone-crushing hugs.

"Hadn't expected to see you here so soon, lad," Da said. "Sit by the fire, do. 'Tis a wet one today."

"It certainly is," Liam answered.

Da shook his head. "You still sound very Dublin, my boy. You should spend a few days out here, see if you can't get a bit of country back in your voice."

"Oddly enough, I'm rather inclined to take up the offer. For the first time in years, I find myself reluctant to go back to Dublin."

Da took up his pipe and leaned back in his chair with a look Liam knew well. He was meant to spill his budget, and do so fully.

There was nothing for it but to talk. "Everything has worked out the way I'd hoped. I finished my schooling, received the honors I was hoping for. I have a chance for a good job in a profession I enjoy. I could settle myself in a nice area of Dublin. Live comfortably. That's everything I wanted."

"But?"

Liam held his hands up in a show of uncertainty. "I'm not as happy about it as I expected to be."

"Why is that, do you suppose?"

Liam rose from the chair he had only just sat in and moved to the fireplace, leaning against the mantle. "I'm not certain. I've been trying to sort it out, but so far, I don't have a lot of answers."

Da didn't look the least concerned. Liam knew his father was not an unfeeling person, which meant he must not have thought the problem was as large as it loomed in front of Liam.

"And what happened with the confusing colleen you spoke to me about last time you were here?" Da asked.

"She went home," Liam said.

"And where is home?"

Liam paced away. "A little village called Kinnelow in County Wicklow."

"Could it be that Dublin's lost its appeal because your heart has wandered out to the country?"

Liam shook his head as he paced. "We don't know each other as well as all that," he said. "I spent a few afternoons in her company, that's all. Enough to be intrigued and interested, perhaps, but not enough to be in love."

"That's city talk, that. I knew I loved your ma the second time I saw her. Granted, I didn't know how much. But I was full aware that she'd found a place in m' heart, and until I sorted what that place looked like and how large it might grow, how permanent it might be, nothing in m' life was satisfying any longer. That question rested heavy on my soul. And a soul that's weighed down can't be at peace."

"You're telling me that having all my dreams come true feels shallow because I'm not sure if I love Winnie?"

Da scratched at the hair on the back of his head. "You know, for having had such a fine education, you emerged an utter muttonhead."

His father never was one to mince words. But what was it he found so thickheaded about Liam's approach to his current predicament?

"I founded a student club on campus for people who solve problems and mysteries, who find clues to puzzles and can unravel riddles easily. I'm struggling with this one, and you're not proving overly helpful at the moment."

"Perhaps that's because you're not proving very willing to listen."

While it wasn't a pleasant accusation, Liam couldn't argue it wasn't at least somewhat justified. He sat in his chair once more, facing his father. "Help me sort it. I may simply be too close to the riddle to see the answer."

"Let me tell you a story, my boy." Father worked at his pipe as he spoke. "When I was younger than you, I met a lass. She was beautiful, clever, the sort who turned all the boys' heads. I met her at a county hiring fair. We were both looking for work and both managed to find it. The position she found would've taken her away from home, and she was heartbroken at the idea. The one I secured would've placed me far from her, which I found decidedly uncomfortable. Yes, I'd only met her the day before. We'd only spent together the previous afternoon and the morning we were hired, but 'twas enough to know there was something that hung in the air between us. It was something I didn't want to let go of. In the end, she couldn't bear to accept the job she'd been offered, and she returned home. I did what most would consider remarkably foolish and refused the job I had received."

"You gave up a position?"

Father nodded. "And I followed her home."

"Are we talking of Ma, then?"

Again, he nodded. "She was from Howth. And while I knew very little of the sea, I took up work on a fishing boat. I learned what I could and made a place for myself, all the while coming to know her better. In time, I courted her properly. It wasn't what I expected to make of m' life or where I expected to live. But I knew, no matter where I went, that if it wasn't with her, I'd never be truly happy."

"Are you telling me that I should give up the offers in Dublin to go to Kinnelow? The town is too small for me to do anything there."

"I'm not telling you what to do, son. I'm telling you what I did, and that I don't regret it. You fancy yourself a solver of mysteries, but this lass keeps confounding you. You tend to think that a mystery has only one answer. And I keep telling you that, with people, 'tis never that simple. Think beyond what you've let yourself imagine. The answer lies in those gray areas you tend to forget exist."

Liam thought on that as the evening went on. He spun the idea in his mind as they ate their supper of fresh-caught fish. He reminisced with his father about the people they knew and the things they'd seen in the days he'd been with him out on the sea. And even as they spoke, Liam thought and pondered. Lying on a cot in the loft of his family cottage, the first inklings of an idea began to form.

Kinnelow, as he understood it, was not terribly far from Bray. The new railroad ran from Dublin to Bray. And while Bray didn't rival the size or opportunities of Dublin, it was not a tiny country village. With the arrival of the railroad, the town was growing. They would need builders and architects and engineers. It would not pay what a position in Dublin would. It certainly would not be so prestigious. But he would inarguably enjoy it. Being part of a town that was growing rather than one that was established would be exciting.

Being in Bray would place him nearer to Kinnelow, nearer to Winnie. Being close by would allow them the opportunity to discover if there was a reason to believe they could build a life together. He didn't have that answer, but maybe he didn't need it yet. Maybe he simply needed to take a step closer.

Father had followed the woman he loved to the place where she needed to be. Fate had done the rest.

Liam didn't know if he would be so fortunate, but he was absolutely certain that, unless he tried, he would live the rest of his life wondering what might have been.

Chapter Thirteen

Kinnelow was nothing short of heaven. How Winnifred had missed it during the four years she'd been in Dublin. She'd not been back even once, fearing she'd never convince herself to return to the city. Here, she was loved and welcomed and valued. Here, she was herself.

She'd been back in her home village for nearly a month and had already put her education to good use. She had a little house just off the market cross. The village had set it up for her. When she'd arrived, it already had furnishings and was ready for her to move in. The village hadn't known what she would need to do her doctoring, but they'd done their best. She had made a trip to Bray a week after arriving and obtained the rest of the things she was in need of. Now she had her own place to live and was building a new life.

The people of the village had kept Winnie busy the past few weeks. They didn't bother attempting to affix "doctor" to her name in any way. They knew she had the skills she needed. They knew she had the ability to treat them. But she was still Winnie, their friend and neighbor, the brave and determined orphan who had taken such a monumental risk for their sakes.

The Crimean War was over; all the young men who were going to return from that conflict had. The number was two. Only two. The future of Kinnelow was a little uncertain with so few young men there and so many villagers having been lost in such a short amount of time. But there was hope that others would come. They had already had a couple of families arrive to settle on farms that had been left empty. And those families, despite not having known Winnifred growing up, had come to trust her very quickly upon her return from Dublin. In this little corner of Ireland, she was afforded something she could not have found anywhere else: the chance, as a woman, to be a doctor.

She was happy, content, fulfilled. But there was part of her that felt a stab of regret. Her mind, of its own accord, often wandered back to Liam and their strolls through Dublin, their pleasant conversations, their shared interests. She often thought about how easy it would've been for him to reveal her secret and earn himself an extra degree of approval from two very important men. But he hadn't. He was a deeply good and compassionate person. It could take a lifetime to discover that about someone. She felt she had been given a glimpse at the person he truly was, and it had only added to her admiration of him.

Her heart didn't feel whole. She wasn't sure it ever would. But on that last afternoon in Dublin, when she'd hoped he would express some interest in trying to build something together, or at least speak of some regret at being separated, he hadn't. Not truly.

For a month now, she had attempted to pull her head out of the clouds and plant her feet on the ground. For the most part, she had succeeded. But now and then, the longings of her fickle heart caught up to her.

"Keep your arm in the sling," she told Mrs. Devon, "and you'll be feeling right as rain soon enough."

The woman nodded, taking her medical advice as seriously as everyone else in the town did. They trusted her with their well-being, and that meant a lot.

"Would be a fine thing if we had a parcel of young men move to the village," Mrs. Devon said. "You and the other young girls are facing slim pickings, you are."

"'Twould take an odd sort of young man to overlook the strangeness of a woman doctor. I'm not certain we'd find one."

"Oh, there must be one somewhere," Mrs. Devon said.

There was. In Dublin. But that felt worlds away.

Mrs. Devon slipped out and went on her way. Winnifred put away the items she had pulled out for the visit, knowing there would be another soon enough. Kinnelow wasn't a large village, but she found she was needed more than she would've anticipated. Many of these good people had left off seeing to their ailments for years, waiting for someone to arrive who knew how to help them.

She heard the door open and footsteps approach. Another patient already.

"I'll be with you straight off," she called as she set out her medical tools.

"I'm in no hurry." She knew that deep, rumbling voice with a heavy hint of the city and the tiniest remnants of a country upbringing.

Slowly, she turned around, trying not to get her hopes up, but all the while praying it really was Liam.

He smiled when their eyes met, and her heart jumped to her throat.

"Liam, what is it you're doing here?"

"I heard Kinnelow had a new doctor. I wanted to come see for myself."

"You're a far piece from Dublin," she said.

He nodded. "I am."

"Are you meaning to stay long?"

He tucked his hands in the pocket of his jacket. "That, I don't know yet."

She motioned for him to sit. She sat as well. For a moment, nothing was said. It was every bit as awkward as the day he'd arrived at her flat as she was packing to leave the city.

"How have you been, Winnie?" he asked after a time.

"Well. The village welcomed me back warmly. I've this house and enough patients to keep me busy and give me an income. I get to be m'self again," she said, motioning to her dress. "I particularly appreciate that part."

"I didn't dislike Fred," Liam said, "but I can't honestly say that I would rather see him here than you."

She smiled. "I, for one, don't miss him."

Again, an uncomfortable silence settled between them. Winnifred felt like she had a million things to say to him, and yet no words came at all. He didn't seem at all sure what to say either. But she could take the same approach he had a moment earlier.

"How have you been since last we met?" she asked.

"Well," he said, echoing her same answer. "I have found a job."

"I didn't doubt for a moment you would. Especially with the recommendation of the provost to speed you along."

He nodded, but there was hesitation in the gesture. "Rev. MacDonnell's support did proffer me several very prestigious internship offerings in Dublin."

"That is a fine dilemma to have," she said. "How did you eventually choose one?"

"I accepted none of their offers," he said. "Instead, I found a much more humble position in a place where I am far more needed."

"And where is that?"

Liam's eyes held hers, his gaze intent and communicative. "I am living and working in Bray."

Bray? "That's only a couple of hours drive from here."

"Which was a great deal of its appeal."

Winnifred didn't know what to say. He had found a job, one without the accolades and opportunities of Dublin, and had chosen it specifically for its proximity to Kinnelow. Dare she hope he was saying what she thought he was?

He rose and moved to her chair, sitting on the ottoman at her feet. "I could not clear my mind of you, Winnie. Every time I passed the shops you and I visited or walked down a street you and I traversed, I thought of you. Again and again, my heart asked, 'What of Winnie? What if she were here? What if you were there?' It happened so often and so powerfully, I could no longer ignore it."

"You missed me?" Her voice was quiet, a little broken with emotion.

"More than I could've imagined," he said. "Dare I hope that you missed me?"

She slipped her hands around his. "More than I could've imagined."

He lifted her hand to his lips and kissed her fingers. "You have no idea how pleased I am to hear that." His voice held a hint of relieved laughter.

"But will you be miserable at this job in Bray? 'Tisn't what you were hoping for."

He kept their hands entwined. Speaking as easily with her as he once had, he said, "The work is very interesting. There's a great deal that needs to be done. Bray is growing. Men with my skills are needed there. That part of it is exciting."

"And you're near enough to Kinnelow that we might see each other now and then."

Again, he kissed her hand. "And *that* part is crucial."

Liam stood, and pulled her to her feet as he did. He set his arms around her, but kept enough of a distance between them to look her in the eye as he spoke. "We have not known each other long, and I'm not asking for you to take so enormous a leap of faith. But I would very much like the opportunity to come to know you better. And if the tenderness that has started between us leads to something more, I want to be near enough that we don't have to give that up."

With every word, he was giving Winnifred hope. But she worried that hope was hollow.

"I cannot leave Kinnelow," she said. "Not only would I not be permitted to practice medicine as myself anywhere else, but also the people of this village paid for my education. Remaining here and serving them is how I am meant to repay that."

Liam pressed a kiss to her forehead. "I know it. And should we decide that building a future together is what we both want, then we will sort that part, I'm certain of it."

"Is the bridge designer suggesting we 'cross that bridge when we come to it'?"

He grinned. "I suppose I am."

"I like that idea," she said. "Very much, indeed."

His expression turned mischievous, and even a little wicked. "Then I suspect you are also going to thoroughly enjoy my next idea."

He kissed her. A warmth she hadn't known but had somehow been longing for filled every inch of her. Her arms wrapped around him, his around her. Their kiss was one of affection, budding love, of promise, and hope. Hope that served as a bridge between a lonely past and a bright future.

Epilogue

Liam Rafferty had gained quite a reputation in Bray. He was not merely a talented engineer, but he was also a problem solver. The unique challenges of a town growing as quickly as it was, thanks to the arrival of the railroad, needed someone with a mind for puzzles and riddles.

Winnifred Fitzsimmons had gained the confidence of not only the village of Kinnelow, but also of many who lived in the surrounding area. Though many wondered how she had gained her knowledge of medicine, no one doubted she had the ability to heal and treat anyone and everyone who came to her.

Three-quarters of a year had passed since Liam had come to County Wicklow. Over the course of those many months, he and Winnie had spent a tremendous amount of time together. He would travel from Bray to Kinnelow on Saturday mornings. Mrs. Devon, a local village favorite, had made room for him in her home. The entire village was cheering on the courtship, hoping all would turn out for the best.

The more time they spent together, the more certain Liam and Winnie were that they were meant to be together; neither knew quite how, but they felt certain they would sort out a way.

And so it was, on a late winter afternoon, Liam arrived at

Winnie's home. He greeted her in the usual manner, with an embrace and a lingering kiss. She held fast to him, declaring she had missed him while he was away.

"As pleased as I always am to see you," she said, "'tis difficult to greet you knowing how soon you'll leave again."

"Then this, Winnie, is bound to be your favorite visit of them all."

She looked into his eyes from within his embrace. "What does that mean?"

"I had a very enlightening conversation with the man I work for in Bray," Liam said. "And I have a very interesting proposition to run past you."

Holding his hand, she led him to the settee where they always sat when catching each other up on the week. She sat beside him and leaned into his one-armed embrace.

"What is this proposition?"

"My employer is aware that I spend my Saturdays and Sundays here in Kinnelow, and he is most certainly aware of why. I told him at the beginning of this week that I can no longer bear to make this journey week after week. I told him it was time I remained here where my heart is."

"And what did he have to say about that?"

Liam could hear the nervousness in Winnie's voice and had no desire to make her suffer by drawing out the explanation.

"I asked him if it was possible for me to switch around the way I am doing this. I told him I wished to live here. I suggested that I could make the journey to Bray once a month and stay there for a day or two, receiving information about our latest projects, turning in my drawings and designs. I told him it doesn't seem necessary for me to be there every day when most of my work is done on my own after receiving the information I need. At first, he wasn't certain. But the more we spoke on it—and we spoke on it over several days—the more he began to see the possibility."

Winnie turned enough in his arms to look directly into his eyes. "What was decided?"

Liam took her hands in his and held them fast. "We believe it can be done, Winnie. If you and I can endure my making a trip back once each month, and on rare occasions an extra one here and there, then I believe I can, at last, stay here. With you."

A smile spread slowly over her lips, and the tiniest sheen of tears shone in her eyes. "I have known since the second visit you paid me here that I wanted you to stay. It has been torture every Sunday saying goodbye. While I will miss you on your trips to Bray, I would far rather have you *gone* occasionally than *here* only occasionally."

"I had so hoped that was what you would say."

Liam slipped his hands from hers and took her face lightly in them. "My father told me he knew very soon after meeting my mother that there was more to their connection than mere coincidence. He followed her home, and they built a life. I have hoped these last months to follow in those footsteps."

Winnie leaned forward and lightly kissed his cheek. "I hope I get to meet him someday."

"I fully intend to invite him to the wedding."

A bit of color touched her cheeks. The look she gave him was more mischief than embarrassment, though. "Don't you think you had best ask the bride for her hand before inviting any guests?"

He slowly set his arms around her, tucking her close to him as they sat together. "I have been meaning to ask her, but it is customary to first ask permission of a woman's closest male relative. I have searched high and low and cannot find her brother anywhere."

Winnie laughed. "I am not resurrecting Fred, not even for you."

"Then I shall skip with the formalities and strike straight at the heart of the matter."

She rolled her eyes theatrically. "I wish you would."

Liam pressed the quickest of kisses to her lips before forcing himself to lean back and do the thing properly. "Dr. Winnifred Fitzsimmons, I have discovered I cannot live my life without you. Every day I'm away from you is a misery. If you would agree to marry me, I promise to live the remainder of my life attempting to be worthy of you."

"You needn't worry on that score. I saw your goodness in Dublin."

"Will you build this bridge with me, Winnie?"

She smiled broadly. "I would love nothing more."

Liam's father had told him that, in matters of people and matters of connections, the answers were not always obvious. Little could he have guessed when stepping into Provost House at Trinity that the answer to the puzzle he was presented with would be the unforeseen opportunity to marry the woman he loved. But that riddle had led him here.

To a new life.

And new opportunities.

And a deep and abiding love.

SARAH M. EDEN is the *USA Today* bestselling author of multiple historical romances, including Foreword Review's 2013 "IndieFab Book of the Year" gold medal winner for Best Romance, Longing for Home, and two-time Whitney Award Winner Longing for Home: Hope Springs. Combining her obsession with history and affinity for tender love stories, Sarah loves crafting witty characters and heartfelt romances. She has thrice served as the Master of Ceremonies for the Storymakers Writers Conference and acted as the Writer in Residence at the Northwest Writers Retreat. Sarah is represented by Pam Victorio at D4EO Literary Agency.

Visit Sarah at www.sarahmeden.com

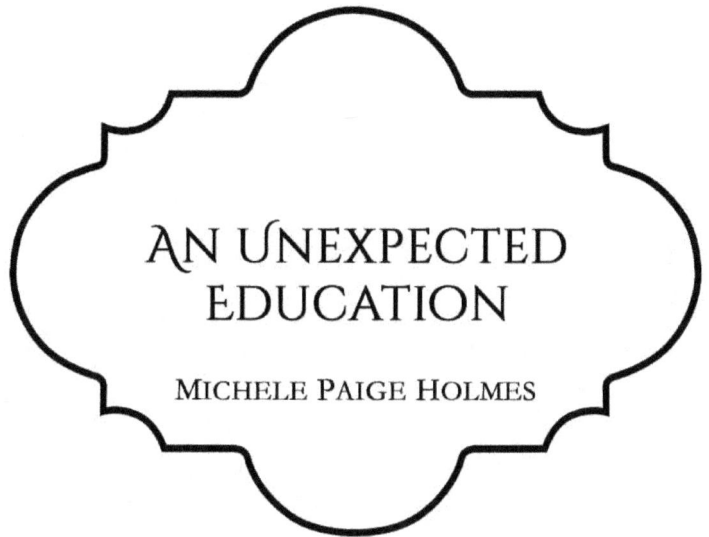

An Unexpected Education

Michele Paige Holmes

Chapter One

Liverpool, England
1851

"It's dry now, Mama." Seven-year-old Esther Sessions stepped back from the fire, a piece of newsprint dangling from her fingertips. Her nose wrinkled at the lingering odor. Herring for dinner—again. She wouldn't dare complain. She wouldn't say anything to her father this evening if she didn't have to. Maybe it would be one of the good nights, when he didn't come home.

"Bring the paper here, darling." Mama's feeble hand stretched out from the cot. "If we're lucky there will be a story about Queen Victoria."

Esther pulled a chair close and spread the paper over her patched skirt. Today they had one of the first pages of a paper that was only a few weeks old. It was so disappointing when the fish came wrapped in the obituaries or a page of advertisements, though she didn't mind the latter too much. She found it interesting to read about all the marvelous items that could be purchased by people who had money. Her parents hardly bought anything—except coal, food, candles now and then, and the bottles of drink that made her father act even worse than usual.

Her mother rolled carefully on her side, so she could see

the paper too. Her eyes scanned the page, and her face lit up. "Let's start with this one." She pointed to a bold headline.

"'The Great Ex—'" Esther frowned, then tried again. "'The Great Ex-hibe—'"

"—The *H* is silent, and the *I* doesn't sound like the *I* in *ice*," Mama corrected gently. Her trembling hand took Esther's and moved it across the words. "The great exhibition."

"What does that mean?" Esther rolled the word around in her mind, liking the important sound of it.

"I don't know," Mama said. "Let's read and find out."

Keeping her finger on the page, Esther started the first line. "'On Friday multi—'"

"—Multitudes," Mama said. "You're doing so well, Esther."

"'Multitudes of people flocked to the Crystal Palace.'" Esther's breath caught as she imagined what a palace made of crystal might look like. She turned to her mother. "Is there really such a place? It sounds like something from a fairytale."

Mama tried to lift her shoulders as if to shrug but only managed a slight movement, accompanied by a wince. "There must be such a place if it's in the papers."

"What does 'flocked' mean?" Esther asked. "Did the people fly? Like a flock of birds?"

Mama shook her head. "I don't think so."

Esther looked down at the paper again. "'The nob—le—'"

"—Noble." Mama smiled sadly. "That means people who are titled."

Esther nodded. People with titles lived in grand houses, had plenty to eat, wore pretty clothes, and rode in fancy carriages. "'The noble, the learned, and the wealthy—'" She knew that word because it was the opposite of what her family was—"'came to parade its long ave—nues.'"

Mama reached and turned the paper so it was angled more toward her. She began reading quietly. "'The exhibits engross the attention of all. Admiration, along with a sense of wonder overcome the observers as they take in the immense number of striking objects on display.'"

Esther's imagination whirred as she and Mama took turns reading about sculptures, fountains, glass, artwork, and inventions.

"'Such a marvel of industry and innovation has never been seen before,'" Mama finished.

They sighed at the same moment.

"I should like to see just one of those marvels," Esther said. An entire crystal palace filled with such treasures was incomprehensible.

"Someday you shall." Mama set the paper aside and clasped Esther's hand. "The world is changing, and you're going to be a part of it. But to do so you must keep reading and learning."

"Then you must be with me." Esther stared down at her lap as her foot swung back and forth, the toe of her worn shoe, handed down from her brother, peeling halfway up each time it caught on the warped floorboards.

"Look at me, Esther."

She lifted her fearful gaze to her mother's loving one.

"I will always be with you. Even if I am not in this room or with you every minute. I will always be right here." Mother's trembling hand reached to touch the spot over Esther's heart.

"Papa says I must go to work soon too." Esther was already older than many children who worked. The only reason she'd been able to stay at home this long was to care for her mother. And that . . . It wouldn't go on forever, as much as she wanted these times, just the two of them together, to last.

Silas had been working in the factory nearly six years now, and he was only four years older than Esther. Her father threatened to take her with him each day—small children were especially prized at the mill—and Esther knew that day was coming fast. Only Mama's illness had allowed both of them to stay home together as long as they had.

Esther worked hard to please her father. She cooked the best meal she could each day, and she kept his clothes clean and mended and the floor swept and the room tidy. Not that there was much to tidy up.

A coughing spell seized Mama, as if to confirm Esther's worst fears. Mama was getting worse, not better.

Esther jumped up and ran to the basin. She returned with it in time to catch the bright red blood that almost always came up now when her mother coughed.

"Thank you, Esther." Mama lay back on the cot, her eyes closed, when her coughing spell was done.

Esther tucked the thin blanket around her, then went outside to dump the basin. When she'd finished, she gave a quick glance back at their door, then down the opposite end of the street to the pump. She would need fresh water to prepare dinner and to help Mama wash. Impulsively she decided to hurry and get the water now, before going home. She hadn't brought her shawl, but it would only take a few minutes, and she'd left Mama resting as comfortably as she could these days.

Esther ran the length of the street, to the pump at the end. Two women and one boy were in line before her, so Esther had to wait, shivering and all the while glancing back toward their door. It wasn't good for Mama to be alone so long, or at all, really. What if she had another coughing fit?

At last it was Esther's turn at the pump. She rinsed the basin, then filled it as high as she dared without spilling.

Thankfully it was tin, not porcelain like some, so it wasn't too heavy for her to carry, though she had to walk slowly this time.

At their door she paused, balancing the basin on her leg and reaching for the knob. The door swung open, and her father loomed over her. Startled, she jumped back, and some of the precious water sloshed over the side of the basin.

Home early. What had he done this time to be fired?

"Where've you been?" He grasped Esther's arm and jerked her forward, spilling more water down the front of her skirt and onto her shoe.

"I—I had to get water for dinner."

"Same old slop," her father snarled. "Not much longer. Tomorrow you start working too."

"But Mama . . ." Esther's protest died on her lips as she stared across the room. "Mama!" She dropped the basin and ran toward the cot and her mother's still form. She took her mother's cold hand in her own and pressed it to her cheek. "Wake up, Mama."

"She's dead," her father said coldly.

"I was only gone a few minutes," Esther sobbed. "Oh, Mama." She pressed her cheek against her mother's still chest.

A rough hand jerked her head back. "Go fry up that fish." Her father pointed his thumb toward the fire. He released her braid and it slapped against her back.

Esther made no move to obey. *Mama can't be dead. She can't.* She shook her mother's shoulder a little, then noticed the blanket wasn't tucked around her as it had been. Esther's eyes shifted to the end of the bed, searching for and not finding the blanket. She found it on the floor beside her father, near the head of the bed and her mother's face.

She looked back at her mother—lips parted, brow scrunched, arm raised as if she'd been—

"You killed her!" Esther whirled on her father, pummeling him with her fists.

He didn't deny it but laughed and shoved her hard away from him. "It's your fault she's dead. You shouldn't have left her here all alone."

Chapter Two

Liverpool, England
June 1863

Esther wrapped the stale bread from the market in a tea towel and placed it near the fire to warm and hopefully soften. With a sigh that was part exhaustion, part lack of enthusiasm for their evening meal, she stirred the soup. The pleasant aromas of meat, vegetables, and fresh bread from the kitchen at Wayburn—the evening meal, for Lady Parker and her servants alike—lingered in her memory, forcing her to quell pangs of both longing and hunger. If only she might take Lady Parker up on her offer to stay for dinner, at least occasionally. But no meal was worth Father's wrath. And if he didn't find Esther here at home, his food hot and ready on the table when he walked in the door, he would be furious.

At least tonight she had managed to purchase a bit of broxy from the butcher, to go along with their usual peelings, and she hoped this would please both her father and brother, as would the dreaded bottles of gin waiting on the table. She hated spending even a few pennies on drink, considering what it did to her father and knowing all the other necessities that money could be used for, but she dared not disobey and neglect to purchase it. At least if he was drunk there was a chance he would fall asleep earlier.

After long days at the factory, both he and her brother were frequently in foul moods, and she was often the recipient of their displeasure. Knowing how the summer heat only intensified their tempers, Esther opened the door wider in the hope some of the hot, stale air would exit their tiny flat.

Turning from the doorway, she debated whether or not she dared steal five minutes to read the book tucked in the basket of mending she'd brought home. Certainly there was time. The distant factory whistle hadn't sounded yet, and once it did she'd at least half an hour before her father and Silas returned. Even if she somehow missed the whistle, she'd know when they were approaching. Of its own volition her body recognized the dreaded time of day, her stomach clenching and head pounding each evening as the hour of their arrival approached.

It took but a second to decide to indulge in a few pages of *Mrs. Perkins's Ball,* so she might imagine it was both a merrier and cooler time of year—as well, of course, as imagining herself attending such an event. Though a ball or any other sort of pleasure did not seem likely to ever happen, she still remembered her mother's promise that reading would lead her to great places. Even if they never turned out to be real places, Esther felt immense gratitude for the journeys her imagination took. They were all that sustained her some days.

Five minutes passed all too quickly, and she was just hiding the volume in the folds of a petticoat when considerable noise out in the alley carried in through the open door.

"Not my Robert!" Mrs. Watson's wail echoed down the narrow passage between the tall buildings.

Oh dear. Esther felt a pang of sympathy for the woman and wondered what ill had befallen her husband. An accident—loss of a limb, as Mr. Sanders had suffered only a few months ago? Like many tenants, he worked at the paper mill..

Oh no. A sick feeling, beyond the usual malaise affecting her at this time of day, started in the pit of Esther's stomach. What if her father had something to do with Mr. Watson's misfortune? She had overheard them arguing recently. What if her father was responsible for whatever had happened? It wouldn't be the first time he'd caused trouble at work or brawled with one of the neighbors.

Esther stood and walked toward the doorway, only to stop upon seeing a constable standing there. With a start of fear, she met his solemn gaze.

"Is this Benjamin Sessions' residence?"

"Aye. What of it?" Esther cringed the second the words fled her mouth. Past experience had her guard up at once, but she hated sounding as rude as her father. Lady Parker would certainly rebuke her if she heard such poor speech.

The constable cleared his throat. Pity, not anger, filled his gaze—an expression she wasn't used to seeing from a man. Even the decent downstairs folk who worked for Lady Parker rarely looked anything but serious and work-weary. Never had any pitied her. *It must be bad.*

Esther forced her feet forward, worrying more with each step that her father had stirred up serious trouble. But if the constable intended to cart her off to prison for her father's crimes, at least he seemed sorry for it. And if he didn't intend to cart her off—well, if Father had landed himself in another mess, this time she might just leave him to stew in it. They had precious few coins in the crock on the shelf, and she hadn't any intention of using those to pay for his misdeeds again.

"You're Miss Sessions?"

She nodded, her throat too dry to respond otherwise.

"Might I step inside a moment?"

A flicker of fear shot through her. She didn't want him to come any closer, but she beckoned him toward the pair of wobbly chairs at their crude table and near the doorway. They'd only two, which meant she had to eat standing when her father and brother were home.

The constable shook his head as he stepped into the room. "You might sit, though," he suggested. "Please," he added when she didn't move.

On legs that felt leaden, Esther moved to the nearest chair and sank into it, her eyes still fixed on him. What had her father done?

"Would you care for some tea?" she asked, belatedly remembering her manners. Not that giving him a drink would alter whatever terrible thing he had come to tell her.

"No thanks, Miss. Have to be off to the next house soon."

The next *house.* This involved more than just her father and Mr. Watson. Perhaps her brother had joined the fray as well and they'd both been carted off to jail. It would explain why neither was home yet. Esther placed her trembling hands in her lap to still them.

After a long moment and a pitying look around the shabby room, then back at Esther, the constable spoke. "This afternoon there was an explosion at the mill. The gas lamps—"

"—An accident?" Relief rushed over her so quickly that she sagged against the back of the chair a second before remembering it was broken. She righted herself hastily before she fell backward and hit the wall. "My father didn't—he wasn't—was he hurt?" For the first time it occurred to her that perhaps the constable hadn't come bearing the sort of bad news she'd been expecting.

"I'm sorry, miss." The pitying expression returned. "There weren't any survivors."

"No—" *None?* Wouldn't she have known—somehow? But she worked on the opposite side of town, and her long walk to the market and then home each evening never took her near the factory district. Thick smoke almost always filled the air here, and the streets were usually crowded and noisy. "My brother—works there as well." Her confused gaze met the constable's once more.

"The whole building went up quickly. Those few who managed to stagger out were badly burned and didn't last long. Most didn't have time to get out."

"I see." She didn't really and brought a hand to her spinning head. "So they're—"

"—Deceased." The constable glanced over his shoulder, as if anxious to be on his way now that the news had been delivered.

"Both of them dead?" she whispered. Tears burned behind her eyes. Could it be true? Esther's hands covered her cheeks, and she winced, having momentarily forgotten the remnants of her father's latest abuse. *Dead. He's gone. He can't hurt me anymore. But Silas.* Her brother hadn't been kind to her, but he was only a few years older—much too young to die.

"There now. It will be all right."

She nodded. Her tears spilled and started tracks down her face. A sob broke free. Esther leaned forward, her arms wrapped around her middle.

The constable's expression crumbled into awkward discomfort. He tipped his hat and stepped back, just outside the doorway. "I'm sorry for your loss."

She pressed a hand to her mouth and nodded. He had no idea that the tears sliding down her cheeks represented relief.

Heaven did not weep for her father's passing. Neither

did Esther. Instead, she maintained a carefully somber expression as she stared at the priest, standing at the head of the caskets, beneath the only shade available as he spoke to those gathered for the paupers' funeral. She wasn't the only one laying someone to rest today. Among the mourners she recognized several other tenants. The explosion had taken many lives, including her father's and brother's. The latter she still had difficulty believing, as there had been no body produced, and her brother seemed all too clever and conniving to perish at such a young age.

That was the nature of the accident, factory owners had explained to those whose loved ones' remains could not be recovered. The explosion and ensuing fire had been swift and all consuming, destroying not only the building where it happened but three others before it had been contained.

Swift and all consuming was an apt description for Esther's feelings of the past three days as well. The news had seemed overwhelming at first—impossible. At any minute she'd expected her father to stomp through the door, angry at being delayed. But she'd eaten alone that night, seated in a chair for the first evening meal that she could remember. Later she'd slept in the bed instead of on the floor.

The sun had risen the next morning, and she with it, to a quiet, peaceful room. He really wasn't coming home. Gradually, minute by minute, hour by hour, the feeling of disbelief had turned to peace, as the fear she'd lived with so long began to recede.

Behind Esther the June sun shone down, its rays easily penetrating the cotton of the most suitable dress she could arrange for mourning—an ugly black thing with a high, itchy collar and sleeves that were both too short and too fitted. An added hem of lace saved the gown, rummaged from the charity box at church, from being embarrassingly short.

At the moment none of this mattered. Even standing in the sun wasn't bothersome. Her face had long since freckled from years of walking outside without a bonnet, and nothing in the way of weather could spoil the hope she felt for a better future.

Staring at the caskets, Esther felt the first inklings of freedom and perhaps—even joy. Hopefully God would not strike her down for such feelings.

"...consign their souls to heaven." The priest finished his brief speech.

Esther pressed her lips together and stared down at her scuffed boots, clearly visible beneath the dress, lace notwithstanding. She didn't know the criteria for heaven, but she very much doubted that her father, at least, was headed that direction. Not after killing his own wife.

Mama. Memory gripped Esther, and it felt as a vice tightening around her heart. She remembered the day vividly—kneeling by the floor, begging her mother to wake. The details appeared in her mind as if it had happened yesterday. Genuine tears squeezed from her eyes.

The workhouse pallbearers stepped forward to lower the pine caskets into the common grave. How easy it would be for grave robbers to harvest the bodies later. A shiver passed through her at the thought. "God rest their souls," she whispered. *And thank you, Lord, for freeing mine.*

Chapter Three

Esther stared into the beady eyes of her landlord and regretted leaving the door open to let in the evening breeze. A stuffy room would have been better than facing the surly man.

"I'm 'ere about the rent," he bellowed, as if she was both deaf and dumb. He offered no expression of sympathy for her loss—not that it would have been sincere, coming from Mr. Kent. Much like her father, he hadn't a kind bone in his body.

"I'll pay it on the first of next month," she said firmly, then reached for the doorknob, eager to end their conversation. She'd already started taking her meals at the Parkers, and with what she was saving not having to purchase food—or gin—she might just have enough to keep her word.

"The first 'as passed, or can't you count?" His lip curled in a sneer. "Rent's late."

Esther's eyes narrowed. "I am aware of the date and that this month's rent was paid in full, on time, by my father." He'd had many faults, but failing to keep a roof over their heads wasn't one of them. They had lived here, in this one room, as long as she could remember, and they had always been on time with the rent.

"You calling me a liar?" Mr. Kent took a step forward, hovering over the threshold so that she would have difficulty closing the door. "'e 'asn't paid, and unless you do, by the week's end, yer out." Mr. Kent jerked a thumb over his shoulder.

He was lying. "Curious that you should come asking for it just now," Esther said, placing a hand on her hip and doing her best to match his bullying tone. She was certain her father had paid this month as he always did, but what could she do? A woman's word against a man's? It wasn't even worth trying to argue or get anyone to believe her. Esther held in all the things she wished to say, eager to be rid of him. She could think what to do later, without Mr. Kent so close that she could practically feel his foul breath on her. "*If* I am unable to pay you, I'll be gone by the week's end." *Two days.* That's all he'd given her.

He faltered, seemingly thrown off balance by her compliance. "Well now . . . Maybe I was a bit 'asty. I think we could work—somethin' out."

The *something* he likely had in mind was easily discerned by the lustful look in his eyes as they raked her over from head to toe. Esther barely suppressed a shudder. He was easily twice her age and had a vile reputation.

Feigning interest in his suggestion, she leaned closer, looking either direction down the alley, as if she were concerned about someone seeing them. The only concern she had was whether or not anyone was around who could and would help her if Mr. Kent became aggressive.

As she'd hoped, his gaze followed hers. She used that split second to jump back and slam the door. She rammed the bolt into place, feeling a slight satisfaction at the oath and cursing that came from the other side of the door. Hopefully, she'd smashed his toes. As an extra precaution, she carried the least broken of the two chairs to the door and shoved it firmly beneath the knob. It wasn't much protection, but the best she could do for now. She grabbed the skillet and held it in both hands, ready to strike if he somehow broke through.

Despicable man. There were far too many of them in this world. It seemed all a woman could do to successfully dodge them. And what was she to do now, with but two days to come up with an impossible sum? There was no help for it, no choice that she could see but to ask the woman she held in highest regard—one who, herself, had managed a life remarkably free of male domineering. Esther would have to explain herself to Lady Parker and throw herself at her mercy.

"I wonder that it took you nearly a week to come to me." Lady Amelia Parker peered down her aristocratic nose at Esther, as a speculative gleam seemed to spark in her eyes. "I suppose it's because you're both stubborn and independent—likely the very traits that have kept you going as long as you have."

"It was the books, actually," Esther said. Others employed in the formidable woman's household wouldn't dare utter so much as a syllable to the stern, aging widow—let alone correct her. But Esther didn't fret. She and Lady Parker had been talking thus since Esther was ten years old, when Lady Parker had discovered it was Esther who was doing the mending and sewing—not her mother, as Esther had led the housekeeper to believe when she had first applied for the position.

It was a book, tucked in the basket of freshly starched collars, that had given Esther away. She'd only just discovered the free public library, and thrilled at being able to bring a book home. However, she had to hide any volume she borrowed, as her father would have disapproved.

He said that women who read were of the devil and

should be punished accordingly. Esther had had Satan beaten out of her too often to risk further punishment over a book. So when one came home it was always carefully hidden, between the folds of this or that garment in the center of the basket in which she transported the sewing.

Lady Parker had discovered the book one day when Esther failed to remove it before a maid took the basket upstairs. Esther had been summoned at once.

"Does this belong to your mother?" Lady Parker held up the treasured library book, Dickens' latest.

Esther remembered feeling frightened. Lady Parker was not a woman to be trifled with. She'd let servants go before for more trivial matters than this. If Esther lost this position, her father might kill her. He nearly had two years before, when she'd been let go from the mill. If her father had known *why* she and the other children her age had been so abruptly dismissed, he would have killed her. Still, her freedom from the terrors of labor amongst the machinery remained one of Esther's proudest accomplishments.

After finding a pamphlet in the street about the Factory Act and realizing that the mill where she worked was violating child labor laws, she had planned and schemed, finally writing an anonymous letter, alerting authorities to the conditions of the mill. It had taken a few months and much stealth for her to acquire paper, ink, and a stamp. Forming the words, copied from the newspaper, had taken even longer, but at last she posted her missive. Another two months had passed, during which she had all but given in to despair, certain that no help would be forthcoming, when one day a team of inspectors had arrived. Their visit couldn't have been more timely.

Once again she had been ordered to climb beneath the machine to retrieve a bobbin. The first time she'd done so she nearly lost a finger, and every occasion since had been terrifying. Her hand had never quite been the same; though her index finger had eventually healed, it bore an ugly scar and no longer lay flat like the others. It throbbed whenever she sewed for any length of time. Thankfully, the day the inspectors came, she and the other children younger than nine years of age had been dismissed straight away. It was the first miracle of her life.

After that Esther had seen to it that her next position was in a home, not a factory. Her mother had given her two gifts—the ability to read and the ability to sew tiny, delicate stitches. Both had served Esther well. She'd read the advertisement in the paper and answered it herself, with a sample of her best sewing—which she claimed was her mother's.

Though she'd been dishonest in acquiring the position, Esther had answered Lady Parker's questions with honesty, summoning courage from her past success.

"It is not my mother's book but mine, borrowed from the free public library."

"And do you dally at this library when you are supposed to be delivering my garments?"

"No, ma'am. I go to the library on my own time, on my way home Fridays." Esther stood ramrod straight and looked Lady Parker directly in the eye, an easier task since the woman was seated and Esther stood.

"You expect me to believe that a seamstress's daughter reads Dickens?" Lady Parker glanced at the volume in question.

Esther nodded. Dickens was one of her favorites. It was easy to see herself in his characters. He understood what it was to be in want of basic necessities like enough food and a warm coat.

"Do you read to your mother while she sews?" Lady Parker asked, a curious expression on her face.

Esther hesitated. "Not anymore," she said at last, her voice lowered to a whisper. "My mother is dead." She swallowed, then hurried on, praying her honesty wasn't about to get her sacked. "*I* do your sewing. I read only after it is all done—and if my father isn't home."

Lady Parker blinked, then broke their gaze. She looked away a long moment, while Esther dreaded her fate. An apology would likely do little to sway the woman in her favor, but she gave one anyway.

"I am sorry to have lied to you." She meant it, though she wasn't sorry for having passed two years in Lady Parker's employ. "I—I needed the work, and I knew I could manage it well."

Lady Parker's attention snapped back to Esther. "Are you saying that your mother was dead *before* you even applied for this position? This *entire* time it was you I entrusted with the care and keeping of my undergarments?"

Esther nodded, then pressed her lips together and fought an absurd urge to giggle at Lady Parker's huff of indignation. Was it so improper that a girl should sew and iron a lady's unmentionables? She saw much worse than chemises and drawers in the alley near her home. Esther wanted to point out that she had never let Lady Parker down. On the contrary, on more than one occasion, the grand woman had given Esther praise to take to her mother for the quality of the work.

Instead of speaking her mind, Esther hung her head, sobered by the shock and disappointment in Lady Parker's expression. Losing her position was nothing to laugh about. Indeed, it was something worth crying over. She already felt the tears building behind her eyes. "I'll leave now." She started to turn away.

"You'll do no such thing until you are dismissed," Lady Parker snapped, her usual, even tone replaced by words that rushed out in a hasty, heated breath. As if realizing this herself, she ran her hand over her lap, smoothing her feelings perhaps more than the invisible wrinkles in her skirt. After a moment she drew in a great breath and began again. "Working in this household, I should think you would have already learned that a servant is not to leave a room in the presence of her employer until asked to do so. It appears your training has been remiss." Lady Parker's stern voice sounded oddly strained. "Come here, child."

Esther shuffled toward her, stopping only when her trembling knees could almost knock against Lady Parker's.

The older woman studied Esther, scowl deepening as her gaze fell upon the purple bruise staining Esther's forehead.

"What happened? Are you as clumsy as you are impertinent?"

As she'd been truthful about everything else, Esther saw no reason to lie about this. "My father was angry and struck me."

"Is he angry often?" Lady Parker asked.

"Aye, ma'am."

"And this mark on your arm?"

"Silas—my brother—twisted it. He gets angry too."

Lady Parker drew in another deep breath and brought a hand to her chin as she continued studying Esther. "Your stitching is very fine for someone so young. Your mother taught you well."

"Thank you," Esther said.

"I wonder, do you read as well as you sew?" Lady Parker held out the book.

After a second's hesitation, Esther took it. "I believe I have much improved since discovering the library. Before that I had only the fish papers to learn from."

"Fish papers?" Lady Parker's nose wrinkled as if she could smell them. "Whatever do you mean?"

"The fishmonger wraps the herring in old newsprint," Esther explained. "Mama and I would always unwrap it carefully and hold it before the fire to dry. Then we would read every word we could. I learned ever so much that way. We even read about the crystal palace filled with wonders that people came to see in London. Mama said that if I keep reading, someday I'll see places like that."

"Did she, now?" It was Lady Parker's turn to purse her lips. Her eyes seemed suddenly brighter than they had been a minute before, and Esther wondered if books or talk of the palace excited her too. But when Lady Parker looked quickly away again, Esther realized she had been mistaken.

"Sit," Lady Parker ordered a moment later. "Open the book and read aloud. Start at the beginning."

"Yes, ma'am." Esther moved aside and perched on the edge of the sofa. She was already halfway through *David Copperfield*, but perhaps Lady Parker had not read it. *Perhaps she cannot read.* Esther glanced up through her lashes and felt a pang of pity for the stern, older woman. Maybe she had never had anyone to teach her.

"'*The Personal History, Adventures, Experience, and Observation of David Copperfield the Younger of Blunderstone Rookery—Which He Never Meant to Publish on Any Account.*'" Esther glanced up. "Isn't that a rousing title? Before I began reading I could imagine all sorts of things, just from the title alone."

"And is it all that you hoped? What you've read so far, that is?"

Esther considered. "Not exactly. There is quite a bit of sadness. David's mother dies, you see. And his stepfather beats him."

"Perhaps there is a happy ending," Lady Parker suggested, her eyes bright again.

"I do hope so," Esther said. She'd cried terribly over Little Nell's death in the last Dickens book she'd read. Then Father had struck her for moping, and she'd cried even more. "Mr. Dickens doesn't always write them that way, but sometimes they end all right."

With the same reverent touch she always gave books, Esther opened to the first chapter and began reading. "Whether I shall turn out to be the hero of my own life . . ."

An hour later Lady Parker had increased Esther's wage and given her a new responsibility—reading aloud to her in the afternoons for two hours each day, as the old woman's eyesight was failing and she could no longer enjoy good literature on her own.

"I suppose it was your books that saw you through these difficult years," Lady Parker remarked now, the hint of a smile easing the stern lines around her mouth. "Still, stubbornness and independence will serve you as well. Of course you may stay here. Do not even think of returning to that wretched flat and landlord. Whatever you lack, we can provide—starting with a dress less horrid than the one you are wearing."

"Thank you, Lady Parker." Esther bobbed in a curtsy. "I shall be happy to take on whatever additional duties you see fit, in return for my lodging. I might read to you in the evenings as well now, if you prefer."

"There is something else I wish of you. Though I hope you will not see it as a duty, but as an opportunity."

"Anything," Esther said, curious as to what this new assignment might be. A large and capable staff already ran the household efficiently.

"Come. Sit." Lady Parker beckoned to the sofa beside her chair, as she had on so many other occasions, though of late her hand seemed to tremble a great deal with even the slightest motion.

Esther crossed the room and sat demurely, as Lady Parker had taught her. Her inclination would have been to sprawl across the sofa while reading, but early on, Lady Parker had insisted that Esther retain a ladylike posture during their afternoons together. The result was often a backache, but Esther wasn't about to complain when she had such happy employment. Her time at the mill was not forgotten.

Lady Parker turned slightly in her seat, her hand reaching out to Esther's as her eyes strained to see. Esther clasped the old woman's hand and, not for the first time, felt a tender affection for her employer.

"Thank you," Esther said again. "For allowing me to stay."

"I will allow it, but only for a short while," Lady Parker said.

"Oh—" Esther closed her mouth abruptly before she could rudely question why. Any time was better than none, and she would be grateful.

Lady Parker *tsk*ed. "Don't fret. Hear me out. I've no intention of sending you back where you came from or any other such unfit place. I want to send you out in the world. It's time you began thinking about seeing your crystal palace."

Esther started at the reference. It had been years since she'd shared the story of her mother's last hour with Lady Parker.

"Did you bring that treasure with you?" she asked, an almost-knowing look in her eye.

Esther nodded. Still dumbfounded, she untied her mother's old reticule and withdrew a hankie with the brittle paper wrapped inside. She handed both to Lady Parker, who unwrapped them with care. The newsprint from 1851 was faded. Even the faint smell of fish no longer lingered, but the dream her mother had for Esther remained the same.

"They keep your palace in the borough of Bromley now," Lady Parker informed her. "It is not so far from London that it should be impossible to visit. Less than a day's drive. We shall have to arrange it for one of your holidays."

Holidays? London? Esther's stomach flipped with equal parts trepidation and excitement. "Do you wish me to be your traveling companion, Lady Parker?"

She laughed—a sound Esther had heard only two other times in all her years of employ with the woman. "This old frame is too frail for travel over rough roads. And I don't trust those locomotives they have steaming all over the country— much too fast for me. But you, my dear, are young and strong and brave—ready to take flight on your own adventures as your precious David Copperfield did."

"I don't understand," Esther said. How could Lady Parker imagine that she could go anywhere?

"My dear, since the day when you first read to me, I have been scheming to spirit you away from your father and help you find a better place in this world. I would have arranged it sooner, save for your loyalty to and hope for your brother. Now I see no reason to postpone. It is time you begin your formal education."

"Education," Esther gasped.

"Close your mouth," Lady Parker snapped. "It is impolite to gape."

Esther obeyed, though her shock had not dissipated.

"Though we've little more than two months before for the next term begins, I have arranged for you to attend Ladies College in Bedford Square—in London. I am well acquainted with Mrs. Elizabeth Reid, the founder, as well as several of the trustees. They are eager to welcome you, and my continued donations, to their school."

"But I haven't—I'm not a lady. I don't know enough to attend college. And I haven't the funds."

Lady Parker waved a hand dismissively. "Trivial matters, all. You do not have to be of the upper class to attend Bedford. You do know enough—not everything, of course, but that is why one goes to school. To *learn*. And you are shortly to come into a great deal of money."

"I am?" Esther glanced around the room to see if any of the other servants were nearby and overhearing their conversation. Would anyone else worry, as Esther was starting to, that Lady Parker might not be herself at present? "May I ask, from whom?" Certainly her father had not left her a penny. She hadn't even any hope of collecting the last of the monies owed to him by his employer.

"You are to inherit from me, of course." Lady Parker's expression grew smug, as if exceedingly pleased with herself. "You have been like the daughter I never had, Esther. I have benefited from our meetings far more than you, of that I am certain. But legally I cannot leave my estate to you. Wayburn has belonged to the Parker family for generations, and I am unable to alter the trust. As I have no offspring of my own, the house and grounds will go to my wastrel nephew, Jackson—who will no doubt gamble the entire place away within a year of my passing. But . . ." She paused, shaking a bony finger toward Esther. "I have figured out a way to beat him at his own game."

Esther stared at her blankly.

"My money is my own. I brought it to my marriage, and I got it back when Arthur died. It was meant to shore up Wayburn, and it has, but no more. I intend to give all of it away—most to you."

"You cannot—you mustn't—"

Lady Parker held up a hand, her entire arm trembling. "I can, and I will. I must give away all that I can before my passing, which is not long in coming, I daresay."

"Don't say that." Esther leaned forward anxiously. "You mustn't think like that. You are more alive than most people half your age." Lady Parker had confided both her age and birthday to Esther some years ago, and Esther had remembered the date each year so they might celebrate the occasion. By her reckoning Lady Parker was seventy-seven years of age. Quite old, yet still full of vigor—particularly this morning.

If Esther was like a daughter to Lady Parker, Lady Parker meant no less to her, as the only figure in her life who cared for her, and for whom Esther herself held a high regard. Esther liked to imagine that Lady Parker was her grandmother, though a somewhat distant and stern one. She was the only person in the world to whom Esther felt she could turn for assistance. The only one she could share her love of stories with. But she had never imagined she would receive anything more from Lady Parker than a wage for work well done.

"You're not going anywhere," Esther said resolutely, as if that would change the outcome. These many years later her mother's death still stung, and she didn't think she could bear it if anything happened to Lady Parker.

"It is you who will be leaving." Lady Parker stabbed her cane into the floor and rose slowly, waving off Esther's help and signaling the end of their conversation. "Two months from today you will take up your new residence at the boarding house attached to the college. Between now and then we have much to do. Beginning Monday you will work with a tutor from eight until four each day, to help fill in the gaps in your preliminary education. Save for learning a foreign language and how to be accomplished with music and art, I believe you will find yourself adequately prepared—thanks to our years of reading together. We shall do the best we can in those subjects. It will not be the end of the world if you, instead, excel elsewhere—for example, in literature and mathematics. Ladies graduating from this college are able to teach, either as governesses or possibly even at these new primary schools springing up all over the place." Lady Parker gave the rope pull a firm tug, summoning a maid.

"By the time you have completed your studies at Bedford, you will have the ability to provide for your own needs. You will not have to be reliant upon a man for your support." Lady Parker's mouth pressed into a serious line. She held a hand out to Esther, who stood and took it so they were facing one another.

"Never again will you need to be at the mercy of someone like your father. You will have independence, Esther. Though you have courage like your namesake, you will no longer need to be like her, serving a man and begging for his favor." Lady Parker gave Esther's hand a gentle squeeze.

Esther nodded and felt tears pricking her eyes. "You are too good to me." She longed to embrace Lady Parker, and to be embraced by her as her mother had used to do, but she knew her place. "Thank you," she said instead. "Thank you."

"Now then." Lady Parker released Esther's hand and stepped away, her usual brusque approach returning. "You shall need a new wardrobe, including everything from parasols to shoes. You will require dancing lessons, as there will no doubt be at least one ball during the term. I have employed a voice instructor. You may not be able to play the pianoforte, but I've heard you humming while you work, and I believe you will be able to sing passably. You will need to work very hard on your penmanship."

A maid entered the room and curtsied.

"Show Miss Sessions to her room," Lady Parker instructed.

"There is an extra bed in the servants' quarters," Esther began, then stopped at the shake of Lady Parker's head.

"You cannot sleep there. You must get used to polite society and its ways. You are no longer a servant but a guest in my home, a woman of refined manners and graces. Consider tonight your first small step toward becoming a gentlewoman scholar."

Chapter Four

London, England
September 1863

Dearest Lady Parker,
The train ride was splendid—not in the least frightening. London, however, is another matter entirely. I fear I shall not venture out much, owing to my misadventure on the way here...

Esther arrived at her lodging in London feeling rumpled and dazed. The journey from Liverpool to Euston Station by train had flown by quickly, and she had enjoyed every thrilling minute of it. The summer had also passed quickly, as if Esther were living a dream and experiencing someone else's life. But a trunk full of pretty clothes accompanied her on this journey, as well as a newly-acquired sophistication and polish she hadn't known she was capable of two months ago.

With the exception of an overly tight corset, and bonnets that, while lovely, tended to block her vision and make it feel as if she were a horse wearing blinders, Esther enjoyed her new wardrobe and the status it seemed to afford her.

Before, on the long walk from her home to Lady Parker's estate in Allerton, she'd been the frequent recipient of disapproving stares from passersby, particularly as she grew closer to the wealthier neighborhood, as people obviously took note of her worn shoes and clothing.

During her hours spent working at Wayburn, Esther wore a uniform that was neat and clean. But that garment always stayed behind; she'd walked to and from work in her own, patched and faded clothing. She had believed that she'd trained herself not to mind the disparaging looks or the unkind remarks about her person. She often used her imagination to pretend she was the heroine in a Dickens novel and all would turn out well for her in the end.

That it had seemed more fairytale than reality. She was now Pip, about to be both elevated in society and provided opportunities she'd never dreamed of. But unlike Pip, Esther's benefactress was not unknown, and there were no skeletons in Lady Parker's cupboard.

"I was not happily married," she'd once confided in Esther. "So when Arthur died, I saw no reason to enter into matrimony a second time." Instead she had managed her income well and enjoyed a largely solitary existence, shunning most social events for many years, as it seemed one man or another was always after her increasing fortune.

And now she was intent on spending it before another man, her nephew, could inherit and lay waste to all she had built. As if the monies Lady Parker had spent the past two months on tutors and lessons, clothing, shoes, bonnets, ribbons, petticoats, and the like for Esther was not enough, Esther carried with her a bank draft in the amount of £2000 for the college. It was a staggering sum, and Lady Parker had promised the same to the school for the next year. No doubt it was her generous donation that allowed Esther one of the coveted spots this semester. To think she was going to a college where Dickens' own daughter had studied!

Great expectations, indeed. Esther felt the weight of Lady

Parker's hope for her success on her shoulders. Being an exemplary student and making Lady Parker proud was the only way Esther had to show her appreciation for her tuition and board. Lady Parker had even seen to it that she had pin money for the next four months. She'd spared no expense on Esther and had seemed herself almost young again during the flurry of preparations over the summer weeks. Esther determined not to let her benefactress down. She would prove herself a capable student—much more than capable, she hoped. But she had very nearly failed already today.

After the train had deposited her at Euston Station, she had hired a hackney to drive her the remainder of the way to the college. This was accomplished easily enough, and her luggage loaded for an agreed-upon extra few shillings. That had been hours ago. Numerous, unscheduled stops later, accompanied by the driver's insistence that she pay more if she wished the journey to continue, she was at last—thanks be to many prayers—arrived at Bedford.

Or so she hoped. He could have driven her elsewhere for all she knew of London. But he had put down the step for her, and, refusing his hand, she had descended the stair to the cobbled street, now bathed in the sun's last rays and the first light of the lamps being lit for the evening.

A modest, three-story building stood before her. Esther tipped her face back, searching the edifice for any sign that she was indeed arrived at the college. The front door opened, silhouetting a middle-aged woman in the glow of the room behind her.

"Miss Sessions?" She descended the stairs toward Esther.

"Yes." Esther nearly sagged with relief at being in the right place.

"We expected you much earlier," the woman said. "I'm Mrs. Lewis. I run the boarding house."

"I'm pleased to meet you," Esther said. The woman had no idea how pleased she was.

"Let me call John to help with your trunk."

"No trunk until I've me shillings," the driver said.

Esther turned on him. "I paid up front for the luggage." She recalled Lady Parker's admonition that she must not speak rudely. It was not polite to disagree in public. But Esther had already parted with far more coin than she'd intended to today. The man had cheated her enough. "And I paid you at each out-of-the-way stop you made as well, though I'd not authorized such, and I dare say we ought to have been here hours ago."

"What's this?" A tall gentleman descended the stairs to join Mrs. Lewis.

Esther glanced up at him, less than eager to have another male to contend with. One was enough at present.

"It sounds as if the driver has overcharged Miss Sessions and now wishes to hold her belongings hostage," Mrs. Lewis said.

"That's not—" the driver began, but the gentleman beside Mrs. Lewis held up his hand. He turned to Esther. "Is this true? What fare is he asking?"

"I have paid it several times over since we set out." Tears of frustration burned behind her eyes. What an impossible way to begin here. She was tired and hungry and so very far from anything familiar.

Esther took a deep breath, then went on to explain about the extra shillings for her trunk and the additional fees requested at each of the four stops they had made throughout the long afternoon.

The gentleman listened without interrupting, then turned to the driver, whose face was screwed up in anger.

"She said it was her first time in London. I was showing her the sights is all."

Esther spoke up again, her voice loud as she stomped her foot. "I did *not* request that of you. And if the stops we made are the best London has to offer, then I shall not be leaving the college even once this term."

The gentleman beside her folded his arms across his middle and leveled his gaze on the driver. "It seems you've already been paid for your services. I'll be taking her trunk down now. And we'll post a letter to your company—" he inclined his head to take in the name on the side of the cab "—about how you're cheating innocent newcomers. We've students coming and going, and you'll be having none of our business in the future." He moved to the back of the carriage and began untying the rope.

After giving the driver one last glare, Esther joined Mrs. Lewis, who was beckoning her.

"You must be exhausted. What an ordeal. I'm so terribly sorry." She extended an arm around Esther's shoulders as she drew close. "Don't fret about your trunk. John will see that it arrives in your room."

Esther glanced over her shoulder as Mrs. Lewis guided her up the stairs toward the front door. The gentleman had succeeded in wresting the trunk from its position and had been joined by a boy who looked to be a few years younger than herself. Together they lowered the trunk, but it was the gentleman who lifted it once more and started toward the house. She would have thought the boy to be the John Mrs. Lewis referred to, not the gentleman, with his fine suit and his brown hair curved in a perfect wave at the top of his forehead.

As if he'd discerned her thoughts, he glanced up at her as she crossed the threshold behind Mrs. Lewis.

Feeling heat flood her cheeks, Esther whirled around and hurried to catch up with her landlady. She had no business noticing anything about him or any other man she might encounter in London. The cab driver had already proved her previous lessons correct. There was no man alive who could be trusted.

Chapter Five

My Dearest Esther,
Do not let the incident with the carriage driver upset you over long. It is as we both know—men are not to be trusted...

She was an imposter in a strange, new world. Esther clutched her books to her chest and made her way down the second-floor hall to her next class. She'd had two thus far this morning, her first day at Bedford, and her head was spinning. She'd believed that her tutor at Lady Parker's house had crammed her mind full of information the past two months, but that was nothing compared to what she'd learned—or tried to learn—this morning.

Mathematics was going to be a problem. She could figure sums quickly in her head, and years of sewing had taught her how to calculate measurements, but there was so much more to mathematics than that. Formulas and equations—problems that took an entire chalkboard to explain and solve. She was going to need some help. Perhaps one of the other girls at the boarding house would agree to tutor her. Thus far they had all been very kind. None had shunned her or even asked much about her background. She'd returned the favor, not asking any personal questions and keeping her thoughts to herself. She liked them all, though it seemed easy enough for her to tell who had come from money and who had not.

Yet, that they were all here attending college said something about each of them. They were tired of living in a man's world. It was time for women to have a say as well. Of course the means to that end—if there was such a conclusion—was through classes taught largely by—men.

A Professor Lind was listed on her schedule next. He taught literature, a subject she hoped to feel far more comfortable with than math.

Esther found the correct classroom and filed in with the other students headed that direction. The professor stood at the board, his back to the door as he wrote. Something about him seemed familiar, and when he turned so that his profile could be seen, she realized where she had seen him before.

John. John Lind. At least she knew his surname now. She hadn't seen him again since he'd helped with her trunk. How odd that a professor should have done so.

He opened class with a quick roll call. When he reached her name, a warm smile lit his face, and his gaze seemed to linger a second longer. Or was it her imagination? She didn't think so. She certainly didn't *want* his gaze lingering on her. Perhaps he'd just been recalling her folly with the driver.

He plunged straight into the lecture, and Esther sat up excitedly when she realized they were going to be studying Greek classics. *The Iliad*, followed by *The Odyssey*, were first on the list, and she felt a little thrill when he passed out copies to each of them. Lady Parker had selected the latter for Esther to read to her a few years earlier, complaining that Esther favored contemporary authors too much and had need of classics as well. Initially Esther had balked at the departure from her usual favorites, but upon reading she had found

Odysseus's adventures thrilling, and even more so the idea that his author had lived so long ago.

"Yours to keep," Professor Lind said as he placed a book on her desk. "You can make notes inside or keep a separate notebook. It doesn't matter. As you read, class, be thinking about..."

Esther ran a hand reverently over the cover and said a silent prayer of thanks for the amazing opportunity to be here in this great city and learning about a great and ancient civilization.

The class passed all too quickly, and it was with reluctance that Esther packed up her belongings and stood to leave with the others.

"Miss Sessions."

Esther looked to the front and Professor Lind.

"Yes?"

A few of the students glanced her way inquiringly as she made her way to the front of the room and the professor's podium.

"Have you recovered from your difficulties the other night?"

"Yes, thank you. I . . . appreciate your assistance." Too late she realized she'd never thanked him. Truthfully, she'd never thought of him again. Mrs. Lewis had whisked her off to a hot meal, followed by the luxury of a warm bath and a decently comfortable bed, and thoughts of any man—even one who had been astonishingly kind—had vanished.

"You're welcome. I'm glad to hear it. Are you settling in all right?"

She nodded. "The classes—your class, at least—is wonderful." She sounded like some of the girls at the boarding house, gushing about this fellow or that. "I love reading," she quickly added, lest he think he was the cause of her exuberance.

"Then you've come to the right place. You'll have your nose in a book most of the day, every day for the next few months."

Esther nodded again, then glanced toward the door, suddenly eager to leave, when only moments before she had wished his lecture about the Greek gods might continue.

"I'm keeping you from your luncheon. I apologize," he said.

Her eyes widened. Never had a man apologized to her before—even when he had done something wrong. And here the professor had done nothing but inquire after her welfare.

"Thank you." She hurried from the room, knowing she had ended the conversation badly, and wondering what she ought to have said and why she felt it mattered at all.

* * *

"Singled out your very first day of class." Esther's roommate Molly leaned her chin on her hands and stared at Esther across the table in the boarding house dining room. "What's your secret?"

"I haven't any," Esther said. It was the truth, save for the enormous one she harbored—that she wasn't like these other women and didn't really belong here.

"He's handsome enough, that's for sure," Charlotte, another student living at the boarding house, added as she sat beside Esther. "And his lecture was—"

"—Not nearly as stimulating as mathematics." Margaret, another of the girls living in the boarding house, entered the room and took the seat at the far end of the table. "I found Professor Hughes' class perfectly exhilarating. I believe he may love numbers as much as I do."

Esther glanced at Margaret, trying to judge if she might

be the sort who would be willing to help another with all those numbers.

"Professor Hughes is married," Molly said. "No fun to be had there."

"Molly!" another admonished. "We're here so we don't *have* to be married."

"So we don't need a man to support us," Esther said. That golden ring of an idea was what would get her through mathematics, music, and anything else she found particularly difficult.

"I know," Molly said offhandedly, making Esther wonder if Molly actually favored the idea of marriage. It wouldn't surprise her at all if she did, given her frequent dissection of any male in her sight.

"Though you'd never have a life of luxury if you married a college professor," Molly continued. "I hear they don't make much at all."

"I'm not marrying anyone," Esther protested. "Professor Lind was kind enough to help me with a difficult situation the night I arrived. He was referring to the incident today. That is all."

"Sure it is." Abigail joined them, dropping her books on the table as if for emphasis. "I'd beware if I were you. It may be he's a gal-sneaker."

"Ladies, we do not slam our books. Nor do we bring them to the table." Mrs. Lewis entered the dining room, followed by two other girls who also boarded here. They were all on a rotation to help with meals and upkeep at the house, the one area Esther felt confident she could excel in.

Mrs. Lewis held a tea service, and the girls held platters of apple charlotte. Esther's mouth watered in anticipation. How quickly she'd become accustomed to this new life and three delicious meals each day.

"How were everyone's classes this morning?" Mrs. Lewis asked.

"Confusing," Molly said. "Thank goodness we have art and music this afternoon. My mind can't take many more hours of book learning."

A couple of the other girls nodded their agreement, while Esther silently dreaded both upcoming classes.

"Some classes were better than others," Abigail added.

"But they were all good," Esther said, not wanting to complain, when the opportunity to be here was so glorious.

"Especially that last class, right?" Charlotte nudged Esther, then looked at their landlady. "Mr. Lind singled Esther out after class."

"To inquire about the incident the other night—with the hackney," Esther clarified quickly at Mrs. Lewis's baffled expression.

"Oh, yes." Mrs. Lewis smiled, though it didn't seem to reach her eyes. "Young women attending the college do not fraternize with the professors," she added, her gaze drifting to each of them around the table, arriving last and lingering longest on Esther. "You are here to learn, not to be courted. Many of you will go on to become governesses. A few may marry, but our intent here is to educate you, so that marriage is not your only option. Is that understood?"

"Yes, Mrs. Lewis," they chorused.

For Esther it was more than understood. It was imperative.

Chapter Six

Dearest Lady Parker,
I've written my very first essay and await my score most anxiously...

John Lind read the last paragraph of the essay and quickly turned the paper over, resisting the urge to move his hand and therefore view the name at the top. He always made a point of reading his students' work before discovering whom that work belonged to. It made for impartial grading and zero chance of discrimination on his part, not that it had been a problem of his in the past. This semester, however, he could see the benefit of the safeguard he'd long ago put in place.

He'd never favored one student over another but was starting to feel differently. One in particular stood out to him—from the moment he'd laid eyes on her, refusing assistance as she exited a carriage and taking in her surroundings with an expression that was part awe, part terror.

Miss Sessions was not like the other women at the college. She was far more serious—less talkative and more contemplative, though a few of his lectures had managed to rouse her enough that the impassioned spirit he'd suspected lay just below the surface had shown itself splendidly.

He guessed that the paper he'd just read belonged to her—he hoped it did. And therein lay the problem. He couldn't start hoping that one of his students excelled beyond the others. He wished for all of their success—equally. Or, at least, he used to.

Setting the paper in question aside in the pile of those to receive the highest marks, John returned to the stack before him and read another hour, until his eyes were tired and his head had begun to ache. He rubbed his bleary eyes as he noted the late hour. Perhaps it was time to see about a pair of spectacles. Or perhaps he was simply getting old, and the life he had chosen starting to weary him.

He leaned back in his chair, contemplating the past decade. At age twenty, he had been a student himself and—unlike his father—eager to do something meaningful with his life. His love for the university and a few, key friendships during his years of study had led to this position at Bedford. *A revolutionary idea,* many had said when learning he was to teach at a college for women. Others had been less complimentary, calling it ludicrous or preposterous, or even a fool's errand.

Women cannot be taught; they must be managed, his father had said. Just one more proof that he hadn't a shred of common sense, much less decency, about him.

Teaching at Bedford was, in fact, rewarding—the most rewarding occupation John could imagine for himself—until recently. Until the day, three weeks ago, when a head of chestnut curls, accompanied by a solemn, wary—yet youthful and innocent—face had emerged from a carriage and done something odd to his heart. He had taught many pretty faces over his six years at Bedford. He worked with fine women closer to his own thirty years than their young students. He'd had ample opportunity to pursue a relationship, yet had chosen not to. Always his teaching had been enough to fulfill him.

Until now. Until Miss Esther Sessions had arrived and awakened something within him that he couldn't quite reckon with. She'd carried her bonnet in her hand instead of on her head, and she'd stood up for herself, seemingly fearless and ready to take on the driver who had cheated her. Her gloveless fingers had curled into fists, which John suspected could have delivered a solid punch if he hadn't intervened.

Part of him had wished to see the scene through, but another part had not wished her first day at Bedford to be marred more than it already had, by her late arrival and the dishonest driver. An urge to protect had propelled him from his usual reserve to an uncharacteristically chivalrous act. Normally he had nothing to do with the ladies outside of his classroom and school hours. Only odd coincidence had placed him at the boardinghouse at the time of Miss Sessions' arrival. He had been speaking with the other John employed at Bedford, the lad who fetched wood for the stoves, posted letters, and took care of errands and odd jobs as needed.

When Mrs. Lewis had gone out to greet the newest arrival, he had glimpsed Miss Sessions and something about her had evoked his attention and response.

Even if she'd had the faintest idea of his interest—he was certain she hadn't—and even if she felt a similar curiosity about him, she was his pupil and he her professor. Breaching that relationship of trust and mentorship in pursuit of a different type of relationship was unthinkable.

Except that seemed to be all he could think about lately. He looked forward to teaching the class she was in more than his other classes. His spirits elevated each time she entered the room. And it had become his goal to coax or goad her into verbal response at least once every class period. Often, once she made her first comment, others followed more easily. She had a brilliant mind for literature, and as much as he enjoyed their conversations in class, he imagined what it would be like, for just the two of them to be seated before a fire reading and discussing the books they both loved together, long into the night.

But such was not to be.

John returned to his stacks of papers, beginning with the pile to receive the lesser marks first and noting in his grade book the score for each pupil. When only three remained to be recorded, he came to the essay he had so enjoyed, the one that had made its points so passionately. He flipped the paper over, this time keeping his hand from covering the top, and was not at all surprised to see Miss Sessions' name.

Esther. An unusual name these days, but so fitting for her. There was something regal and queen-like in her bearing. If she'd been named after the bible heroine, John could easily imagine a resemblance to the brave, heroic figure.

Still, he shouldn't think of her by her given name. It wouldn't do to have a slip like that in class. She must remain Miss Sessions.

He recorded her high mark in the grade book, then looked ruefully at the paper. Never again would he be able to keep himself from recognizing her work. Not only were her thoughts deeper and more insightful than those of most of his other pupils, but her handwriting was distinct—atrocious, actually.

John studied it more carefully and noted that at the beginning of her essay, her letters were stiff and regimented, as if she had taken great pains to form each correctly. But as the essay went on, and she made each of her impassioned points, the writing became sloppier—almost illegible in the places where her arguments were strongest. Ink blotted the page, as if pen had been brought to paper too swiftly, as if she could not write fast enough and cared little for presentation over purpose.

In contrast, almost all of the other papers he read, from this class and others, both past and present, had perfectly scripted letters. These were the pages of gently bred young ladies who'd had governesses and tutors to guide them through the arts, including those of correspondence. Miss Sessions' writing suggested she'd had neither, and perhaps had only come quite recently to do any sort of writing at all. Her script was childlike and awkward.

Much like the woman herself, John mused. He'd witnessed her boldness with the driver, yet he sensed her unease at school, and on those few occasions he'd heard her speak—in settings other than a class discussion—her words and actions had been both stilted and uncertain. If he were a betting man—something he never would be, thanks to his father's poor example—he would have felt confident wagering that Miss Sessions had not been brought up as many of the other women at the college. He doubted she'd ever had a governess to teach her—yet she'd learned somewhere—or had enjoyed any other privileges or obligations of society. She was the proverbial daisy amongst a vase of roses. And, for that, she intrigued him all the more.

Chapter Seven

Dearest Lady Parker,
I wish you might view Bedford's reading room. It has volumes upon volumes, even to far surpass your fine collection of books...

Esther stepped inside the college reading room and took a minute to breathe in the smell of books and ink while gazing in wonder at the wall of crammed shelves just waiting to be discovered. It was all she could do not to pinch herself or skip across the room in joy. *Books!* More than she might possibly read during the years she would study here. Had there ever been any sight so glorious as a library?

Unable to contain her smile, Esther hurried between the pillars and toward the shelves, taking only a second to detour and place her school bag on a table near one of the domed, stained-glass windows. Light shone through, causing colors to dance across the table. Esther's smile broadened. *Such a beautiful room, and mine to enjoy.* Gone were the days of hiding a single, precious library book within a basket of sewing.

After a few minutes' search, Esther located the book her chemistry professor had recommended. Esther had struggled with yesterday's lab and had requested extra reading that might clarify the lesson for her. With the volume in hand, she returned to her seat to begin several hours of study. She'd already told Mrs. Lewis that she would not be taking her dinner in the dining room this evening. She'd eat in the kitchen alone later.

With the exception of one other student, the reading room was vacant this late on a Friday afternoon. After a long, intense week of study, most students were ready for a change of scenery, but Esther needed the weekend to catch up. It had become her habit to stay at the college as late as possible and after that resume her studies downstairs in the residence hall. For while Molly was a fine, friendly roommate, she was not the least inclined to silence—which Esther desperately needed to concentrate and embed in her memory all that she was trying to learn.

Saturdays Esther met with a private tutor for French, as the college offered no French class suitable for beginners. Her French would have to become at least passable if she hoped to ever work as a governess—something she wasn't at all certain she favored.

Much like the idea of marriage, she didn't find the prospect of teaching well-to-do, and likely spoiled, children enticing in the least. Instead, she wished to use her education to do something meaningful, to educate those who needed it most. Those like her, who faced threats like starvation and violence each day. The faces of those children called to her, beckoned her to return from whence she'd come and somehow make their world better.

Her mother had done that for her, giving her the gift of literacy. Could Esther not find a way to do the same for others? "Woman cannot live on books alone."

Esther looked up to find Mrs. Reid, Bedford's founder, standing beside her.

"May I join you, Miss Sessions?"

"Of course." Esther pushed some of her papers aside and checked the impulse to rise and pull out the woman's chair and offer to fetch her tea. "It is good to see you again, Mrs. Reid."

"Ah, you remember me, do you?" She lowered herself into the chair across from Esther. "I suppose you cannot help but remember a person so old."

"That's not it at all," Esther protested. "I was much inspired by your speech the first day of classes."

"Amazing that they still allow me to talk, isn't it," Mrs. Reid said in good humor.

"You founded the college, did you not?" Esther asked. "I should think you are allowed to do anything here that you wish."

"Mostly." Mrs. Reid chuckled. "Tell me, how are you finding chemistry?"

"Difficult," Esther said without hesitation. "I have learned the states of matter but am somewhat confused on changes to those states. For instance, it seems improbable that the union of two gases creates water, yet that has been proved as truth. I find the periodic table is hard to memorize, and until I know the elements better, I am frequently lost during the labs. I'm afraid this is all new to me."

"A few short months ago water was simply water, am I correct?"

Esther nodded. "There were two types, actually—dirty and clean. Lady Parker's residence yielded the latter and mine quite often the former."

Mrs. Reid's expression grew contemplative, her smile somewhat wistful. "And yet, here you are, at the beginning of the finest education a woman can obtain—in the entirety of the world, I daresay. Few believe women capable of learning subjects like chemistry and calculus."

"Let us hope that I am capable," Esther said.

"According to your professors, you are." Mrs. Reid glanced at the papers scattered about the table. "Professor Lind tells me you wrote the most brilliant essay he's ever read in all his years of teaching."

"He did?" A blush crept up Esther's cheeks.

Mrs. Reid nodded. "Though you are not likely to hear it from him. He awards good marks but rarely praises students in class. He does not wish to make those who struggled with an assignment feel poorly, nor does he wish to see his star pupils grow pompous or overconfident."

"Little worry of that." Esther fanned her hand in front of the books on the table. "I've plenty of other subjects to keep me humble." But for the moment chemistry was forgotten, and she allowed herself the pleasure of knowing she had pleased Professor Lind. Of all her classes, his was her favorite. But she had known it would be, from the first. Literature she could relate to. It was the only part of her education that wasn't lacking. And while Professor Lind was no substitute for an evening spent sparring and debating with Lady Parker, Esther greatly enjoyed his lectures and insights into their readings.

"As I said earlier, one cannot live by books alone," Mrs. Reid said. "I promised Lady Parker that I would check in on you from time to time. I've tried, but it seems the last three weeks you've scarce slept in your bed and have missed numerous meals with Mrs. Lewis and the other boarders.

"I'm not used to having three meals every day. And as you know, I'm not like the other boarders. What they learned years ago is largely new to me. I have to study if I am to succeed."

"Oh, I have no doubt you'll succeed." Mrs. Reid rose from her chair. "But you need to live a little—outside of this room—as well. I'll see about arranging a midterm outing for all. Much can be learned from exploring the world as well as reading about it."

Chapter Eight

Dearest Lady Parker,

I hope you will be pleased to know that I received the highest marks on my essay. Professor Lind told Mrs. Reid that mine was the finest he's ever read! I know I have you to thank for that. I wish you might attend Mr. Lind's classes with me, as you would so enjoy the discussions . . .

Esther glanced longingly out the second-floor window for another glimpse at the autumn sky. Though she had yet to venture anywhere in a carriage in the month and a half she'd been at Bedford, she found her frequent walks enjoyable—much more so than her mathematics tutoring sessions. With reluctance she forced her feet down the corridor toward Professor Hughes' classroom. She knocked twice, then pushed open the door as she'd been instructed to do previously.

"Good afternoon, Prof—" Her greeting cut off abruptly at the sight of the man before her—not portly Professor Hughes, but tall Professor Lind. He looked up from the textbook he had been studying and smiled.

"Good afternoon, Miss Sessions. I assume you're here for tutoring."

She nodded but made no move to come farther into the room. She must be mistaken about the time of day, or perhaps had confused the date. As if further proof of her error she noted that Katherine, the other student who received tutoring with her, wasn't here.

Professor Lind answered her unspoken question. "Professor Hughes has, unfortunately, had to leave us temporarily. His wife has become ill, and her doctors advised that he move her to a better climate as soon as possible. He will not be returning to us this semester."

"Oh." Once again Esther's tongue seemed bound in Professor Lind's presence. What was she to do now? Professor Hughes' tutoring hadn't exactly been helping her improve her marks or her understanding of the subject, but she had hoped he might pass her anyway, given her continued efforts.

"The other professors and I will be covering his classes until we can find a more suitable replacement." Professor Lind closed the textbook—a math book—pushed it aside, and beckoned her to come in. "He showed me where you left off. I've just gone over the material myself as a quick refresher."

Esther raised her brows at this. If she'd believed she was in trouble with mathematics before, she suspected her situation had just taken a turn for the worse. How was a teacher of literature supposed to help her understand complex algebraic equations?

Holding in a sigh, she walked into the room, then slid into the nearest seat. Professor Lind rose from his and went to the board, which already held a row of the most recent problems she'd been struggling with. He stepped to the side, so she might better see.

"It always helped me to think of solving for x—or whatever variable is being sought—as a mystery that required a precise path to be solved. One misstep, and I take the wrong direction and inevitably give the wrong answer. I've gone over your assignments and have concluded where, and quite likely why, your missteps are occurring."

Esther's face warmed with something akin to shame. Surely Professor Lind would know her for the imposter she was. She hadn't cared so much what Professor Hughes believed of her. But Mr. Lind had praised her work and made her feel as if she might actually belong here. To have him realize how incapable she was made her want to cry. And that made her furious. Why should she care what he thought—what any man thought?

"Miss Sessions?" He was looking at her oddly, and she realized she'd been staring blankly at the wall behind him, and perhaps even gaping at him while her mind revolved through numerous emotions.

She pursed her lips and sat up straighter. "I'm sorry, Professor. Please continue."

"If at any point in my explanations you feel lost, you must let me know. Algebra can seem like a foreign language to one unacquainted with it."

Did he know of her struggles learning French as well? Esther gave a weak nod, and he began again.

"Following the correct path can be difficult if one does not know the right way to proceed. I suspect you've never been shown the order which must be followed when tackling problems of this sort."

Esther soon found Professor Lind's voice and explanation nearly as mesmerizing as she did during his other lectures. He started at the very beginning, breaking each problem down, showing her step by step which must be solved first, second, and so on. She'd had no idea that the order in which she worked the sums and products and dividends was so terribly important. He helped her understand coefficients and reviewed the various rules for multiplication and division, yet she was not made to feel inferior. On the contrary, he praised her as she was able to repeat steps back to him and explain each of the seemingly simple, yet important mathematical properties.

An hour passed quickly, and Professor Lind continued, though the bell for luncheon rang. He made no move to leave, and Esther found she didn't want to either. A new kind of excitement was building in her, a confidence she hadn't experienced before—akin to the way she felt in his literature class. She could do this!

When, at last, Professor Lind invited her to the board to work the problems herself, she felt eager to test her abilities. He handed her the chalk, his fingers brushing hers. Their eyes met, and her heartbeat escalated—not in fear, her usual response to any man's proximity, but with some other, unfamiliar, *pleasant* sensation.

It was gratitude, she quickly decided. She felt good in his presence because she was so grateful for his help.

She turned to the board and tried to focus her attention on the first problem. After a moment her concentration returned, and she spent the next several minutes carefully following the steps he had outlined. She worked each problem slowly, rechecking her work at every step, all the while aware of Professor Lind a short distance away, leaning against the desk, arms folded across his middle, as he watched her.

Esther had finished only two of the lengthy problems when her hand began its familiar ache. Writing on the chalkboard proved even more difficult than writing on paper. She placed the chalk on the tray and paused to massage her hand before proceeding to the next problem.

"Let's see how you've done." Professor Lind pushed off the desk and moved closer. "Describe to me each step you took and why you took it."

Esther hadn't expected this. Professor Hughes merely checked her work and—most often—told her she was wrong, followed by a confusing explanation as to why. She began with the first problem, rethinking each step and verbalizing. When she'd finished some minutes later—without being interrupted by Professor Lind—she paused, waiting nervously to hear she was wrong. It took courage to turn to meet his gaze. She desperately wanted to please him, to repay his inexplicable faith in her. Yet another new, and wholly unexpected, feeling.

He beamed at her, his smile making his already pleasant face even more so. "Excellent."

Relief fluttered within her, an almost ethereal joy. Esther returned his smile with one of her own. No one had ever proclaimed her mathematical abilities were anything close to excellent. *Hopeless* and *remedial* were the terms she'd heard most recently from Professor Hughes.

She went through the steps to the next problem and found that answer correct as well.

"I believe you've got it," Professor Lind said, sounding genuinely excited—perhaps as much for himself that he had been able to teach her.

She wondered if he was nervous at all, taking over Professor Hughes' classes.

"I'll work the other two now." Esther faced the board and picked up the chalk, gripping it awkwardly, as her finger had stiffened and refused to curve as it should.

"Allow me." Professor Lind's hand again brushed hers briefly, and he took the chalk from her. "You tell me what to do, and I will write it down."

Heat rose in Esther's cheeks—whether from his unexpected touch or her shame over her disfigured hand, she wasn't certain. She clasped it behind her and faced the board.

Her voice wobbled a bit when she spoke. "We'll begin

with the numbers in the parentheses. First, seven squared becomes forty-nine. Subtract fifteen from that, and you get thirty-four."

He wrote the answer as she'd instructed. "You figure numbers quickly for one with little mathematical experience."

"I've been doing sums in my head for a long time," Esther said. "Since I was a little girl working—" She stopped abruptly, too late realizing she had just given herself away.

"In a factory?" Professor Lind turned from the board to look at her.

She nodded. What would he think of her now?

"Is that where your hand was injured?" His gaze dropped to her arm.

Esther nodded but did not offer more. She'd embarrassed herself enough already.

"It pains you when you write." It was not a question, but a statement. He had noticed.

Esther frowned, concerned there were other idiosyncrasies about herself that she'd also not hidden as well as she'd believed. Oddly, he didn't seem bothered to know he was teaching a woman who'd spent her life in poverty. A fragile stem of trust bridged between them.

"My finger was nearly crushed when I was seven years old. It was never treated properly and did not heal well."

"May I look at it?"

Esther hesitated. She did not often dwell on her bent finger, except to be grateful that she still had a finger at all. Still, exposing its ugliness—the disfiguring, hardened flesh that mounded between her second and third knuckles—for examination to an acquaintance, and a man no less, brought a different sort of discomfort.

"Please," he added. "I promise to be gentle. I am curious to know if there is something that might be done to improve its function and lessen your pain."

With reluctance Esther surrendered her hand. He took it in both of his, tracing his finger gently along the scar before probing at the bone beneath. His hands were warm, his touch gentle, as promised. A wave of sensation swept from where his fingers touched her skin to her other senses, threatening her balance.

His head, bent close, showed off the perfectly styled wave she'd noticed the night they met. He smelled pleasant, perhaps of some cologne. And his eyes, when they looked up at hers, were a piercing blue that seemed to reach within her, crumbling the carefully constructed walls that his previous kindnesses had nearly breached.

"Have you ever had a physician examine it?"

Esther held back a bitter laugh. "No. The harm was done by the time I began work for Lady Parker—or she might have thought of it, kind as she's been to me. She had my wrist set when it was broken." Esther held out her other arm as she withdrew her hand from his. "It healed well."

"How was your wrist broken?" Professor Lind lifted his gaze to hers.

"My brother twisted it. He didn't intend to do that much harm."

"Yet he *did* mean to harm you?" Professor Lind's voice held reproach.

"He meant to have the only piece of bread in the house. We were both hungry, and hunger does odd things to people." Though not nearly so bad as what alcohol did. "Silas was merely following our father's example—doing what men do." She heard the chill and censure in her voice, and felt it as it sped through her veins to her heart. She froze, staring up at Professor Lind, at once realizing their proximity and that they were alone. What kind of fool was she, trusting him with her past? And worse, with her person? Who knew but that he had arranged for Katherine to not be here today so they would be alone.

Esther stepped back suddenly, then turned and rushed around the other side of the desk. She collected her books and hurried toward the door. "The time for my tutoring session has passed. Thank you, Professor."

"Esther—"

Hand on the doorknob, she stopped. Had he just—

"Forgive my use of your given name, Miss Sessions. I only meant to get your attention, to assure you that not all men are like those in your family. I apologize if I have made you uncomfortable. My only wish is to help my pupils achieve success."

Her hand drooped on the knob. She wanted to believe his words, to feel both safe and relieved. How grand it would be to return to Professor Lind and his kindness, to the way she'd felt just moments before. At the least, she ought to express appropriate gratitude for all he had done for her. He had helped her so much today, far more than Professor Hughes.

But fear anchored Esther in place. For all his apparent goodness and sincerity, Professor Lind was a man. And life had taught her that men must not be trusted.

"Thank you for your help, Professor," she managed, then twisted the knob and opened the door, leaving him alone, as she had found him.

Chapter Nine

Dearest Lady Parker,

For better or worse, I have completed midterm examinations. I feel that I have done my very best and am confident in the outcome...

There was a chill in the air the morning of the Bedford College outing. As promised, Mrs. Reid had arranged for an excursion around London the Saturday after midterm exams.

After so many weeks of intense studying, Esther felt relieved to have a weekend off. As much as she loved Bedford's reading room, it was nice not to be in it today.

With the exception of chemistry, she felt she had done well on her exams. Though she had not returned for additional tutoring for mathematics, her understanding and scores had steadily improved since the afternoon Professor Lind had demystified the mathematical properties and proper order for working a problem. Her algebra homework still took a great deal of time to complete, but no longer was it akin to a foreign language. Esther even had hope that someday she might be able to take the calculus course offered at Bedford.

"Come sit with me, Esther." Molly's gloved hand tugged her toward the first of several, open-top carriages. "Professor

Lind is riding up front, so he can tell us the history of all the sights we are to see."

Esther ignored the little pang of joyous angst, as she'd come to consider it, that she felt whenever attending Professor Lind's classes. She so looked forward to his lectures and insights. She loved the readings he assigned and enjoyed writing the essays. At the same time she dreaded seeing him. His kindness confused her and threatened her long-held stance that men were vile creatures, not to be trusted but rather tolerated and generally given as wide a berth as possible. Yet Professor Lind seemed to draw her to him like a moth to flame.

And she knew what happened to those poor, unfortunate moths that succumbed.

Molly's incessant chatter would be Esther's safety net today. She wasn't sure how Professor Lind was supposed to narrate anything with Molly along in his carriage. He would be fortunate to get a word in edgewise.

He smiled when he saw them approaching. "Just the two ladies I was looking for."

"You were?" Molly's breathless answer and accompanying blush embarrassed Esther, who then felt her own face warm.

"I've been given a special charge to make sure those new to London receive the grand tour today. That includes the two of you."

Molly nudged Esther with her elbow. "Never have I been so grateful to be from Cambridge."

Professor Lind held his hand out, as humble as any footman or gallant as any knight, but Esther hesitated to take it. She'd accepted no help from any man while boarding and exiting both train and carriage on her journey to London, and she hadn't thought to start the habit now. But neither did she wish to offend the professor.

Molly nudged her again, and after an additional second's hesitation, Esther placed her hand in Professor Lind's.

As if realizing the act of faith and trust that was, his fingers curved gently around hers, bringing to mind the last time he had held her hand and the unexpected pleasantness of it.

"I hope you have a most enjoyable day, Miss Sessions."

"Thank you, Professor." She stepped into the carriage and slid to the far side of the two forward-facing seats. Abigail already sat in the one across from them, with the empty seat beside her assumedly for the professor. Gushing and giggling, the ever-exuberant Molly took the seat beside Esther.

Behind them the other carriages began filling, and happy chatter carried through the air. It was the perfect autumn day, the weather cool enough to require a short jacket, but not so cold as to necessitate a closed carriage and cloaks. Esther felt particularly smart in her ensemble, having had it confirmed by Molly earlier that her navy jacket trimmed in black braid and the matching bonnet were of the latest style. Esther had no doubt of this, as Lady Parker had sent them, along with a dozen other items she'd deemed necessary for the upcoming autumn and winter.

While Esther appreciated the finery, she doubted the bonnet would stay on her head all day—not when it restricted her view, and there were so many things to take in as they drove.

Professor Lind stepped up into the carriage and stood tall as he spoke through a large paper cone that amplified his voice so those in the other carriages might hear as well.

"Our first stop this morning will be the Theatre Royal. The board of trustees has arranged for us to see a rehearsal of the ballet *La Sylphide.*"

Joyous exclamations followed this announcement. He

took his seat, and the driver flicked the reins. The horses started forward, and Esther felt the same anticipatory flutter that she'd felt upon boarding the train for London. Though the carriage did not travel nearly as fast, it felt thrilling nonetheless. She'd never ridden in an open-top carriage before and, previous to the summer spent with Lady Parker, had not ridden in a carriage at all. How strange and wonderful it was to be one of the grand women driving in one, after so many years walking the great distance from Lady Parker's home to hers, in every type of weather.

They left Bedford Square and headed down Bloomsbury Street, toward the imposing buildings of the British Museum that Esther had passed on her walks. They were not stopping there today, but Professor Lind had promised his literature classes a field trip to the museum upon the conclusion of their study of Greek literature.

"The museum, intended to emulate Greek architecture, as well as being worthy of the treasures housed inside, was completed in 1852," Professor Lind informed them as they drove past the entrance.

"It's as close to the Parthenon as I'll ever get," Molly said, her head tilted back as she took in the immense columns fronting the building.

"I wouldn't go there even if I could," the more reserved Abigail added.

Esther silently agreed. Greece, while fascinating to study, seemed far beyond her reach. A castle she didn't dream of, though perhaps she should. But for today, being here in this splendid city was thrilling enough.

Long before their arrival at the theater, her bonnet lay in her lap, the breeze blowing strands of her hair loose from their pins as she leaned out the side, trying to take in as much of London as she possibly could. She was content with merely seeing it all, but occasionally Professor Lind commented about the buildings they passed. As Esther had suspected, Molly's constant stream of exclamations didn't allow for him to do much more.

"Ooh. Look at that." She tugged on Esther's arm.

Esther shifted in her seat to see what had Molly so excited now. As she turned, her gaze collided with Professor Lind's, and Esther had the uncomfortable feeling that he had been watching her. His almost guilty smile and quickly averted gaze, along with the curious way Abigail was looking between her and Professor Lind practically confirmed it.

But why?

Both the beauty of the music and the grace of the dancers in the ballet held Esther spellbound, but she found the way *La Sylphide* ended sobering. The free-spirited sylph was caught by the man pursuing her, her wings crushed in the scarf that bound her to him.

"Wasn't that the most tragically romantic story you've ever seen," Molly gushed as they left the theatre.

"It was tragic," Esther agreed. "And insensible. Isn't it just like a man to capture a woman, crush her spirit, then kill her."

"But he didn't mean to," Molly protested, hurrying to catch up to Esther's angry strides. "James was sad at the end too."

Esther made no reply. Her father *had* meant to kill her mother, and the reminder left her shaken.

Westminster Abbey's Gothic architecture and stained glass soothed her. To think that she was walking where the queen had at her coronation. Her spirits lifted further at the glimpse of Buckingham Palace as they drove past. She almost asked Molly to pinch her, to make sure this day and outing were real. To think that Queen Victoria was in there somewhere, just on the other side of those gates!

As their carriage rolled past the palace, Professor Lind stood once more. "For our last stop today we will be picnicking at Hyde Park."

Esther pulled her eyes from the Buckingham guards and sat up straight.

"It was established by Henry VIII in 1536, originally for use as a hunting ground. In 1637 it opened to the public and has tragically been the locale of several duels involving members of the nobility. In 1851 Prince Albert oversaw the building of —"

"—the Crystal Palace," Esther blurted.

"Yes." Professor Lind looked down and smiled warmly, seemingly not bothered by her interruption. He returned to speaking through the cone that magnified his voice. "A feat in and of itself, at three times the size of St. Paul's Cathedral, it housed the more than 14,000 exhibits from around the world for The Great Exhibition."

He continued on, sharing other facts about the park, but Esther had no care for those. Though the Crystal Palace was no longer here, she *was*—at the very place she and her mother had read about so many years ago. She could hardly contain herself until the carriages stopped. As the baskets and blankets for their picnic were being unloaded, Esther slipped off in search of that sacred bit of ground. She wanted a few minutes there by herself, without talkative Molly or any of the other girls, to think of, and thank, her mother.

A few minutes soon turned to several, and Esther realized that, like many of the other sites in London, Hyde Park was immense. Twice she asked directions of strangers—women, of course—until at last she reached the southern end of the park and found the vast field near the Serpentine River where the palace had stood. Esther imagined that she could still see the faint lines in the grass all these years later, and when she closed her eyes she imagined the palace itself looming before her.

"I'm here, Mama," she whispered. "You were right. I kept reading, and now I'm here. I wish—" Her voice faltered. "I wish you were with me." How unfair it was that her mother had never seen anything beyond Liverpool's slums. She'd had only her mind in which to travel, never a fine carriage, never an opportunity to be all that she might have been.

Leaves crunched behind her, and Esther turned to see two women, deep in earnest conversation, strolling arm in arm. One appeared several years older than the other, and the way their heads bent close tugged at her heart. *Mother and daughter?* Did they realize how fortunate they were to have each other—an arm to clasp, a confidant, a friend? As kind as Lady Parker had been to her, Esther still lacked the affection these two women obviously shared. Lady Parker was not the type for hugs, nor one to talk about anything personal. *No matter,* Esther told herself, even as tears stung her eyes. She'd been incredibly blessed, and if there was still that constant pang of loneliness in her life, well, so be it. She was far better off than most.

As the women moved out of her line of vision, Professor Lind entered it, from his position leaning against a nearby tree. Their eyes met across the distance, and with a look of chagrin he started toward her.

"I am sorry to disturb you," he began, once more apologizing when he had scarce done anything to merit such. "I am charged with keeping all of the Bedford College students safe this day, and when we discovered you to be missing . . ." He glanced at the field where the Crystal Palace had once stood. "I thought I might find you here." He paused once more, considering her. "This place means something to you."

Yet again he had observed more than she had intended to reveal. But today this did not bother her, and Esther even found herself wanting to share the reason this spot of grass felt almost sacred. "It means a great deal," she began, pausing to wipe a lone tear from the corner of her eye. "My mother and I read of it long ago. It was she who taught me to read." For the next several minutes the story tumbled from her, and Esther found herself able to tell of her last minutes with her mother without the tearful bitterness she had experienced in the past. The expression of horror upon Professor Lind's face, when she told of her father's actions, followed by his bowed spine and the acute sorrow reflected in his steady gaze led her to believe she had not erred in telling him—though she had just done the unthinkable in trusting a man.

"Your mother must be happy to know you are here," Professor Lind said when Esther had finished. He cleared his throat, as if there was a tickle in it. "I am sure God has allowed her a peek from heaven today, to see her daughter grown."

Esther had not considered this before but found she liked the idea very much. "I hope so," she said. "I want so badly to make her and Lady Parker proud."

"In the short time that I have known you, you have made me proud," he said, surprising her. "In all my years of teaching, I have never seen a student try so hard or work so diligently."

"Now you see why I must," Esther said. "I fear that at any moment I shall lose my place. I am not like the other women at Bedford."

"No, you are not." Professor Lind glanced at the bonnet dangling from her fingertips. "And I am glad of it." His smile reached his eyes and ignited a pleasant warmth deep within her. Before she might savor the feeling, panic followed on its heels. What was she doing, speaking alone with him like this? She took a step backward.

"Neither am I like your father," Professor Lind hastened, as if he had divined her thoughts. "Or the character James in this morning's ballet."

Esther flushed. He must have overheard her earlier.

"I teach at a women's college because I respect women. I value them. I value you, Miss Sessions."

"Thank you," she said simply. He was not like her father or brother, her cruel boss at the mill, or her past landlord. *Still, he is a man.*

But it was her own feelings she felt most distrustful of at present. She could no longer explain what she felt toward Professor Lind as mere gratitude. This growing feeling within was something else—something more. *Brotherly love?* Yes, she decided, that was it. Professor Lind treated her as she had always wished her brother would have. Professor Lind looked out for her and helped her like an older brother should.

And because of that she cared for him.

That realization had her taking another step back. She must not care for him. He was not her brother and never would be. It would be entirely inappropriate for her to think of him as such, to come to rely upon him in any degree.

Professor Lind's brows drew together. "I've done it again—made you uncomfortable."

She did not deny it but clasped her bonnet tight in her hands and looked past him. "It is no fault of yours. In addition to being continually haunted by the demons of my past, I am as unfamiliar with social etiquette as I am with French conjugation and chemical reactions."

"Would that I might banish your demons," he said quietly.

She wanted to believe that he could. But even if he did, what then? She wasn't like Molly, who wanted both an education and a husband. Esther had no reason to overcome her distrust of men, no reason to pursue even a friendship with Professor Lind—except that she wanted to. More than anything else at Bedford, she looked forward to his classes. Even algebra had become a favorite, during those weeks he substituted. She enjoyed his company, and a part of her wished to be free to enjoy it now, this very minute. If Molly were here with him, she certainly would and would know what to do and say.

"As for your inexperience with French, chemical reactions, and social etiquette . . ." Professor Lind's smile returned, wider this time and with a hint of mischief. "I find that all utterly delightful. The ability to converse with a woman as unpretentious as yourself is a relief to a stuffy professor like me, who is often only able to string together words having to do with a piece of literature."

"But I love to talk of literature," Esther exclaimed. "And I don't find you stuffy at all."

"In that case, will you allow me to accompany you on the long walk back to our carriage?" He turned aside and extended his elbow for her to take.

Esther hesitated. Was such a thing proper for a student and professor? Was his offer born of pity, because he had seen her watching the two women stroll thus? Was she not a fool to even consider being so close to him, to any man? Precious seconds passed, and his arm began to droop before she came to what she hoped was a reasonable compromise—one that would neither offend him too much nor put her in any real danger.

Hands still clasping her bonnet, Esther stepped slightly closer but made no move to take his arm. "I shall be grateful for the company. I believe we did not conclude our previous discussion about Pandora's Box."

His brow lifted at this, and she felt the irony of her statement. Was she not opening her own, figurative box of trouble in allowing any sort of personal friendship with Professor Lind? *John.* Esther recalled her first night at Bedford and how he had come gallantly to her rescue. He had been doing the same ever since. Perhaps he did so for other students as well, and it was her own, skewed perception that made it seem his attention to her went beyond the ordinary. Of course he would come looking for her today and would escort her back to the carriage. She was his responsibility, nothing more.

"We were at an impasse, I believe." Professor Lind began walking, arms swinging at his sides, as if that had been his intent all along. "Some members of the class felt that hope left imprisoned in the box was a further curse, in addition to the many evils Pandora released into the world. I, however, have always seen this differently. The evils released, while trials of sorrow, to be certain, also have the ability to make stronger characters of us—something highly valued in Greek culture. The gods, in their wisdom, would have known this to be the outcome of unleashing such evils. We would be forced to conquer, to rise above them."

"How does hope fit in with that theory?" Esther asked, walking beside him, near enough that they could converse easily, but far enough away that her unease faded. She thought him wrong on those points but wanted to understand his side, all the same.

"Its place at the bottom of the box was purposeful, so that in the event the box was opened—and it had to be, if we cast Pandora as analogous to Eve—hope would not be released, but kept safe, where it might not fade away and be lost, as the other items released must eventually. For even the sting of death is ultimately relinquished."

"It is there we disagree," Esther said. "The sting of my mother's death is still sharp these many years later. I felt it today—was feeling it keenly when you came upon me."

"So I believed." Professor Lind cast a somber glance at her. "Yet, have you not hope? Has the loss of your mother not made you stronger—made you into the fine woman that you have become? She had hope for you, and have you not had the same for yourself? Do you not have it still?"

Esther made no reply but walked in silence, considering. Perhaps he was right—partly. She did have hope, had carried it with her always as a sort of armor against the evils of her dismal station. Her mother had promised that if she continued to read, doors would be opened to her. Esther had clung to that promise, and it had come true.

"I do not expect that many will agree with me on this," he said. "The notion of Pandora's Box as a punishment from the gods has long been established. I only wished to propose the essay question—particularly regarding hope. Is its imprisonment within the box of evils a benefit for humanity, or was hope withheld as a further curse? I must admit I am eager to read your thoughts on the subject, Miss Sessions."

"As am I." Esther laughed. "*I* must admit to conflicted feelings on the matter, now that you have presented the other side so thoroughly."

"Then I have done my job well," he said. "The greatest learning takes place when our ideas are challenged and our horizons expanded."

"You have done remarkably well in that endeavor," Esther concurred, thinking more of the ways he was challenging her beliefs about men and expanding her horizon to include feelings she had never imagined or even known existed beyond the written word.

Chapter Ten

Dearest Lady Parker,

I so enjoy my midday walks around the square and beyond. The hour for luncheon immediately follows Professor Lind's literature class. I find that walking during this time allows me to ponder his lectures and digest them more thoroughly. What a treat they are!

John dismissed his last morning class, continuing his recently formed habit of bidding farewell to each of his students as they filed out—simply so he might have the opportunity for a few seconds' interaction with the one who intrigued him the most.

"Good day, Miss Sessions." He nodded as she crossed in front of him.

"Good day, Professor." She favored him with a smile, and then she was gone, out into the hall with the others.

His gaze wanted to follow her, but he forced himself not to look that direction and instead continued his acknowledgement of each of his other pupils. When the last had gone, he closed the door, then strode to the window, hoping for a glance of Miss Sessions as she made her way to the boarding house next door. Most days he was afforded one. But today she did not appear, and after several minutes, when the trickle of students exiting the building had concluded, he left the window and returned to his desk.

He sat before a stack of papers waiting to be read and graded—another meal alone with only his students' work to keep him company. Today he didn't even have Miss Sessions' essay to look forward to, among those he needed to grade. He had read her class's essays first, saving hers for the last among them, so as not to set the bar impossibly high for her peers. Her ideas and writing continued to inspire him, and it was impossible not to recognize her slanted, uneven script—equally impossible not to remember her grimace as she'd clenched the chalk and worked at the board. How he wished he might do something to ease her discomfort. But even had he known of a surgeon able to help her, it wasn't his place to suggest such a thing, and he didn't wish to cause her more anguish by once again bringing attention to her disfigured hand.

He had noted that she was conscious of it and, when not writing, kept that hand tucked out of sight in the folds of her skirts. He'd never heard any of the other students say anything disparaging about her injured finger, but that didn't mean that they hadn't. Whether they had or not, it seemed likely that Esther considered her hand just one more item on the long list that made her different from the other students at Bedford.

He unwrapped a cold meat pie and selected the top essay to read. As he leaned forward, reaching for pen and ink, his eyes fell upon a paper beneath the seat Miss Sessions had occupied. He stared at it a moment before deciding to investigate. John rose from his chair and walked to the third row of desks. He bent and reached beneath the one that was Miss Sessions', retrieving a single sheet.

Dearest Lady Parker,

John paused, knowing he ought not read the letter but

should return it to its owner at first opportunity. His eyes skimmed the page, searching for a signature and instead landed on his own name.

Professor Lind has challenged my perception on many subjects, not the least of which is—

He forced his eyes from the sentence to the bottom of the page and the signature he had expected, though the handwriting was somewhat improved over the papers he was used to from her.

— Yours ever gratefully, Esther.

He folded the paper quickly before he could give into temptation to read more. He would return the letter this very minute. His meat pie forgotten, John retrieved his hat and coat from the rack near the door, tucked the folded letter into a pocket, and strode from the room, eager for the opportunity to do something for Miss Sessions, to be of some minute assistance during her struggle here.

And it *was* a struggle for her. He'd spoken with the other professors and realized that her ability to express herself with the written word did not translate to the mathematical or scientific. French frustrated her. She found music impossible. He'd counted up the hours she spent each week in extra tutoring. He'd seen how long it took her to labor over words and sentences, with her hand cramping as it did.

She did not need a misplaced letter on top of everything else, particularly one that had likely taken her a great deal of time to write, somewhat neatly penned as it was.

John left the college and made the short walk next door to the boarding house. He was admitted by the housekeeper and shown to the dining room where Mrs. Lewis and her boarders—all but Miss Sessions—were enjoying a lively luncheon.

John apologized for interrupting and inquired as to her

whereabouts, stating clearly that he had something of hers to return.

Several sets of eyes—Mrs. Lewis's included—leveled on him. For a few seconds no one spoke.

"She's out on her noon walk. She goes most every day," Miss Williams said.

"She doesn't care much for our company," Miss Taylor added.

"That's not true," Miss Williams said. "Esther says she needs the cool air to clear her mind. Algebra makes it stuffy. Before she came to Bedford she used to walk several miles each day—of necessity. Continuing that habit now is no different from those of you who still go riding regularly or employ other habits you are accustomed to."

John shone an appreciative gaze upon her. Though her prattle on their outing and in class had, at times, annoyed him, he felt grateful for her many words just now, grateful that she had come to Esther's defense.

"If, during her long walks, Miss Sessions is able to clear her mind and formulate her thoughts for the marvelous essays she produces, then may I suggest you all consider joining her in stretching your legs." He tipped his hat and left them, wearing the coat which still held her unsent letter inside.

* * *

John guessed at which way she had gone and, after three quarters of an hour without a glimpse of Miss Sessions, knew he had guessed wrong. Disappointed, he returned to Bedford with barely time to gulp down his cold pie and begin his next class. The afternoon lingered, the hours passing more slowly than he could ever remember. He felt the letter—or the opportunity it could provide for him to see and perhaps briefly converse with Miss Sessions—beckoning him. His usual passion for the subject matter waned beneath its pull, and for the first time he questioned whether or not he ought to continue teaching.

At last the final bell rang and the students filed out. He forced himself to the door to bid them farewell, striving to give each class and pupil equal time and attention. He was trying—and failing as he never had. What was it about Esther Sessions that had upended his world so completely? The more time he spent with her, the more he wished to spend with her. The more he learned of her, the more fascinated he became.

It wasn't like him to be so interested in his students, so—*obsessed.* It wasn't natural—or was it? Were the feelings he was experiencing that most noble of all emotions that poets and playwrights had been writing of for centuries? *Love.* He'd never scoffed at the notion of romantic love, but neither had he experienced it. And if he was now, what was he to do about it? Miss Sessions was a pupil, in her first year at Bedford, no less, and he her professor and senior by many years. Such matches were not impossible, yet would this one not be? How could he remain at Bedford and hope to court her? Would she even wish to be courted by him? By any man? He knew her thoughts on the male sex. Her distrust and disdain rang through more than one of her essays. She cared not for men—past or present, fictitious or real. Yet she had not treated him poorly, but had gradually trusted him with little pieces of herself, from her injured hand to her—heart?

Suddenly he had to know what it was he had challenged her beliefs on. Had she merely been writing of Pandora's Box or any of the other Greek stories he had turned on their heads, encouraging his students to view the ancient myths from many different angles, or had she been speaking of something ... more?

He closed his classroom door and, instead of donning his coat, withdrew the folded paper from the pocket within. His hand trembled slightly as he carried it to his desk. With his chair facing toward the window, he unfolded the letter and began to read.

Dearest Lady Parker,

He wished he knew more about Esther's benefactress. What had she done—aside from providing educational opportunity to Esther—to earn the title "dearest"? *What might* I *do to earn it?*

Not wishing to read the entirety of the letter—he was wrong enough in his actions already—John's eyes skimmed to the paragraph where he had seen his name.

You asked that I tell you more of this Professor Lind whom I have mentioned frequently in my letters. Professor Lind has challenged my perception on many subjects, not the least of which is my belief that all men are evil creatures. I still believe that most are inherently short of temper and prone to violence. Most regard women as little more than property which they may abuse at their leisure. But I can no longer state unequivocally that all men are representative of such traits. Professor Lind is living proof. He is the antithesis of these men. He is soft-spoken and kind. He is a good listener and knows how to argue a point without being argumentative. He cares deeply for all of his students and does all in his power to help them succeed. I have never met anyone like him.

Though I am still resolved in my course to live independently and never marry, I feel I might change my mind, were circumstances different, and I had the opportunity to be courted by a good man like Professor Lind. I am grateful to know there are at least a few in this world. Mrs. Reid tells me her husband was also one of them.

As for your unwritten—yet still felt—concern, you need not worry. All is well at Bedford. My mind is focused where it ought to be, and if Professor Lind has touched my heart, it is no fault of his, but merely my astonishment at seeing a man so completely different from any I had met previously. I will endeavor to mention less of him in my letters and perhaps more of my amusing roommate, Molly.

John folded the letter before he could intrude anymore on Esther's privacy. He was wrong to have read what he did, yet he could not feel entirely bad for it. He had wondered if the connection he felt with Esther was at all reciprocated, or if he was simply getting old and his long-dormant heart had finally sprung to life, awoken by a most unusual woman. A strong and courageous woman. One who deserved love more than anyone he could imagine.

Were circumstances different...

Did she really mean it? And if so, what did that mean for him? He could not continue on at Bedford and hope to take her on so much as a drive around London. But Bedford had been his life and livelihood for so long. Teaching was all he knew, and despite his restlessness this afternoon, it was all he loved. All he had loved—until now.

Chapter Eleven

My Dear Esther,

I was most pleased (though not at all surprised) to hear you were selected to recite at the upcoming concert. There is no need to fret over your lack of musical ability when you have the gift of bringing poetry to life so beautifully. I regret that I cannot accept your invitation to attend. London is too far, and these bones of mine too old and frail . . .

"I've just the baubles for you." Molly dug through the top drawer of her bureau excitedly. She produced a set of amber teardrop earrings that were a close match to Esther's gown. She stepped close and fastened one on each of Esther's earlobes. "There. Look in the mirror and see if they aren't perfect."

Still wincing from the unexpected pinch of the earrings, Esther stepped to the bureau and peered into the narrow mirror atop it. The woman staring back at her was hardly recognizable, her eyes more golden than brown, and with her hair parted down the middle and swept back into a chignon from which clusters of small curls emerged. A bit of fancy lace topped off the elegant style. The teardrop earrings did match the gown, which shimmered in the light streaming from the lamp on her desk.

"One thing more." Molly took Esther by the shoulders and turned her so they were facing one another. "A touch of face powder, to cover your freckles."

"I won't look like myself," Esther protested, but Molly was already busy dabbing her cheeks. When she'd finished, Esther turned to the mirror once more, surprised again at the woman staring back at her. Molly's application had been subtle, and Esther couldn't deny that it was a nice addition. She'd never minded her freckles, but without them she looked more like the other women at Bedford. Perhaps she would have to take some of her pin money and purchase some face powders of her own.

"Thank you," she said, turning once more to Molly. "Without your help I'd be a mess."

Molly shook her head. "Nothing about you is a mess, Esther Sessions. You have a quiet grace about you that doesn't require a fancy gown or curls. Just be yourself tonight, and you'll outshine us all."

Esther laughed. "I've no intention of doing any such thing, nor is it possible. I've heard you sing and Charlotte's pianoforte."

"At least hold your head up and be proud," Molly insisted. "There are many kinds of art, and yours will be a beautiful contribution." She blew out the lamp, then followed Esther out to the hallway.

Outside their room the other residents were talking excitedly, fancy gowns and crinolines swishing this way and that as they made for the stairs.

"Aren't we the jammiest bits of jam," Molly exclaimed, twirling in a circle in a crimson gown that seemed to match her bold personality.

"I think I should prefer to be considered afternoonified," Abigail said, looking as solemn as Esther felt.

Her stomach churned as if a dozen frogs were leaping about in a frenzy of nerves. She was frightened and excited—both in ways she'd never experienced before. In the past her fear had been of physical danger. She'd been afraid of her father's temper and his hand. She'd been afraid when walking alone on the streets after dark. She'd been afraid of starving or freezing during those long weekends when her father spent all their money on drink instead of food or coal.

Her fear tonight should have paled in comparison, and she told herself it must, reminding herself that she had endured many difficult experiences, and reciting in front of a crowd need not be one of them. Indeed, it ranked as trivial. Yet her nerves would not be quelled.

Bedford's packed hall did not help. The students had each been allowed to invite two guests to the evening's performance, and it appeared that most of them had. Esther felt torn between wishing Lady Parker was here to see her, to being grateful she was not—in the event the evening ended in disaster.

The concert began, and it became impossible not to be caught up in the performances. Molly's voice was indeed angelic, and the keys of the pianoforte trilled with the most glorious music imaginable. Esther sat spellbound, enraptured with it all, until a gentle nudge from Mrs. Lewis reminded her that it was almost her turn to go on.

Pretending composure that she did not feel, Esther rose from her seat and made her way to the side of the room, awaiting her turn on the dais. When it came—all too soon—she calmly ascended the steps, holding up the heavy skirt of the fine gown Lady Parker had sent for the occasion.

Esther faced the audience, a sea of faces both familiar and strange, took a deep breath, and began. "'Aurora Leigh, be humble. Shall I hope / To speak my poems in mysterious tune

/ With man and nature..."' She had chosen to recite from the fifth book of Elizabeth Barrett Browning's *Aurora Leigh*. It had seemed appropriate to select a piece written by a woman, as Bedford was a women's college, and Esther loved the lilt and sway of Browning's poetic tale. She identified with the characters—Aurora, who had lost her mother at an early age, and Marian, who was both abused and self-taught.

"'In token of the harvest-time of flowers?

> With winters and with autumns—and beyond
> With the human heart's large seasons, when it hopes

And fears, joys, grieves, and loves?'"

The lines that came next made her grateful for the face powder, as she felt a flush creep up her cheeks at the intimate words. Esther's gaze drifted from the back of the large room to the front and caught Professor Lind's stare—what she could only describe as enraptured—as he looked up at her from the middle of the front row. Her voice faltered a moment, then continued strong, her mind withdrawing from her surroundings and into the depths of the poem. Her voice infused with passion as she spoke Browning's words.

> "'We women are too apt to look to One,
> Which proves a certain impotence in art.
> We strain our natures at doing something great,
> Far less because it's something great to do,
> Than, haply, that we, so, commend ourselves
> As being not small, and more appreciable
> To some one friend.'"

Professor Lind's eyes held hers in a second of

recognition, as if to say he appreciated her efforts and would be honored if she would consider him a friend. She continued on, her heart practically singing the memorized lines.

> "'How dreary 't is for women to sit still
> On winter nights by solitary fires
> And hear the nations praising them far off,
> Too far! Ay, praising our quick sense of love,
> Our very heart of passionate womanhood,
> Which could not beat so in the verse without
> Being present also in the unkissed lips,
> And eyes undried because there's none to ask
> The reason they grew moist.'"

Her own eyes were moist and her mouth dry by the time she finished. When Professor Lind jumped from his seat and began clapping vigorously, and the audience followed, Esther felt her tears spill over. She curtsied gracefully, then hurried from the stage, making her way to the back of the room, as the strains of violin began. She sagged against the back wall in relief. She had done it. She had performed in front of not only the women and professors of Bedford College, but their families as well. And they had clapped for her.

"As I knew you would, you stole the stage this evening."

Esther stiffened at the familiar, *male* voice so close behind her. What did Professor Lind mean, approaching her like that? He knew her previous discomfort at being too close to him. And couldn't he see that she was being included in a cluster of other students as she hadn't been previously—not since those first few, awkward days when they had discovered there was something odd—or many things odd—about her?

Since then, of necessity and to ease her discomfort, Esther had spent most of her free time in the reading room, in tutoring sessions, or studying by herself at the residence hall. Molly alone had seemed to realize that Esther wasn't standoffish. She'd merely been trying to survive in a world so dissimilar to what she was accustomed to.

But tonight she had thrived. The long hours, days, and weeks spent memorizing this evening's recitation had paid off, and she was receiving as much praise as the others who had performed.

She sensed Professor Lind's continued presence behind her, imagined that dizzying feeling sweeping her up was due to the enticing aroma of his cologne, and that his gaze bore the same intensity she had witnessed during her performance. Her heart thundered at the thought of it. She couldn't ignore him. She didn't want to and had him to thank for even being allowed to participate tonight. As politely and discreetly as possible, she excused herself from the conversation between three of the other students and their guests.

"Professor." She gave a nod of acknowledgment as she faced him and felt the thread of tension reach out and snag her. He *was* looking at her as he had earlier this evening. The blue of his eyes appeared deeper, and the smile that made him look closer to her own age was nowhere to be seen. His expression, while not somber, might be called peculiar—anxious, perhaps, yet at the same time insistent. She'd no idea what to make of it.

He spoke in an odd tone as well. "I was beginning to think I would have to wait until Monday's class to congratulate you on an outstanding performance."

His approving smile at the end of her recitation, along with his standing ovation, had been congratulations enough.

"Any success is owed to you and Lady Parker—she for

constant corrections to my pronunciation and speech during the many years I read to her, and to you for the opportunity to perform this evening. Charlotte told me it was you who argued that I should be given the chance." Gratitude swelled within Esther once more, yet it did not make up the whole of feelings encompassing her heart, encircling it and infusing her with warmth. The thread of tension between them tightened and arced. Something felt—different. Altered from their previous interactions, both in the classroom and without.

"You deserved to be given every chance, to be given everything." Professor Lind's expression remained serious. "Would that I might offer it. I cannot, and yet neither can I help my—" He broke off as another student and her guest moved past. Leaning closer to Esther, he asked, "I wonder if I might have a word with you—privately."

She nodded, more curious as to what he had been about to say than fearful of being alone with him. Surely he didn't mean to take her far.

But he did take her hand—rather boldly—and pulled her off to the far corner of the room, away from the clusters of people visiting, away from the table of refreshments that had been set out. Once there he released her and placed himself in the corner, with Esther on the outside—a courtesy she both noted and appreciated. She wasn't trapped here, and they weren't truly alone. She was in no danger. Or none of a physical nature, at least.

Professor Lind lowered his voice. "Tonight when you spoke, it felt as if you were addressing me and no one else. Am I imagining this, Esther?"

Cornered or not, she felt caught. The use of her given name made her wish she'd a bonnet to grasp onto and hold out as armor. "I saw you up front," she offered feebly.

"You saw *through* me," he corrected. "Through the

professor and into the man, the one who has not been able to keep you from his mind since he first laid eyes upon you."

Esther's lips parted in astonishment at his confession, but she had no idea how to respond.

"*Never* have I felt about another student—about any other woman, student or not—the way I feel about you. You inspire me to try to be better than I am in every way possible. I stand in awe of your strength and all that you have overcome. I look forward to every word you speak and every sentence you write. And tonight, with your selection, it seemed—I felt—" He broke off, but there was an almost pleading look in his eyes. "If I have been mistaken, I apologize, and I will not bother you again. I only wish to know. I must know if you feel the same about me. Perhaps not as intently, but enough that you might consider—"

"Professor, you mustn't keep this evening's star all to yourself. There are others here who wish to meet her." Mrs. Reid appeared at Esther's side, saving her from having to answer and from herself. Professor Lind's confession had been near to prompting one of her own—that she *had* been thinking of him tonight, that she thought of him often and looked forward to his lectures in a way that, even in her limited experience, seemed not natural or usual for a student.

What it meant, she wasn't entirely certain. But where it could lead was absolute. Disaster and heartache, if not something much worse, might await her if she started down that slippery slope. She must not—must not think of him, or care for him, must not trust either of their feelings. *A passing fancy, nothing more,* Lady Parker would surely say—after she'd had Esther's head for even contemplating the idea of a relationship with him. Esther would do well to remember that she had been sent to Bedford for an education, to forge a future in which she might provide for herself.

Alone. Without any man to complicate her life or condemn her to the misery her mother had known. *He would not—* She abandoned the thought before it could fully form. Of course Professor Lind would not act as her father had. She had been observing him for three months and had never seen any sign of temper. But to imagine possibilities of happiness would only serve to make her more miserable than she suddenly felt. She had been wrong to indulge her feelings at all.

"Excuse us, Professor." Esther tried to convey both regret and rejection with her eyes. Then, with her spine stiffened and without a backward glance at him, she allowed Mrs. Reid to lead her to the group of trustees gathered near the stage.

Chapter Twelve

"Have you heard?" Abigail slipped onto the stool beside Esther at the long counter in the chemistry laboratory.

"That I failed last week's lab?" Esther frowned at the list of ingredients on the paper in front of her. She was doing better on exams—she could memorize even if she didn't completely understand—but continued to struggle with the weekly experiments. She might recall the properties of the various substances and liquids but often incorrectly predicted what would happen when combining them.

"You didn't fail. It was just a little messy, that's all," Abigail said—a gross understatement of the overflowing disaster Esther had caused by accidentally switching two ingredients. "I meant, have you heard the news about Professor Lind?"

Esther felt her heart lurch. She swiveled on her seat to face Abigail.

"He's left Bedford. He's not teaching here anymore."

"What?" Esther gripped the counter, afraid she might fall off her stool.

Abigail nodded. "He'd been here over six years too. But he gave his resignation after the concert Friday night. No one knows why."

Esther knew why. Or she thought she did. If Mrs. Reid had overheard him—if she had believed he was pursuing a relationship with a student . . . What if he hadn't resigned at all? What if he had been dismissed?

Professor Adams entered the room and called the class to attention. Esther gathered her materials in silence, all while fighting a sick feeling in the pit of her stomach and wanting to go somewhere by herself so she could cry. He couldn't be gone. He hadn't even said goodbye.

But then, neither had she when she'd left him standing alone in a corner Friday night.

The remaining three weeks of the term seemed to pass more slowly than the first three months had. Literature class went from being her favorite to her least favorite, as the guest lecturers lacked the passion and excitement that Professor Lind's had.

Twice Esther had nearly approached Mrs. Reid, to confess her part in Professor Lind's dismissal, for Esther felt certain that he had been dismissed. He loved teaching and would not have given it up so abruptly. She felt guilty and responsible, though she hadn't exactly done anything wrong. Neither had Professor Lind. His brief words the evening of the concert had been only that—words. Neither of them had acted on whatever it was they had supposed they felt. Feelings that Esther was dismayed to find did not diminish during the last lonely weeks of term, though she tried to banish them by throwing every bit of herself into her studies.

"Come with us," Molly had pled one Saturday afternoon in mid December. "We're going Christmas shopping. It will cheer you up. You've had the morbs far too long."

Esther had shaken her head. She had no one to shop for

except Lady Parker, and the best gift she could give her was to do well on exams.

It was with great relief and excellent marks in nearly every subject that Esther boarded the train to Liverpool a few days before Christmas. While the other students spoke excitedly of going home to see their families, friends, and even beaus, Esther did not feel any great sentiment toward Liverpool or Wayburn. Her room at Bedford felt as much a home as any place ever had, with Molly more of a friend than she'd ever been blessed with before.

The train arrived at three o'clock in the afternoon, and a carriage was waiting to drive her to Wayburn. When she alighted in front of the house, Esther still wore her bonnet and even accepted assistance from the footman. Lady Parker stood on the front step, leaning not on her cane, but on two servants, one on either side. She met Esther's gaze with a look of approval, and Esther felt a rush of gratitude for her benefactress. Lady Parker had never been particularly affectionate toward her, but she had demonstrated love and generosity.

Forgetting decorum, Esther gathered her skirts in her gloved hands and hurried up the steps. She paused in front of Lady Parker and leaned forward, placing a kiss upon the old woman's cheek.

"What's this?" she exclaimed. "Taught you how to kiss at that college, have they?"

Esther nearly laughed. It wasn't like Lady Parker to jest. "Of course not. I'm just happy to see you."

"You'd best get me inside before you're seeing me on my knees. I haven't been outside since you left."

"Not at all?" Esther stepped back as the servants turned Lady Parker around and assisted her into the house. Her legs moved very slowly, and she seemed to tremble more with each step. Once inside, they helped her into the parlor, into a chair lined with large, fluffy pillows.

Lady Parker's hands shook as they rested on the arms of the chair. "I've had a telegram from Mrs. Reid apprising me of your first-term grades."

Esther held back a scowl, wishing she might have been the one to share that news. "Chemistry is not my forte." She had passed, but barely.

"Perhaps not, but it seems nearly every other subject is. Your marks were all quite good, even French and algebra improved, I was pleased to see."

"I worked hard," Esther said, relieved Lady Parker did not seem disappointed in her.

"So I've heard. Mrs. Reid says you are the finest of students, and she is exceptionally pleased to have you at Bedford. As you know, your acceptance there was on a trial basis and as a personal favor to me."

Esther hadn't known and felt grateful for that. She couldn't have imagined feeling more pressure to succeed than she'd felt already.

"But now the trial is over, and you have passed." Lady Parker seemed to sag in her chair, as if her speech had sapped the last of her strength.

Esther stood and reached for one of the blankets frequently draped over the arm of the sofa when they read. The high-ceilinged room was notoriously drafty, its lone fireplace too far removed from the furniture to provide any real warmth.

With a start, Esther realized much of that furniture was missing. The blankets, too, were gone. She looked slowly around the room, noticing the bare walls and floors. Even the large rugs were missing.

"Lady Parker," Esther said, alarmed.

Lady Parker's eyes flickered open. "What is it?"

"Where have your belongings gone? The furniture and paintings and rugs?"

An Unexpected Education

"Sold." Lady Parker's mouth puckered smugly. "All of them. Just a few essentials left for that nephew of mine to inherit. I'd do without those if I could. The money has gone too—most to the college, though I have set aside enough for your expenses until you have completed your education. I decided not to leave you more than that."

"You don't have to leave me anything." Esther hadn't really believed Lady Parker when she had promised an inheritance several months ago. "And if my education is so costly that you must give your possessions away, then I should prefer not to return to Bedford."

"Of course you will return," Lady Parker scolded. "Enough podsnappery. A gentlewoman does not argue. I can do what I wish with my money, and I have. Do not be ungrateful for it. After I'm gone my nephew will get the estate and everything tied to it. I'm simply ensuring that precious little is left when I go."

"But surely you want to live in comfort until then," Esther pled.

"Comfort is knowing Jackson won't get it and that no man will pursue you for your money. Besides, I'm not long for this world."

"Don't say that." Esther rushed to her side. "You've just missed my reading is all. You wait and see, I'll have you up and about and arguing with me about Dickens in no time." She clasped Lady Parker's frail hand in hers, disbelieving. How had the woman aged so in only a few months?

"Time to dress for dinner," Lady Parker said, ignoring Esther's protests. "We have guests, and I've a surprise for you, so wear something nice—the dress you wore to the concert. It's time you meet the man who is going to inherit Wayburn."

Chapter Thirteen

Esther dressed for dinner with care, looking much as she had the night of the concert, with the exception of Molly's earrings. She didn't mind their absence. Her earlobes had been sore for two days after.

From the maid who attended her, Esther had learned that Lady Parker had invited her nephew to come tonight, so that he would be aware of the condition of the estate and all that he would *not* be receiving upon her death.

"She doesn't want any trouble for you after she's gone," Lily said in a hushed tone. "Or for any of the rest of us. She's already given us letters of reference and set aside a year's salary for each—can you believe it? An entire *year*. We're not to receive it until she passes. The steward has our envelopes now. Then we're each to be dismissed, so as to not have to work for her nephew. Downstairs is abuzz with talk of the man. We all cannot wait to see him. From Lady Parker's description, you'd think he has horns like the devil."

Esther took all this in quietly, her reflection in the dressing table mirror contemplative. "Surely Lady Parker does not think to leave us anytime soon."

"Her shaking palsy has only worsened since you left us. The doctor said the medicines are no longer working—and there's nothing more can be done. She seems to have lost her will to overcome it since you left."

"I should never have gone to London." Esther winced as Lily tucked another pin in her hair. "I should have stayed here and kept her company, kept reading to her."

"She has missed that. She might have advertised for another companion, seeing as none of us belowstairs can read as you can. But she never did. It's you she fancies."

Esther turned in her seat and clasped Lily's hands. "I have been most fortunate, but I do not count myself better than anyone in this house—above or belowstairs. You do know that, don't you?"

The maid nodded slowly. "I do, Miss, but others talk..." Esther sighed. She had suspected as much, had felt the undercurrent of tension between her and her former, fellow employees during the summer months when Lady Parker lavished tutors and attention upon her. Esther had loathed seeing the footman carrying the boxes of her new wardrobe up to her room, had felt ashamed and traitorous when the maids assisted the dressmaker during her visits. It was wrong to do so for her. She was an imposter all over again—an even worse one than she had been at school. At least at Bedford, in the end, she had been able to prove she belonged.

Dreading the evening to come, she descended the stairs, unable to enjoy the opportunity to wear the beautiful gown once more, and not appreciating the heavenly aromas wafting from the kitchen. A year ago she wouldn't have believed this possible, would have given much for one simple end of a fresh loaf. How was it she could feel miserable when she was now so richly blessed?

There seemed only one solution to remedy her spirit. She must not return to Bedford, but must resume her prior position here and care for Lady Parker. To have had one, glorious term at school was more than she ever could have dreamed of. She had not seen the Crystal Palace, but she had walked where it once stood. She had not been brave enough to return Professor Lind's kindnesses, but she had felt them. It was enough. It would have to be, and she would be content. She would tell Lady Parker of her decision tonight, after her nephew had left. Perhaps with Esther's care, Lady Parker would not be turning her estate over to him as soon as she believed.

Two gentlemen, both facing away from her, were seated in the drawing room when Esther entered. Lady Parker looked up to greet her, and one rose at once, turning toward Esther.

She gasped, as did he.

"Professor—"

"Miss Sessions."

She reached for the nearest chair to steady herself as Lady Parker's shrewd gaze drifted between them.

"May I present my nephew, Jackson Lind—and his son, John. Though, it seems, you may already be acquainted with one another."

"I—had the honor of teaching Miss Sessions this semester." The professor's voice seemed to match the tremble of Lady Parker's hands. "She was a most remarkable student."

Professor Lind is Lady Parker's loathsome nephew's son. Disappointment—no, despair swept through Esther. She glanced at Lady Parker and caught the look of satisfaction upon her face.

She knew. Esther thought of all the times she had mentioned Professor Lind in her letters and felt grateful that at least the one in which she had come closest to confessing her feelings about him had never been sent. That she had misplaced it now seemed most fortunate, though, at the time, it had been troubling. And thank goodness she had not answered Professor Lind's plea the night of the concert.

He had played her for the fool enough already. Despite his look of astonishment, he had to have known who she was. She had mentioned Lady Parker to him on more than one occasion. He had to have known about her—and her money.

What was it Lady Parker had said this afternoon after telling Esther she was not going to leave her an inheritance after all? *No man will pursue you for your money.*

Somehow Lady Parker had known John Lind was attempting to do just that.

"It is a pleasure, Miss Sessions." Jackson Lind had finally risen from his seat and now bowed his head low before her—mocking, no doubt. When he rose once more and gazed upon her, she felt both revulsion and fear. His eyes, yellowed and bloodshot, held the same look her father's had when he had been drinking. His smirk made her want to scream.

Did they realize how close to success their scheme had come? If she had given into her feelings for Professor Lind, if—heaven forbid—he had courted her and she had agreed to marry him, then the inheritance she would have had—Lady Parker's money—would have become his.

Or perhaps they had not been that close to success at all. Lady Parker had not forgotten what men were. It was Esther who had nearly succumbed, who might have ruined her life had she completely trusted Professor Lind. He had never cared for her at all. She'd merely been a means to an end—to his great aunt and her fortune.

Esther could feel no satisfaction that he had failed. Instead, to her great dismay, she felt tears building behind her eyes. Her throat had swollen, so that she could hardly swallow, let alone speak. She could not endure another minute, let alone hours, in this company.

"Please excuse me. I am unwell." Disregarding all that Lady Parker had taught her about decorum and manners, Esther turned and fled the room.

Chapter Fourteen

My Dearest Esther,
I have done something I hope you will not have cause to regret...

Esther ran toward the stairs, wanting an entire floor and a locked door between herself and Jackson and John Lind.

"Miss Sessions—Esther—please wait!"

The sound of her name from John Lind's mouth hastened her tears. Her room wasn't far enough away. She needed to be out of this house, away from him entirely. She needed to be far from anywhere the charlatan Professor Lind was. Her heart felt as if it was breaking all over again, fragile and bruised as it had been since he had left the school without saying goodbye. Of course he had left his post abruptly—in pursuit of other, more lucrative financial ventures.

What she wouldn't give now to have never seen him again, to have never known of his deception.

Esther ran to the front hall, then out the door and down the steps.

"Your carriage is ready, Miss," the footman said.

She hadn't called for a carriage—perhaps Lady Parker had ordered it to take the vile nephew and his son back where they had come from. They would have to take another.

Esther hurried across the drive and into the waiting

vehicle. The door closed behind her, and shivering, she took up the blanket waiting on the seat. She hadn't thought to bring a cloak—hadn't planned on going out.

The carriage lingered another minute or two, all the while she sat worrying she would be found out. At last it lurched forward, then stopped again briefly, rocked, and started once more. She had no idea where it was taking her, and she didn't care. She had escaped Professor Lind and his confused, concerned gaze. How good he was at lying! Even now she wanted to believe he was innocent and that he had not known who she was. *Impossible.* Esther buried her face in her hands and wept.

A great deal of time—enough that her tears were spent—passed before the carriage stopped. Esther parted the curtains and peered out, dismayed to see the front of Liverpool's St. George's Hall.

"Bother." She frowned and waited for the door to open. She would simply tell the driver to take her back to Wayburn again. At the least she could hope that Lady Parker's guests had departed before her return.

The step lowered, and the door opened.

"Miss Sessions?" *His* voice.

Esther pressed against the seat, sinking into the darkness.

A hand appeared, holding a lantern, illuminating the inside of the carriage. A second later Professor Lind's head followed.

"Lady Parker asked me to give this to you." He extended the hand with the lantern inside the carriage, her cloak draped over it.

Esther took it from him and wrapped it around herself but did not say anything. It seemed highly doubtful that Lady Parker would trust him with so much as a button, let alone

Esther's cloak. So how had he come to have it? What was he doing here, anyway? And how had he arrived? Had he followed her?

"May I assist you?"

"You may close the door. I am not going anywhere."

He paused. "Are you certain? I was led to believe you were to attend a reading from Dickens this evening?"

Esther's eyes widened. Then she looked up at him sharply. Another trick of his, no doubt.

"Lady Parker said to tell you the tickets are in the carriage. In an envelope on the seat, I believe."

"I've seen no envelope." She wasn't going to be fooled by him again.

He held the lantern higher, as if to help her search. "There—on the floor near your feet."

Esther looked down and saw that he was right. A folded paper lay beside her on the far side of the carriage—too far away from the door for him to have placed it there. She still didn't trust him.

She bent, picked up the paper and unfolded it. Two tickets for *A Christmas Carol* fell into her lap. She lifted one closer to the light and read—incredulously—that Dickens himself was to play the part of Scrooge. She clutched the tickets to her heart, overcome with the prospect of seeing him on stage and hearing from his lips one of her favorite stories. It was one of Lady Parker's as well.

"But where is she?" Esther stared at him. "Where is Lady Parker? What have you done with her? There are two tickets here."

He hesitated before answering. "I am to accompany you."

Esther shook her head. "She would never do such a thing. She does not trust men." *Wisely.*

"She also said that you would say that. I am to tell you to

read the letter that came with the tickets." He nodded to the paper still open on her lap.

Esther leaned toward the lantern, but he withdrew. "May I join you inside? It is a cold night, and it was quite a miserable drive up top."

For the first time she noted that his hair and shirt and tie were damp. It appeared he had no hat or overcoat with him. Behind him snowflakes drifted down in the light of the streetlamps in front of the theatre.

"You may come in," she said. She was not fond of the idea but did not wish to be responsible for his freezing to death. She scooted to the far side of the carriage, and he climbed in, pulling the door shut behind him and shivering.

She offered the blanket. "I have my cloak now."

He hesitated, but she thrust it at him. It was large enough they could have shared, but she was already compromised enough, being alone in a carriage with him.

"Read your letter," he urged, teeth chattering as he held the lantern out for her. She took it from him, so as not to be so near to him, and began to read.

My Dearest Esther,

I have done something I hope you will not have cause to regret. With Elizabeth Reid's assistance I have spent the past month and a half investigating your Mr. Lind. Imagine my surprise when I learned of his familial ties! I had not known Jackson was a father, and indeed it seems he was not much of one. At the time I requested that he and his son visit, he had not spoken to John in several years. By all accounts, it would seem John is the opposite of his father—much like you are the opposite of yours—and is a good man who works hard at his profession.

Still not in favor of the attention he seemed to be giving you or of your growing attraction, I asked Mrs. Reid to intervene, to keep an eye out for you. I did not want you to suffer as your mother or I had, did not want to see your opportunities thrown away. Elizabeth did as I requested, interrupting what she believed to be a rather intimate and important conversation the night of the concert. She later confronted your Mr. Lind regarding it, and he confessed to her his love for you. He resigned his post that very night, planning to pursue other employment so he might be free in the future to seek a courtship with you.

Elizabeth shared all of this with me, and still I disapproved, certain he knew of the inheritance I planned to leave you. I felt vastly relieved he had left Bedford until she reported to me your melancholy the last weeks of school. So great was her concern that you were not sleeping or eating and would work yourself to death trying to please me and forget Professor Lind, that she paid me a visit—came all the way to Liverpool by train, and her an old woman like me.

She has convinced me of John Lind's true character and that—as you so eloquently wrote in the letter she brought to me—all men are not the vile creatures of our previous experiences.

Perhaps, as with Scrooge in Mr. Dickens' story, I had a lesson to learn. Before you came into my life, it was empty and bleak, in spite of my wealth. I was safe, secure—and very lonely. My hopes and dreams for you gave me new life and a purpose for which to exist. But I have filled that now, and I am soon to leave this world—and you. And I do not wish to leave you alone. I wish for you to have the happiness Elizabeth knew in her marriage, to have love. I believe you will find this with your Professor Lind, and I give you my blessing to do so.

Enjoy the play. I expect you both to give me a full report at breakfast tomorrow. I have sent Jackson packing but invited John to stay for Christmas.

Your ever grateful friend,
Lady Amelia Parker

P.S. I suspect you may not believe that your Mr. Lind is an innocent in this. So I have changed my will, leaving you nothing but the means, already entrusted to the school, to continue your education. Should Mr. Lind realize this—and still profess and prove his devotion to you—I should think that a good indication of his character. I was wrong, Esther. Not all men are evil. You were right. A few, like your Mr. Lind, are kind and good.

Esther read the letter twice, too shocked the first time to completely grasp what Lady Parker was telling her. Even with a second reading, it did not seem possible. The coincidence was too great. He could not be innocent.

"Lady Parker writes to share with me that these tickets are my Christmas present. She is not leaving me any funds whatsoever."

"I am sorry to hear that," Professor Lind said.

"Of course you are. You wished to have those monies, but she has withdrawn them so no man will ever pursue me for my inheritance." Esther leaned forward and made to move past him out of the carriage, but his arm across the door barred her way.

"What do you mean to do?" she demanded, giving him her coldest glare. "Will you hold me hostage in Lady Parker's carriage? Ransom me? Do you think to get her money in that way?"

"I do not wish to take anyone's money," he said somberly, while still blocking the door. "I knew nothing of Lady Parker before yesterday morn, when a summons came for me. I did not know of your association with her until this evening. I was as much surprised as you. Perhaps more so when she bade me follow you and 'win your heart.'"

Esther sank back onto her seat, arms folded across her middle, letter and tickets clutched in her hand. "How am I to believe that?"

"I do not know." His voice was quiet. "I have only my word to prove my innocence, only my past deeds to convince you of my character—and there is one deed I must confess."

Esther stared at him, wondering what his confession might be when she had already seen, with her own eyes, that he had tricked her.

"I found a letter you had written to Lady Parker, and I read it." He closed his eyes, as if he could not bear to see her reaction to such news.

"What letter? What did it say?" Esther demanded, though she believed she knew. There was only the one she had lost . . .

"You wrote to Lady Parker that I had changed your perception about many things—including men. You said that if circumstances were different, you might consider—you might wish to be courted by me."

"Someone like you," Esther corrected, curtly. "I believe that was the phrasing I used." He had read her letter! The most private letter she had ever penned.

"I am sorry," he said. "It was wrong of me. I have no excuse but that I wished to know if I had any hope, if there was any possibility that you returned my feelings."

A few short weeks ago she had. But now . . . she wasn't certain. Her past had reared its head again, and she was frightened.

"Esther." He leaned forward in earnest appeal. "May I call you that, please? It is a lovely, noble name."

"My father said I was named after a woman who groveled before a king and did what women do best—fed a man and plied him for favors with her body."

"No." John drew back, as if shocked at such blasphemous

interpretation. "Esther is a true heroine. Her courage saved her people from death. She was wise, faithful, and brave—very much like you."

Esther had believed she was all cried out, but a fresh set of tears gathered in her eyes at his tender words. "Thank you," she whispered. *John.* His name was that of a biblical hero too, a follower of Christ, a fisher of men, a doer of good. Until now she had believed it fit him so well. "I would like to save my people. I wish I could."

"What do you mean?" He was leaning forward again, and this time she did not wish him away.

"I want to help the very poor, those like me who face death every day, from the factories, the cold, the hunger. They are doomed to a life of misery, with no way out—unless someone teaches them to read, as my mother taught me."

"Are you thinking of a school?" he asked, excitement and possibility in his voice. "A school for the poorest children—boys and girls?"

"Yes. I think so," Esther said. She had thought of this before but had never formulated a plan completely.

"And you would teach," he continued. "You *would* save your people. You *will.*"

She shrugged. "It is only a dream." She looked up at him sharply. "I have no funds for a school."

"Thanks to me." He sounded sorry—not for himself, but for her.

"And you have no employment—thanks to me." Was she, too, not a little guilty of wrongdoing? What would have happened, had she given him an honest answer, one that came from the center of her heart and being, that night?

A half smile lit his face, and her heart caught. She had missed those smiles, had missed him. How she wished they could go back to when he was simply Professor Lind, and she his student, and there had been no connection to Lady Parker.

"I will find another position," he said. "But I fear I will never find another woman . . . like you, Esther." His face wore that same vulnerable, anxious expression it had the night of the concert. Suddenly she wished she *could* go back and tell him that she cared for him.

"Mr. Dickens will not wait all night," John said, glancing at the tickets in her hand. "Will you allow me to accompany you? For this night, at least? After that, if you wish it, I will leave and never return to bother you again."

"You do not bother. You have never bothered." She bit her lip. To admit she cared for him was to take a terrible risk. *Much as he has taken in leaving his position at Bedford? At following me here, after I ran away from him?* Esther swallowed and tried to summon her namesake's courage. "I would like it very much if you would accompany me tonight—John."

His answering smile warmed her as nothing else might. After throwing aside the blanket, he grasped the handle and pushed open the door, then stepped out as Esther fastened her cloak. When he offered her his hand she accepted it. And when he kept it, tucking it into the crook of his arm, she did not object.

Chapter Fifteen

"He was the most amazing Scrooge." Esther tried her best, for the third time in as many days, to explain Dickens' voice and his mannerisms and expressions to Lady Parker. "It was as if—he had written the character himself!"

"Indeed," Lady Parker said, a twinkle in her eye that had not been there a few days ago. Though she had not attended the play with them, she seemed to enjoy Esther's excited retelling of it very much. John's imitations of Marley and The Ghost of Christmas Past had seemed to please her immensely too, as did the long, literary discussions and debates the three of them had enjoyed.

Esther laughed, then threw up her hands in defeat. "Dickens was simply too marvelous for words. Now that I realize he reads at Liverpool, next year you shall have to come and see him yourself."

"Next year . . ." Lady Parker's voice trailed off. "Is a long time away. And I am a tired old woman. I'll leave you now. These bones must be off to bed."

At her words, the two manservants waiting by the door sprang into motion, moving swiftly toward her and lifting either side of her chair.

"Goodnight," Esther called.

"Thank you for a lovely Christmas," John added.

"It isn't over yet," Lady Parker said, tilting her head and looking toward the ceiling near the doorway as they carted her off. Esther followed her gaze to the sprig of mistletoe hung there. When she glanced at John, in the chair beside her, she saw that his eyes were upon it too.

"I wonder where that came from," he said, standing and tugging Esther up beside him.

"I am certain I don't know," she said. "Lady Parker is too practical for such nonsense and superstition."

"Nonsense?" He pulled back, looking at Esther askance. "You do realize that the tradition of kissing under the mistletoe dates back to ancient Greece."

She hadn't known. It wasn't the sort of thing that had ever come up in the many books she and Lady Parker had read over the years.

"During the Roman era, enemies reconciled beneath mistletoe," John continued.

"Did they?" she murmured as he took her hand and gently pulled her toward the doorway. "Pity we aren't Greek or Roman—or enemies."

"But we have had some difficulties—a few days ago. Perhaps a reconciliation is in order."

They had not spoken of those difficulties since the night of the play, of the awful shock of their unknown connection in Lady Parker or of the mistrust that had so quickly filled Esther's mind, nearly shutting out the past four months of John's kindnesses to her. She had not apologized for doubting him, for allowing fear to overtake her courage and what her heart knew to be true.

She turned to him now and allowed him to take both of her hands in his.

"I am sorry, John," she said, apologizing to him this time. "I was wrong to mistrust you, when you had been nothing but good to me."

He frowned. "You do not need to be sorry. Indeed, I hope I never give you cause to feel sorry about anything ever again."

"*Ever* is quite ambitious," Esther said, enjoying the way his fingers caressed the back of her hands.

"Yet not long enough, either," he complained. "But I am hopeful that in the future you will agree to not feeling sorry for the rest of your life, at least." His eyes, filled with hopeful trepidation, sought hers. His voice lowered, and he released her hands but pulled her close, his arms circling her waist. "What do you think you might say to that?"

Esther looked up to his beautiful face and that perfect wave atop his head. Her hands rested against the front of his shirt, and though they trembled slightly, she felt no fear, only a heart overflowing with love.

"I suppose I shall say—that I surrender." And she did, to a very, exceptionally good man.

MICHELE PAIGE HOLMES spent her childhood and youth in Arizona and Northern California, often curled up with a good book instead of out enjoying the sunshine. She graduated from Brigham Young University with a degree in Elementary Education and found it an excellent major in which to indulge her love of children's literature.

She is the author of fifteen published romance novels, including the HOLIDAY HARBOR contemporary series, HEARTHFIRE HISTORICALS, and the FOREVER AFTER series. She is also the author of four novellas in the TIMELESS ROMANCE and TIMELESS VICTORIAN COLLECTIONS.

You can find Michele on the web: MichelePaigeHolmes.com
Facebook: Michele Holmes
Twitter: @MichelePHolmes

Good Heir Hunting

Nancy Campbell Allen

Chapter One

Graham Lucas sat at the bedside of his dying childhood friend in the large manor house that had been home to Baron Francis's family as long as Graham had been alive. Bertram Francis, or Bertie, had been out of his head in delirium for two weeks, and the doctor had told Graham and Bertie's father, the baron, that any time now the angel of death would arrive to carry Bertie home to his eternal reward.

The baron looked upon his son with a mixture of dismay and sadness. Graham looked upon Bertie with frustration and not a little regret. If only Bertie had listened, even once, to Graham's admonition to temper his hedonistic lifestyle, they might not be here now. The doctor had said Bertie's ultimate downfall was due to a poisoned liver from too much hard drink and an illness contracted from places better left from polite conversation.

Bertie drifted in and out of consciousness, at times calling for his long dead mother, and at other times mumbling about someone named "Mary." Graham looked at the baron, for whom Graham's own father had acted as solicitor for over thirty years. That duty now fell to Graham, and he'd performed well in the two years since his father's death.

"May I ring for tea, sir? Or would you care for a drink?"

Baron Francis looked at Graham, his eyes red-rimmed and tired. "We did try, did we not, young Master Graham?"

Graham swallowed and nodded at the man who had always been more like an uncle than employer. "We did, sir." He looked back at the man in the bed, much too young at 32 to be breathing his last. Graham and Bertie had lived side-by-side since birth, the difference in their stations never mattering to the baron or the baroness, who had passed a few years back.

"Mary!" Bertie thrashed in his bedcoverings and coughed hideously. The baron rushed to brace his son's head and tip a cup against his lips.

"Who is Mary, son?"

Graham did not expect a coherent response from his friend. They'd not run in the same social circles for nearly a decade, so this "Mary" would not be someone known to Graham. He doubted she was even an actual person. The amount of laudanum the doctor had given Bertie in the past weeks would have made the Archbishop of Canterbury mutter nonsensically. Mother Mary, Mary Queen of Scots, Mary Quite Contrary—any one of them could have been the object of Bertie's obsession and Graham and the baron would never know.

Bertie's eyes flickered open and he looked at his father. He blinked, and then looked at Graham, who moved his chair closer to the bed. To his astonishment, Bertie's expression was clear.

"Dying, am I not?" he said, his voice hoarse.

Graham winced, and Bertie looked up again at his father, who still braced his head.

"You must rest, son," the baron said. "You're ill, nothing more."

Bertie grasped his father's shirtfront, which hadn't been changed in two days. "I have a son, Father."

The baron blinked, and Graham's brow creased in confusion. A son?

"What are you saying?" The baron shook his head. "I do not understand."

Bertie licked his dry lips. "Five years ago, when I pursued the business venture in Liverpool, you remember? Mama had just passed, and I..."

Graham nodded. While Bertie had gone off to Liverpool and subsequently been fleeced of a fair amount of money, Graham had been steadily building his clientele as a solicitor. All he'd known of Bertie's endeavors was that he had returned home defeated. He'd never pushed for details, and Bertie hadn't offered any.

"There was a woman...a young woman, a railway worker's daughter. She and I...we..." He glanced up at his father again and looked away. "I was quite enamored of the girl, but I couldn't very well marry her now, could I? How could I bring home the daughter of a railway worker?"

The baron stared at his son. "Bertram, your mother was the daughter of a professor, not a king! *My* father was a humble rector; the majority of this estate I built and earned myself! We are hardly the sort to judge a person's worth by his lineage."

Bertie's face fell, and for a moment, he was the young boy who'd taken tumbles out of trees or broken his toys. Graham couldn't help but be moved to pity. "Tell us about this son," Graham said.

"The girl's name is Mary, and she has written sporadically." His face flushed. "I did send money when I could, but funds were often..."

Graham nodded. Bertie's funds were often gambled away.

"Son, you ought to have told me," the baron said. "I'd have helped you make it right."

"You always make it right, Father, and it was a shame I couldn't bear to drop at your feet." He coughed again, and the baron gave him another sip of tea. "At any rate, the last I heard from her, they were still in Liverpool, but her parents had disowned her when the boy was born, and she had lost her job as a seamstress."

Graham briefly closed his eyes. "When was this last contact from her?"

"A year ago."

"And the child is how old? Five?"

"Nearly." Bertie rested against his father and sighed raggedly. "I thought you should know, since I'll likely be dead by morning."

"Do not say it. You'll rally and be strong as ever." The older man met Graham's eyes, grief visible on his features. Graham saw no harm in repeating the lie.

"You require a good night's sleep, Bertie, that's all." Graham managed a smile, and acknowledged that beneath his frustration lay a well of sadness. Bertie was his oldest friend, whose obsession with class and appearance had evolved with adulthood. It had not touched the memory of their friendship.

Gratitude flashed in the baron's face and he managed a small smile for Graham. "What is Mary's surname, Bertram?"

Bertie glanced up at his father again. "Smith. Father, I do not ask you to bear responsibility for this, I only. . .I thought you should know." He coughed again, harshly, and small flecks of blood appeared on his lip.

The baron held a handkerchief to Bertie's mouth and when the fit subsided, gave him another drink from the teacup. Graham looked out the window at the dark night. Rain had been threatening all day, and it finally splashed against the glass. His heart was heavy, and he wished things could be different.

"Do you still have the letters from Mary?" the baron now asked.

Graham pulled his attention back to his dying friend.

Settled in the big bed, propped against his father's arm, Bertie looked very much like a child himself.

Bertie nodded. "They are in the rosewood box in my bedchamber. There are only three, and as I said, the last was a year ago. She never lives in one place for long, and I do not know where she is now."

Graham sat back in his chair and emitted a quiet sigh. How on earth were they to locate a woman named Mary Smith in Liverpool, if indeed she was still there? There were likely dozens by that name. He knew the baron would insist upon it, and he also knew that as the man's solicitor, the duty would fall to him.

The night stretched on, and the three men remained in place, two keeping vigil over the one as his breath began to rattle, and then finally ceased. Graham swallowed past the lump in his throat as a single tear tracked down the baron's cheek. He kissed Bertie's forehead one last time and then met Graham's tired gaze.

The silence stretched, and Graham finally said, "I'll send for the doctor; he'll take the proceedings from here." He rose from the chair, stiff from sitting so long. "What can I bring you, sir? Anything?"

The baron shook his head. "Thank you, Graham. I'll remain here until the doctor arrives."

Graham nodded. "Sir, I am so very sorry."

"You have been the best friend a young man could ever hope to find. Bertram was fortunate, indeed."

Graham looked one more time at the still form of his friend, and as his eyes began to burn, he turned away and left the room, closing the door softly with a quiet click.

Chapter Two

Eloise Anne Perkins stood in her office at Perkins Kindergarten School and stared at the letter her secretary had just received by messenger.

"What does it say, Miss Perkins?" Miss Jeffries' curiosity was both her most endearing and most irritating trait, and Ellie knew the younger woman was using enormous will to keep from reading over Ellie's shoulder.

"It says my new teacher for the additional class is no longer available for employment." Ellie looked up from the paper. "She married and moved to Ireland."

Miss Jeffries blinked. "She. . .she married and moved?" Her dumbfounded expression mirrored Ellie's emotions perfectly.

"She married and moved." Ellie rubbed her forehead and tossed the letter on her desk. "And today is the first day of school. The children from the new orphanage will arrive in less than thirty minutes and their teacher is not here."

Miss Jeffries straightened her shoulders. "What would you like me to do, Miss Perkins?"

"Are the children's files complete?"

"Yes, Miss. Finished two days ago."

"And you've completed any tasks requested by the other three teachers?"

"Yes, Miss. Well, Miss Drake did request an additional chair for her Discipline Corner, but I've had to order that from the supply warehouse." Her brow wrinkled. "I cannot imagine how many Discipline Corners the woman will need."

Ellie refrained from comment. Miss Drake was a seasoned teacher two decades her senior, and was slow to embrace the newer philosophies Ellie brought with her from abroad. The year before, Miss Drake had made use of a Discipline Stage, where she'd placed the offending child on an uncomfortable stool for peer ridicule. That she now compromised and employed a Discipline Corner instead was an improvement.

Miss Jeffries looked stricken for a moment. "Ought I to have consulted you first, Miss Perkins? I ought to have consulted you first."

"Miss Jeffries, put your mind at ease. We can always use an additional chair." She smiled at the younger woman, who was new to her position, but actually quite efficient. "Notify me in the future for purchases beyond the most basic of supplies."

She nodded. "Yes, Miss, absolutely."

Ellie sighed and escorted the secretary from her office and into the outer office that was Miss Jeffries' domain. "I don't suppose you've experience teaching four- and five-year-old children?"

"Mercy, no, Miss! What I know of teaching wouldn't fill a thimble!"

"Fret not, Miss Jeffries, I was only teasing. I will take the class for today. You must draft an advertisement for the teaching position; see it's delivered to the *Gazette*, and to Almhurst and Warwick Women's Colleges. Along with the notice to Almhurst, send an additional message to Mrs. Crowden, explaining the situation in more detail." With any luck, Mrs. Crowden, Ellie's mentor and the director at Almhurst, would have a few viable candidates to suggest.

Ellie left Miss Jeffries to her task and made her way down the hallway of the old school building she'd been graciously granted by the private board of directors. The process of establishing her own kindergarten school had been fraught with obstacles, from the city leaders to the directors of the education system.

The school provided education, uniforms, and two meals daily for three of the city's orphanages. Youngblood and Larkin orphanages were sending a new group of children for the school's second year of operation, along with a handful of students Ellie felt would benefit from an additional year at Perkins Kindergarten. Benchley Orphanage, which she had just added to the mix, comprised the newest addition.

She poked her head inside the first of four classrooms just as the front doors opened and the sound of small feet and enthusiastic voices echoed into the hall. She smiled at Miss Rose, a fresh teacher Ellie had hired the year before, and gave her a wink. "All ready, then?"

Miss Rose smiled, looking only a bit less nervous than she had the first day of school last year. "I do hope so."

"You will be wonderful, Miss Rose." She smiled as the children from Youngblood Orphanage neared, her heart turning over at the sight of them. She'd visited each orphanage in the weeks leading up to this first day, always reminding herself of the reasons she'd pursued her passion of opening a school for children who would likely not receive an education.

Despite her instructions beforehand, the students were often excited and fairly loud with it on the first day of school. She stepped forward to meet the swarm of small people dressed in identical brown uniforms.

"Students," Ellie said, putting on her stern-but-kind face.

"Let us return to the door and enter again." She shooed the bewildered children back. "When we enter the building, we walk, we form a queue against the wall, and we are quiet until Miss Rose welcomes you into the classroom."

The children obediently lined up as she showed them, and as another round of voices sounded at the entrance, Miss Rose took charge of her group.

Ellie met the larger group from Larkin Orphanage now entering and gave the same instructions. The children were a motley little bunch dressed in dark gray uniforms, scrubbed, and fed. Recent orphanage reform had seen significant improvements over the former squalor many of them typified.

Ellie preferred to keep the children together in their "families," but Larkin was a much larger orphanage. The group of thirty now entering was split into two classes, and Miss Brophy and Miss Drake now met her at the doors to gather their students and proceed farther down the hall.

As she waited for the last group to arrive, she considered how she might restructure her day. The board of directors required continual documentation of the school's activities, and copious amounts of paperwork usually dominated much of her time. Other schools where she'd trained in Switzerland also maintained contact with parents or guardians, but these children were orphans, and orphanage directors were kept busy enough without worrying about how a small segment of their population fared at school.

She spied the hired omnibus as it rounded the corner—an expense she convinced the board was necessary for each orphanage—carrying the children from Benchley. To her dismay, behind it rolled the carriage belonging to one of the board's most difficult members. Mr. Twizzle was bombastic and condescending when his wife accompanied his visits to the school, and when she did not accompany him, he was bombastic, condescending, and lecherous. She simply did not have time for him today. And yet...his pockets were deep, and his wife could be moved to compassion. It was a game Ellie had learned to play well.

A gust of wind brushed up against the building, and Ellie smelled rain heavy in the air. She pushed a strand of deep mahogany-colored hair away from her eyes and strained to see who was inside the carriage, hoping desperately it was both man and wife.

The orphanage omnibus came to a stop, and the driver helped the children hop down. Last year's successes with her kindergarten classes had impressed the board enough that they approved one additional class. It had seemed like a good idea then, but she'd not known her new teacher would marry and move.

Miss Jeffries appeared at her side, envelopes in hand. "I've sent for an errand boy. He'll have the messages delivered within the hour."

"Very good." Ellie nodded at her, but then sighed when she noted the second carriage's occupant.

"Mr. Twizzle?" Miss Jeffries looked at the man in surprise, and then her brow drew together in a frown. "Whyever is he here on the first day of school?"

Why, indeed? And he was, regrettably, sans wife. He climbed down from the carriage, his lumbering form rocking the conveyance dangerously.

"Fortunate the carriage is so well sprung," Miss Jeffries muttered.

Ellie's lips twitched and she held back a laugh, but she said, "Now, Miss Jeffries, we must look kindly upon our benefactors."

"Yes, Miss," she muttered. "He is just so very...very..."

"I know." Ellie looked at her employee. "Some things in life are inevitable."

The children gathered close, dressed in their matching blue uniforms. Ellie smiled and said, "Welcome to Perkins Kindergarten, students! Please remember the instructions I gave when I visited you last, and I shall lead the way to your classroom."

"Uh, Miss Perkins," Mr. Twizzle interrupted, climbing the few stairs to reach her side. "I require a moment of your time."

"Sir," Ellie said quietly, "perhaps your visit might wait? I've encountered a problem only this morning with a staff member, and—"

"You have lost control of the staff, have you?" His pale eyes narrowed and his cheeks, ruddy from cold and veiny from many nights of "retiring to the lounge with the gentlemen," did little to enhance his appearance. His lips firmed, and he raised his eyebrows at her, the chastisement clear.

She managed a tight smile and turned to her secretary. "Miss Jeffries, please lead the children to their classroom whilst I consult with Mr. Twizzle."

Miss Jeffries' mouth dropped open in dismay. "B-b-but, Miss, I—"

Ellie took the envelopes from the girl's suddenly slack fingers and leaned close to whisper, "I'll be along straight away. Simply seat them in a circle as you've seen me do, and learn their names. Ask them what sorts of things they hope to do at school."

Ellie gave her shoulder a brisk pat and said to the children, "You will follow Miss Jeffries, and she will begin your day."

Fifteen serious faces looked from her to Miss Jeffries, who seemed infinitely more terrified than her charges. The girl was alarmingly pale, but cleared her throat and said, "Very well, follow me, children."

Miss Jeffries entered the building and Ellie held the door

open as the students followed. Ellie waved at the omnibus driver and orphanage employee, and then glancing at Mr. Twizzle, entered.

He followed, and as she led the way to her office, she said, "You'll forgive if I seem abrupt, of course, but the first days and weeks of school require my full attention. I hope there is not an emergency, Mr. Twizzle?"

"Certainly not an emergency, although I should think the prospect of bringing more money into your school would be of paramount importance."

Ellie stopped when they reached the outer office and indicated a pair of chairs opposite Miss Jeffries' desk. She benefitted from the fact that he was on the shorter side for men, and she was taller than most women. He did not tower over her, and she was grateful for small advantages. Her unwelcome guest looked at the door leading to her office, but Ellie sat in one of the chairs and placed her hands in her lap, consciously refraining from clenching her fingers.

Mr. Twizzle hesitated, but finally sat. He removed his hat and held it, along with his walking stick, across his knees. She did not offer to take them for him.

"You mentioned money for the school, sir?" She smiled, but worried it didn't look genuine.

"Miss Perkins, it has occurred to me that your undertaking here is immense. You are performing a task that has traditionally belonged to men, and according to the best academic minds, too much time spent acquiring knowledge in masculine fields actually alters not only a woman's features, but the feminine. . .well. . ." He glanced at her abdomen.

Ellie counted to five, and then to ten. "How is it, Mr. Twizzle, you propose to prevent my falling victim to such a fate?"

He smiled and visibly relaxed. "You ought to meet with

me weekly, perhaps twice weekly, in the evenings, to review your accounts, the minutiae of your paperwork. Allow me to help shoulder the burden. We could meet here, in your office, or perhaps at one of my clubs. We have private rooms where we would be guaranteed to remain undisturbed."

Ellie knew a moment of true weariness. Would there ever come a day when she would not be forced to smile when she wanted to slap? She had lost count of the number of similar propositions—and insults—she had received in her twenty-five years.

"Mr. Twizzle, you already have unfettered access to the accounting ledgers, minutes of meetings, all of my documentation concerning the day-to-day happenings of this business as well as quarterly and yearly reports. If your desire is to enact better oversight, I can hardly see how that might be improved upon."

"No, Miss Perkins, I mean to help *you*. Shoulder the burden for *you*. Provide the role of masculine guidance in your life. You've not a husband to look after you, and lost your father at a young age, I understand." He smiled and scooted forward on his chair, moving his knee toward hers. "If I were to have a more involved hand in your affairs, I'm certain I could be prevailed upon to enrich the school's coffers above and beyond that which the board deems necessary. Think of the good you could do for your little urchins."

She immediately slid back, putting several inches between them. "Mr. Twizzle, I am certain your wife would wish to be part of whatever business meetings you might conduct where she also has a stake. Her name is affixed to the board of directors as firmly as is yours."

He flushed and opened his mouth.

"Furthermore," she continued, "I've no need of assistance in my business affairs, masculine or feminine. I have been well educated for this position and have all aspects of this endeavor in hand. The name of this institution and its curriculum are legally my own—" she took a breath, smiling to soften the sharp edges of her delivery, "—and as much as I have dared to venture into masculine territory, I hope you'll agree that my face is as lovely as ever."

He blinked, his cheeks still red.

"I do not mean to boast," she said, tilting her head just so, "but I was quite a pretty girl and have been complimented many times since crossing into adulthood. I suppose I am of the fortunate few who have not grown facial hair from the rigors of earning a college education."

She chuckled as though they shared a joke and placed her hands on her knees, signaling her intent to stand. "Although," she said, smiling still and leaning as if taking him into her confidence, "those moustaches you sport are quite the thing!" She touched her fingertip to her lip and added, "I do believe you men have been keeping secrets all this time—style icons, the lot of you!"

He smiled weakly and stood as she did, managing a light chuckle. "I don't know about all that," he said as she led him from the office and out toward the main doors. "I say, Miss Perkins, I do not—"

"I understand," she said, nodding as she opened the front door and stepped out, holding it for him and bracing against the wind and first few raindrops. "Your offer of help, while unnecessary, is greatly appreciated. Please do extend my thanks to Mrs. Twizzle, sir. In fact," she said as he stepped past her and donned his hat, "perhaps I shall pen a note of thanks to her—"

"No, no," he chuckled, "no need for all that trouble. I'll pass along your, er, gratitude."

"Good." She smiled as he made his way toward his

carriage, looking very much out of sorts. She was turning back into the building when another carriage appeared around the corner and passed Mr. Twizzle as he left.

She took a deep breath, her heart hammering in frustration as she allowed the false smile to drop away. His insinuations were insulting in the extreme, and her face was hot with anger. She watched as the other carriage came to a stop, wondering absently if she'd managed to keep the scales balanced. Maintain good relations with board members who had the power to convince the others to close her doors, while still defending her own sense of honor and ability to run her school.

The carriage door opened, and a man who was completely Mr. Twizzle's opposite in appearance descended the steps and paid the driver. He was tall, and as he neared her and removed his hat, she saw he bore a head of dark blonde hair and tawny colored eyes. The difference was striking in such an academic way that Ellie found herself blinking in confusion. It was as though the universe had balanced scales of its own, and hustled away an odious man by replacing him with an Adonis.

"Miss Perkins, is it?" the man said. "I wonder if I might have a moment of your time. It is a matter of some delicacy."

She finally pulled herself from the baffled stupor and shook her head. The rain was coming harder now, and she opened the door wider. "Please, come in," she said, "but I really haven't time at the moment for anything complicated. I am missing a teacher. . ." She led the way up the stairs and glanced down the hallway to her right, hearing some noise coming from the end of the hall where Miss Jeffries had probably been tied to a stake. As there was a notable absence of distressed screaming, she decided she could spare the gentleman five minutes, no longer.

She again returned to the reception area, but this time took a seat behind Miss Jeffries' desk and indicated the chairs opposite for the stranger. He nodded and took a seat, running a hand through rain dampened hair.

"How may I be of assistance, Mr. . . .."

"Lucas. Graham Lucas. I am a solicitor, Miss Perkins, and I am looking for a child."

Chapter Three

To say that the headmistress seemed distracted was an understatement. She looked at him in some confusion, and he had to assume that the hectic nature of the first day of school was to blame. He remembered the hullabaloo of his own school days and couldn't imagine a profession worse than attempting to educate children.

"I am sorry, Mr. Lucas, is it? Are you looking for a specific child? This is hardly a department store, you cannot simply walk in and choose one."

"Oh, no! No, madam, I am searching for a specific child, a boy, who is my employer's heir. Unfortunately, the trail I followed led me to several orphanages who housed five-year-old males named Stephen Smith. I believe I've narrowed the search to Benchley Orphanage, yet there are still two boys bearing that name, and both records show birth mothers named 'Mary.'"

Miss Perkins frowned, nodding. She reached for a neat stack of files on the desk and selected a few. "There are indeed two Stephens in classroom four this year." She looked up at him and pinned him with a direct blue gaze worthy of a fierce nun. "I am rather busy this morning, and fairly distracted, sir. Otherwise, I should never have entertained this conversation for a moment without demanding some credentials, some proof of your identity and authority. These children are wards of the state and I'll not see them come to harm."

He reached into his jacket pocket and produced the packet he'd been carrying for over a month. He unwound the twine and produced his documentation, his photographs of the baron and Bertie, and a certified letter of intent from Baron Francis. He handed the items to her across the desk, and he noted her ink-stained fingers, evidence of her work.

"My hope was to find the boy and his mother; Baron Francis intended to invite them to visit and potentially live at his estate in Wyndomshire. The trail I followed, however, led me to unfortunate news. The child's mother passed away last year and her son was sent through a series of orphanages, finally landing, I hope, at Benchley."

Miss Perkins scanned the letter, absently tucking a curl of rich brown hair behind her ear. The lady was lovely. And stressed, if the crease on her forehead were any indication. She rubbed her temple with a fingertip and finally looked up from the documentation.

"What are your intentions, Mr. Lucas? Are you going to interview the boys to see if one might be your employer's heir? I do not know how familiar you are with small children, and there are nuances involved. I'll not allow any student of this school to be arbitrarily carried off, no matter how rosy the prospect. This will require time."

"Certainly, I would not dream of bringing the child distress." Graham sighed and sat back in the hard chair. "Honestly, madam, I've no plan as yet. I have encountered so many false starts and dead ends that I am amazed to have tracked the child thus far." He was being polite; his frustration throughout the process of looking for Mary Smith and her son had grown to unbelievable heights. If he could snatch up both Stephen Smiths that very day and deliver them to the baron, he'd have done so, gladly. His patience with the whole affair was quite at an end. Even in death, poor Bertie was leading Graham in circles.

Miss Perkins' eyes turned speculative, narrowing on him in thought. He wasn't certain he would like whatever she seemed to be considering. "Have you ever taught children, Mr. Lucas?"

He laughed. "No, I have certainly never taught children, Miss Perkins. I shall bow to your wisdom concerning whatever course of action I ought to pursue."

She shook her head. "I ask genuinely. I am in need of a teacher for the next week, at least, until I can find a permanent one. Do you imagine you might handle a group of fifteen children while you try and determine which Stephen is the correct one?"

He chuckled again, but sobered when he realized she'd put forth the question in earnest. "I...madam, I—"

He turned at the sound of a cry far down the hall, and then running footsteps. Miss Perkins jumped up from the chair and was around the desk and to the door when another young woman appeared in the room, cradling a hand to her chest.

"Miss Jeffries! What is it?"

"He, he bit me!"

Miss Perkins looked out into the hall and back at the young woman. "One of the children, I presume?"

"Yes!" Miss Jeffries' eyes filmed over.

Miss Perkins held out her hand, glancing again out into the hallway, and Miss Jeffries extended the wounded limb for inspection.

"Ah, yes, teeth marks indeed." Miss Perkins nodded and patted the hand softly. "At least no blood."

"It will bruise!"

"Yes, I would say so."

"And leave scars!"

Miss Perkins shook her head. "I would say unlikely. It will hurt for a time, but I daresay there will come a day when even the bruises are a distant memory."

Graham watched the exchange and bit back a smile. The headmistress struck just the right chord between sympathy and no-nonsense. He'd dare one of the little urchins to bite *him*. That Miss Perkins even suggested he rule the roost in a classroom full of those was ridiculous.

"You clean yourself up and see to your other duties for the day," Miss Perkins told the distraught secretary. "Mr. Lucas, would you be so kind as to follow me?"

The secretary looked at him as though noting his presence for the first time. "Mr. Lucas?" she repeated.

"Mr. Lucas is going to help us with the children in classroom four until I can find a suitable replacement. The advertisements you drafted have yet to be delivered; I left them on your desk."

"Yes, Miss." Miss Jeffries sniffled as Graham looked at Miss Perkins in disbelief.

"*Madam*, I do not possess the faintest inkling—"

She began walking out the door and motioned with her head. He caught up to her as she briskly made her way down the hall. "Those are my terms, Mr. Lucas. You help me with this class for a day or two and I shall allow you to interact with the children to find your young heir."

He opened his mouth to deliver a sharp response, but as they came to a stop at the door labeled "4," he looked at her and the words died on his lips. Color was high on her cheeks, her eyes blazed, and she was slightly winded.

She was lovely, seemed quite capable, and she was very much in a predicament. He imagined the gentleman he'd seen leaving upon his own arrival had not been a welcome visitor. Her demeanor had been tight, guarded. That she was a woman attempting to live in a man's world deserved some applause, and certainly he could manage a class of fifteen children. It would be a charming role-reversal, and he was sure he could manage a woman's task of teaching little children as well as Miss Perkins handled the masculine role of administration.

He smiled. "Very well. Consider this class temporarily staffed."

Her shoulders relaxed. "I'll be in and out all day long, you needn't worry I'm simply throwing you to the wolves. I do have a specific curriculum, but just for now, we'll manage."

Screaming and laughter came from within the room and she smiled. It was the first honest expression of humor or lightness he'd seen yet.

"Shall I begin with the alphabet?" he asked.

"Mr. Lucas, students at Perkins Kindergarten learn to play."

He raised his brows high. "Oh? Well then, lead on."

She hesitated, smiled again, and opened the door. The lightness on her face vanished and she replaced it with a stern expression he'd seen on more than one professor in his lifetime. He wondered if it was taught in their schooling. Introductory Studies on Developing and Maintaining Stern Expressions. Given the ruckus in the room, he figured it wouldn't be long before he developed the skill on his own.

"Ladies and gentlemen," she said firmly, and all movement in the room immediately ceased. "I am quite certain I explained last week on my visit to you that behavior involving running and yelling is to be done only at certain times during the day, and certainly not if your teacher has stepped from the room." She looked at each child, and one by one, little faces dropped and little feet shuffled uncomfortably.

"Did Miss Jeffries show you where to sit when you arrived?"

Many nodding heads.

"And where was that?"

A few hands pointed to the other side of the room, where a large rug lay on the floor.

"I suggest you go there immediately." One arched brow punctuated her statement, and Graham was quite ready to follow the children obediently to the squares of fabric arranged in a half circle on the big rug.

She walked behind the little students and said, "For now, you may choose your circle-time square."

The children settled down on the fabric squares, which he now saw were thick, quilted affairs decorated with embroidered animals. Aside from a minor tussle between two boys who fought for the same square, the process was painless.

Miss Perkins retrieved a chair from a nearby table and placed it at the head of the semi-circle. She sat down and looked for a moment at the solemn little faces. "Children, I understand this morning has been unusual. Your teacher for a little while will be Mr. Lucas," she extended her hand to Graham, "and he will take good care of you. I expect you will be very respectful in return."

Most of them nodded, a few scratched their heads, and one had a finger in his nose. Graham felt the first true stirrings of apprehension when Miss Perkins rose from her chair. "You will remain here with Mr. Lucas, and I shall speak with the person who had the altercation with Miss Jeffries."

The children, as a unit, looked at one little boy who slowly straightened on his circle-time square.

"Mr. Crispin, is it?"

He nodded and cleared his throat. "Yes, miss," he managed. "I did not mean—"

Miss Perkins held up one hand. "We shall discuss it in my office. Mr. Lucas, the class is yours." She motioned to him and walked to a cupboard in the corner. "There are manipulatives for teaching purposes on these shelves here, and I'll explain later how they're to be used. These, here, are traditional toys, and a very good set of building blocks. I suggest you begin there."

He nodded and tried to remember his earlier sense of bravado. He looked at the curious faces seated on the floor and felt utterly at sea.

Miss Perkins' lips twitched. "Will you require smelling salts?"

He straightened his cravat, along with his resolve, and matched her earlier stern expression. "I shall manage."

She turned slightly but then back again, close to his ear. He lowered his head, and she whispered, "I understand your purpose here, but do be subtle. These children have known more than their fair share of difficult life. Some do not remember families before the orphanage, but many do. The separation is incredibly painful, as I'm sure you can imagine. Please do not open an inquisition on the two boys with the name you seek."

He nodded. "Of course," he whispered.

She stepped away, and then returned again. "Also, remember that boys are children, not just short men. They are allowed to be children here, with no lectures on maintaining a stiff upper lip."

"Yes, miss." He nodded, and she narrowed her eyes. He made a shooing motion and she finally left him, making her way to the biter.

"Mr. Crispin," she said, and the boy followed her to the door. She opened it, looked back at Graham, pausing and for the first time looking uncertain about leaving the class in his hands.

"Excellent," he said to the children, and took the chair she'd vacated. "Let us introduce ourselves, shall we?"

The next time he looked up, the door was quietly closing, and he was on his own.

Chapter Four

Ellie walked the length of the hallway with young Edward Crispin and shortened her stride to match his. In the space of an hour, she had been notified one teacher was leaving without notice, been propositioned most hideously, dealt with a bitten staff member, and turned over an entire class to a man she didn't know, who was on his own quest. She was grateful that sort of chaos hadn't greeted her the year before; she'd had a time of it convincing the board to support her school and allow her to manage it. They'd have closed her doors, without doubt.

She led the little boy through the reception area, where Miss Jeffries glared at him, and into her office. She had a small sofa against one wall, next to a side table and lamp. She indicated for Edward to take a seat and waited until he scooted back so that his feet hung off the edge.

She sat next to him, perched on the edge and turned toward him, and took in the huge blue eyes that were almost too big for his little face. His dark hair was cut in the perfunctory style adopted by every orphanage she'd ever visited, and his uniform shirt was perhaps a half size too big on his thin little shoulders.

"Mr. Crispin, are you aware that we do not bite at school? It is strictly forbidden to do harm to another student or adult."

He nodded, solemn. "I weren't trying to hurt 'er. She said we could play zoo, and I was a mighty tiger."

"I see. What led to the biting incident?"

"She asked what mighty tigers do." He lifted a shoulder, as if his explanation covered it.

"So you bit Miss Jeffries?"

"Well, not right at first. First I growled, like this." He made a growling noise, twisting his nose and lifting his hands just slightly from his lap to form claws.

"Continue." Ellie nodded, her heart melting but expression professional.

"She said I was very fierce indeed, and what else did tigers do. She petted my 'ead, and if a tiger is petted, 'e bites."

"I see. Well, Edward, it is true that a fierce tiger would likely bite someone who attempted to touch it. At school, however, we cannot bite or do anything that will hurt another person. Do you understand, now?"

He nodded. "Oughtn't to play zoo then, really."

She considered the matter, and said, "Perhaps we could still play zoo, but refrain from approaching the animals. Would that be more sensible?"

He nodded and scratched his nose. One foot bounced just slightly against the edge of the sofa, and she knew her teaching moment was nearly up. "However," she added, "even if a zookeeper attempts to pet an animal in the future, that animal will *not* bite, am I clear?"

"Yes, Miss."

She gave him a small smile. "Are we ready to rejoin the class?"

The corners of his eyes crinkled as he smiled back, and she found herself quite charmed.

"I truly did not mean to 'urt 'er," he said, and Ellie believed him.

"You may apologize to her on our way back to class." She nodded, and after a moment, he did the same.

She stood and waited as he slid off the sofa, and then led him back out to the reception area. "Miss Jeffries, Mr. Crispin has something he would like to say to you."

He stepped forward and said, "Miss, I meant no 'arm. I 'pologize for biting you."

Ellie wondered if Miss Jeffries was going to snub the boy when she finally nodded and said, "Thank you for the apology, Mr. Crispin. I accept it."

Edward's face brightened. "That's very good. I don't like to make anyone angry with me."

The corner of Miss Jeffries' mouth lifted. "I quite understand. I do not like to make anyone angry with me, either."

"I shall never bite you again."

"I am glad to hear it."

"Or anyone else," Ellie added.

"Or anyone else," the boy agreed. "Unless someone grabs me in the street. Then I'll bite."

Ellie briefly closed her eyes. And there it was, the reason she had been so determined to carry on her Swiss maternal grandfather's mission of a new kind of school for the poorer classes of children. The thought that little Edward had experience with being grabbed in the street made her feel ill.

"If someone seeks to harm you, Edward, you are certainly justified in defending yourself." She smiled, holding her hand toward the door for him to precede her. "I'll escort you to class." On her way out, she glanced at Miss Jeffries, who looked stricken. Every now and again, one of the children would say something that served as a stark reminder of the difficulties they faced every day.

They reached the classroom, and Ellie opened the door

quietly and peered inside. Mr. Lucas was seated on the floor with the children, reading one of the storybooks from the cupboard. She whispered for Edward to join the others, giving his shoulder a little squeeze as she sent him off. He rejoined the others and took his place on the circle-time square, settling in quietly.

Hoping that would be the last of the day's drama, Ellie nodded at Mr. Lucas when he glanced up, and then quietly closed the door. She needed to peer into the other three classrooms to assess first day lessons, and coordinate with the cooks who worked part of the day to serve tea and then a late luncheon to the children and staff. Ideally, each of those things would be underway and close to finished if the day had gone according to plan. Telling herself to be grateful the children hadn't tied Mr. Lucas to his chair and then run amok, she hurried to the next task.

Chapter Five

Graham realized his error too late; he'd softened his tone too quickly, giving the little herd of monsters the impression that he was not the same firm taskmaster as the headmistress. They'd behaved well throughout story time, but he realized he was losing them when they began to fidget.

The wheels then fell off the metaphorical cart. Two children said they needed to "wee." Another four proclaimed themselves "starving," which may actually have been true, he was sad to realize. Two boys—ironically the two Stephen Smiths—tussled over the set of blocks he'd removed from the toy cupboard, and three little girls held hands, skipped in a circle, and sang nursery rhymes. The last wasn't so bad in theory, but their circle kept drifting into the other children, who protested loudly.

Little Edward Crispin, who seemed duly chastened after his visit to the headmistress' office, attempted to establish peace between the two block-fighters, and was summarily shoved down out of the way. He got to his feet, clearly offended, and said, "Stop that!"

Now there were three boys fighting over the blocks. The box spilled open, dumping wooden squares and triangles everywhere. One of the Stephens grabbed a block and conked the other one on the head with it, eliciting a howl that echoed through the room.

Graham took the little offender under the arms and lifted him high in the air so they were face-to-face. "You must *not* do that again, am I clear?"

The boy's face fell and his lips trembled at the corners. Miss Perkins' theory about boys being children and not little men was all well and good, but Graham had half a mind to show the little terror what it felt like to get brained in the head with a block.

It was on the tip of his tongue to tell the lad as much when the door flew open and a woman he'd not seen before stared at the scene in open shock.

"What is the *meaning* of this? And who are you?" Now here was a woman with the look of a schoolteacher. Her pinched, disapproving face spoke all the words she didn't verbalize beyond her initial salvo.

"Miss Drake," a voice said outside the room, and then Miss Perkins appeared, flushed as though having run quickly, "I shall deal with this. Thank you, and apologies for disturbing your class."

Miss Drake stared at the headmistress, and Graham, belatedly realizing he still held a child aloft, slowly lowered him to the ground.

"Where is Miss Lovelace?" Miss Drake asked, looking again at the room.

The children slowly gathered around him, and Graham decided if they were looking to him for protection from the dragon lady, they were not going to receive it. Traitors, the lot of them.

"Miss Lovelace is now Mrs. Brecken and she has moved away. This is Mr. Lucas, and he is joining us for a few days while I interview for replacements."

Miss Drake looked Graham up and down, and he felt oddly violated. The children gathered closer still, and he decided to forgive them. A little hand brushed against his, and he looked down to see one of the nursery rhyme singers holding his fingers.

"Does he come with qualifications?" Miss Drake demanded.

Miss Perkins straightened slowly, and if Miss Drake didn't see her misstep, Graham certainly did. "You may return to your students, Miss Drake."

Miss Drake shot another look at Graham and his herd of sheep, now clustered very closely around him for warmth. As she finally took her leave, Graham thought he heard a little voice at his side muttering something about playing zoo with "that one."

Miss Perkins entered and quietly closed the door. She examined the scene, hands clasped loosely at her midsection. Her eyes traveled over the children and rested on him, and he fought to keep from squirming along with the students.

"My goodness," she finally said. "We seem to have forgotten how to behave as proper students ought. As it happens, teatime is in twenty minutes. We've just enough time now to tidy the room and wash up."

The little herd of children stayed in place, quiet, and Miss Perkins looked at him.

"Right, then." He clapped his hands and directed them to pick up the scattered blocks and a stack of books knocked over by the spinning nursery rhyme singers. They followed his instructions, and at the sound of muttering, he sternly added, "Silently."

They finished cleaning the room quietly, and Graham put away the storybooks he'd read. He finally approached Miss Perkins, who watched him with an unreadable expression. One side of her mouth finally twitched, and he felt oddly relieved. He'd been sent to the headmaster's office on a few occasions—very few—and while he didn't relish the thought of repeating it, of all the people to deliver punishment, he figured Miss Perkins might be the most desirable.

"Have you found your heir?" she asked quietly.

"I do not know which boy is Bertie's son." He lifted a shoulder. "I hope further observation might lend some clues."

"Very curious that a titled gentleman would seek to legitimize a grandson he does not know. One born in unfortunate circumstances, at that."

"Baron Francis is unique. He is very kind."

Her smile broadened, even as she tipped her head in curiosity. "Are most titled gentlemen unkind?"

He paused. He knew nothing of her background and did not seek to offend. His work as a solicitor, however, had indeed shown him an element of meanness—at the very least, indifference—possessed by those whose circumstances of birth had given them much. "I was raised alongside the baron's household; I grew accustomed to his generosity of spirit. I suppose I naively assumed he was the standard bearer."

Her smile manifested in her eyes, and he sensed he'd gained her approval. "I am glad for whichever child your heir turns out to be. Your baron is the sort worthy to have the gift of one of these children in his life."

Who was this woman who considered a wealthy man the more fortunate for adopting an illegitimate orphan? Suddenly the thought of solving the riddle of Miss Perkins was equally as important as learning which Stephen Smith was *the* Stephen Smith.

She looked at the classroom as the children finished and he stepped aside for her next instructions. They spent the following several minutes washing for tea, practicing forming an orderly queue without talking, and maintaining that orderly line as they walked up and down the hallway. If one of the children so much as whispered, they all went back to the room and began again.

Finally, they achieved success, and Miss Perkins directed them to wait as the other three classroom doors opened, offering up additional queues of exceptionally well-behaved children. Miss Drake took her class first, throwing Graham a stern look as she passed, and then two younger women followed in turn with their students. Miss Perkins nodded to the class and they fell in line after the last group.

Miss Perkins led them, and Graham headed back to the end of the line behind the two Stephen Smiths, one of whom, he had learned, answered to a differing variation of the name. He was called "Stevie," and the other used the more formal "Stephen." They were truly similar in coloring, stature, and general demeanor, giving him no clues as to which was Bertie's child. He wasn't sure what he'd expected; he supposed he'd hoped to enter the school, spy a miniature version of Bertie, and leave with the fortunate child in tow. As he looked down the short hallway at Miss Perkins, he realized he was glad for the delay in identifying the proper child.

The line turned, and they entered a large room where four tables with long benches sat neatly arranged. The other three teachers stood at the head of the tables where their charges settled onto the benches, so Graham followed suit, freeing Miss Perkins to direct the cooking staff.

Roughly sixty small faces looked eagerly on as tea and sandwiches were distributed, and he felt a pang in the region of his heart at the delight in their eyes as they received the food. The other three teachers, however, were managing their charges with efficiency and calm, so he refrained from bursting into tears and instead helped one little girl retrieve the fabric serviette that had fallen to the floor. He brushed it off and placed it on her lap, and she smiled at him, showing one missing tooth. He found himself hopelessly charmed.

"Grace, is it?" he asked.

She nodded. "Mama called me 'Gracie.'"

He smiled. "Do you prefer to be called Gracie?"

She nodded again.

"Gracie it shall be, then." He looked down the table at the rest of his little group, who ate with relish and spoke very little. He noted, with some relief, that several children at the other tables were quietly conversing, and their teachers allowed it. The thought of passing the entire meal in silence felt unnatural to him and was reminiscent of workhouses that, until the last two decades, had required meals taken without a word spoken.

Mealtime finished, and the teachers each took their students outside for a moment to stretch their legs. "Getting the wiggles out before quiet time," was Miss Perkins' explanation, and it made sense. He wondered why he'd never assumed small children would require exercise as much as he had with his peers in school. There had been classes that had felt so interminably long it'd been all he could manage to keep from jumping from his seat. Finally getting outside afterward had been like escaping from prison.

Once the wiggles were all exorcised, or mostly so, they returned to their classrooms and Miss Perkins managed the instruction for the remainder of the day. He helped when she asked, and observed her masterful management of the unruly littles, who were actually endearing and a little heartbreaking. Comments offered casually spoke of lives of want, both physical and emotional.

He was so enthralled with Miss Perkins, both in general

awe and conscientious effort to remember her skills for the next day when he would attempt the class again on his own, that he had to force himself to study the Stephens. When he did, he wondered how he would ever determine the correct one, which allowed his mind to wander back to Miss Perkins. The cycle repeated itself into the afternoon hours, past rest time, music lessons, toy play time, and counting lessons. They had another, bigger, meal followed again by outdoor wiggle time.

Finally, the hour came to bundle the children into their respective omnibuses for their return to the orphanages, and exhausting as they were, Graham found himself reluctant to see them go. Gracie's missing tooth had not left her in the natural course of things; an older child at the orphanage had fought with her and knocked it out. Edward Crispin, the zoo tiger, was already hungry again. Stevie Smith had carefully folded a piece of paper he'd drawn his numbers on and put it in his pocket to look at later, hoping nobody took it from him. Stephen Smith, who had fallen down hard during wiggle time, clutched the white cloth Miss Jeffries had procured from the medicine cabinet. He dabbed the scraped knee periodically with a wince, and took the cloth with him when they left.

Miss Perkins seemed surprised when he lingered after the children had gone. She waited until the other teachers reentered the school to tidy their rooms before turning to him and asking, "You're not going to follow the children back to the orphanage? I thought you needed more time to observe the boys?"

He nodded as they approached the door. "I do, but I fear following them around and making a nuisance of myself at the orphanage might prove irksome to the staff."

She smiled. "Some of them are rather. . .easily irked. Might I assume you'll return again tomorrow to help us?"

He nodded and opened the door, shielding her from a blast of cold wind. She folded her arms tightly and hurried inside, and he walked with her back to her office. "If you'll allow it, I appreciate the opportunity."

She chuckled. "Now that you've experienced a full day here, I am surprised you find it within yourself to repeat it."

"I am made of stern stuff." He smiled. "Now that I know the reins must be kept tight, I suspect we'll see more success tomorrow."

The other teachers were talking with Miss Jeffries in the outer office, and fell silent when he and Miss Perkins entered. Miss Perkins formally introduced him to the others, and he nodded politely to Miss Drake, the dragon lady, and the two younger teachers, Miss Brophy and Miss Rose. They eyed him in open curiosity, but accepted Miss Perkins' explanation of his presence there as a longtime family acquaintance who had agreed to help until a new teacher could be hired.

"Miss Perkins," Miss Jeffries said, "I've heard from Almhurst College, and they are sending two candidates tomorrow for interviews. They are set to graduate in two months' time."

Miss Perkins nodded. "Very good, Miss Jeffries." She looked at the other three ladies. "And how was the first day?"

Miss Drake glanced at him, but nodded. "Well enough."

Miss Rose also nodded her agreement. "I believe this class will be easier than last year's."

Miss Perkins smiled at her and accepted a few small sheets of paper Miss Jeffries passed to her across the desk, murmuring, "Messages." "Miss Rose, you are no longer a first-year teacher—that may account for the ease you feel about this class."

"Fewer boys," Miss Brophy added wryly. "We each have more girls than boys this year—I suspect that also accounts for some of it."

"What say you, Mr. Lucas?" Miss Perkins turned to him with a smile. "Are boys more troublesome than girls, do you suppose?"

"Most definitely." He nodded, remembering himself and Bertie at that age. "I cannot speak to specific circumstances, but I imagine girls are most likely better behaved."

"That certainly would not account for your students' behavior today," Miss Drake said with a sniff.

He nodded, speaking before Miss Perkins could smooth over the awkwardness. "I imagine I could learn more than a few things by observing you at work, Miss Drake. You carry yourself with the grace of one experienced in educating young children."

She blinked, momentarily stunned, and then her cheeks lightly flushed. "I have taught for a number of years." She didn't exactly smile, but her scowl disappeared. "You may feel free to ask for my advice tomorrow, should you need it. If you'll excuse me."

Miss Drake left the room, and the others stared at her retreating form. Miss Rose, whose mouth had dropped open, closed it. Miss Brophy exchanged a half-smile with Miss Jeffries, who then busied herself with the papers on her desk.

Miss Perkins looked down the hallway at Miss Drake's retreating form, and then eyed him speculatively as she crossed the room to her office door. "Miracles do occur," he heard her murmur, and then she raised her voice as she addressed him. "Mr. Lucas, I have work here that will occupy me for a time before leaving, but am happy to answer any questions you might have for tomorrow." She paused at the door and smiled at the two young teachers. "First day well done, ladies. Tidy up and be finished for the day. You've worked long hours; get some rest tonight."

"Miss." Both younger women nodded their thanks to

Miss Perkins and left the office together, sneaking a look at Graham as they left. Graham hid a satisfied smile. A man could certainly do worse than spend a day in the company of only women.

"Miss Perkins," Miss Jeffries said, and Miss Perkins paused. "I have three of the periodicals you requested for your lecture tomorrow evening at Almhurst College. The other two will be available tomorrow at the library and museum. I can retrieve them any time after the noon hour."

Miss Perkins knit her brow in thought. "Perhaps an impromptu excursion tomorrow would be enjoyable for Mr. Lucas' class. We'll walk there after lunch and I will collect the periodicals myself. I have paperwork for Mr. Crowden, as it happens. We'll make an afternoon of it."

"Yes, Miss. Will you require the use of an omnibus?"

"No, it isn't far. Barring bad weather, we shall enjoy the walk." Miss Perkins nodded at her secretary with a smile. "You're free to leave for the day whenever you wish. You've also done more than your share of work in the last few weeks."

"I am grateful for it, Miss Perkins." Miss Jeffries nodded, and then turned back to her desk. "I apologize for my inability to handle the class for even a short time this morning." She stacked some papers, not looking up.

"Nonsense, you did well. Besides, Mr. Lucas had impeccable timing." Miss Perkins smiled at the young woman, who was still clearly embarrassed and focused on the very neat stack of papers she kept tapping. "Fret not; I hired you to be my right hand, not a teacher. You make a very good and capable right hand."

Miss Jeffries glanced up, flushed, but managed a small smile. "Thank you, Miss."

Miss Perkins entered her office and indicated the chair opposite her desk. Graham waited until she sank into her own chair with a small sigh before taking his seat. He made an attempt to summon his manly strength and refrain from sighing, himself. He failed.

Chapter Six

Ellie smiled at Mr. Lucas, whose tired sigh matched her own. "They are a lively bunch of small people, are they not?"

He nodded his handsome blonde head and tilted his mouth at one corner. "I was quite convinced they would be no match for me. I find that humility and humiliation are a hair's breadth apart today."

"You're very amiable, and your help was a blessing for me, I admit freely. Hopefully I'll be able to spend more time in the classroom for the next few days so that you might better observe the children." She paused. "What will you do if you cannot ascertain which boy is the baron's grandson?"

He frowned. "I shall reason it through, somehow. I watched them all day, hoping to see a trace of Bertie somewhere. The child must resemble the mother, I suppose."

Ellie nodded and turned her attention to the messages Miss Jeffries had given her. She sorted through, making a mental note of when each item would need attention. While she worked, she said, "Are you staying nearby, Mr. Lucas?"

When he remained silent, she glanced up. He blinked, then frowned. "I'm sorry?"

He'd been looking at her in a way that was fairly familiar to her, but this marked the first time she felt a stirring of interest in return. As she regarded him for a long moment, it was then her turn to blink back to the moment.

"Are you staying nearby, one of the inns around the corner, perhaps?"

He nodded. "Fairfax. And what of you? Do you live nearby?"

"Close enough that I sometimes walk. I pass the Fairfax on my way home, and had thought I'd walk today."

"Will you allow me to join you? I have no other plans aside from supper, which I'll take at the pub next to the inn." He paused. "Perhaps you'll dine with me there? I owe you a debt of gratitude for humoring me today, on your most busy of days."

She laughed. "Perhaps the debt of gratitude is mutual, then. As it happens, I am available for an early supper, if you're comfortable waiting until I finish here. Thirty more minutes."

He nodded once. "Absolutely. May I peruse your bookshelves?" He pointed to her bookshelf behind her desk, which was full to bursting. She had another piece of shelving furniture on order from a local artisan.

"Please." She waved him to it and turned her attention to the list in her notebook. She crossed off several items that had either been completed or become obsolete, and jotted notes for the next day. She became, regrettably, distracted by the man who stood close to her chair. Although he wasn't looking at her, she felt heat suffuse her cheeks all the same. He was different than most men who showed an interest in her. He was oddly respectful, did not speak to her condescendingly as did many, especially when they learned not only had she earned a college degree, but had then pursued a career.

Ellie forced herself to focus on the task at hand, which became increasingly difficult when she heard him sliding and replacing books from the shelves. She wanted to look over her shoulder and see which ones were of interest to him. That he'd even asked to look at the books as a way to pass time—even if he *was* just looking for something to pass the time—went a long way toward endearing him to her heart.

He returned to his seat with a book in his hands, and she couldn't help but peer at the title. He'd chosen her new copy of *The Origin of the Species* by Charles Darwin, and she lifted her brows in surprise. She'd not had time to delve into it herself, and she wondered if he was aware it was fairly controversial.

He glanced up at her and gestured with the book. "I'm nearly finished with my copy, but I left it in my room at the inn. I hope you don't mind?"

"No, certainly not. Are you enjoying it, then?"

He nodded. "Fascinating, really. What did you make of it?"

"I've not had a chance to begin it, unfortunately." She offered a wry smile. "Many of my former college friends have given it rave reviews, although I confess we are all probably drawn to it because of its unconventional reputation."

He chuckled and flipped through the pages until he reached the last quarter of the book, where he stopped and began reading. She realized she was staring at him and finally turned back to her paperwork.

She finished much more quickly than she'd anticipated, and when she stretched in her chair, he looked up.

"Ready?"

She nodded and straightened a stack of papers. "I am. Shall we?" She spied the portfolio on the side of her desk and hesitated. "I know you'll not be with us for an extended amount of time, but would you care to look over this material tonight at your leisure? It is a copy of my curriculum I provide to new teachers."

He raised his brows, clearly surprised. "Of course, I would find it most informative. Perhaps tomorrow I'll not be chastised by Miss Drake, if I can learn something."

She smiled. "She is firm and fairly set in some of her opinions, but she is a seasoned teacher and appreciates the kindergarten model."

"She had me quite cowed, I readily confess. I do not know who she affected more profoundly, the students or me."

He took the packet from her and accompanied her as she checked the building before locking the door for the evening. The sky was cloudy and darkening, but there was mercifully no rain. She grasped her portmanteau and gathered her coat collar close at her throat. They left the school grounds and rounded a corner when she noted a hitch in Mr. Lucas' step.

"Is something wrong?"

He angled her subtly toward the storefronts, away from the street, and said in a low voice, "There is a man who was standing just beyond the school property, and I believe he has been following me for the better part of three weeks. I've seen him now too many times to discount it. If you'll look just there, in the window, you might see his reflection."

As they walked, she smiled at a woman who passed between them and an apothecary window. Turning her head as though greeting the woman, she glanced at the glass and saw a man who was crossing the street behind them. He was nondescript, slight of build and plain in dress. She could not say she had ever seen him before; if she had, there was nothing about him to remain fixed in her memory.

"Are you certain?"

He nodded. "The next time I see him, I will confront him."

"Why not now?"

He glanced down at her and offered his elbow. She

threaded her hand through his arm, wrapping her gloved fingers around his bicep. He was solid both in temperament and body, she realized.

"I'll not put you in harm's way. He may not have nefarious motives, but I do find it odd that he's made a habit of skulking around behind me, day after day."

She tried to focus on his words, but they melted into the air as she became very aware of the nearness of him, the sense of strength in his arm, the casual way in which they walked as though they'd been associates for a very long time instead of a handful of hours.

They reached the pub and entered, and she pointed toward a small, square table near the hearth where a warm fire blazed cheerily. He followed as she skirted a larger table in the center of the room where most of the patrons were seated. When they reached their table, Mr. Lucas took her coat and seated her before settling into the chair adjacent to hers.

As he laid his coat and hat next to hers on an empty seat, she looked out the window and thought she caught a glimpse of the stranger Mr. Lucas had brought to her attention. The streets were full of pedestrians and carriages, all moving quickly and with purpose. She frowned, hoping she'd not misread Mr. Lucas; what purpose would he have to alert her to a man who supposedly was following him? Could they be working in tandem toward some nefarious end?

He must have read her expression, because he smiled, looking sheepish. "You're thinking I am mad, or perhaps untrustworthy, and I wonder if anything I say will assure you that I am neither, and my purpose here in the city is indeed an innocent one."

"Who do you suppose that gentleman might be?" she asked him instead of addressing his comment directly.

"I've honestly no idea. That is why I intend to ascertain his motives tomorrow, once and for all."

"Have you enemies? Or perhaps the baron?"

He shook his head. "Not to my knowledge. Bertie was. . ." He frowned. "He was an interesting fellow. Known him all my life, was raised and educated right by his side, as a matter of fact. In his adult years, he led a rather chaotic existence, and I am afraid I wouldn't know if he'd accumulated any enemies."

She nodded and smiled up at a maid who brought them both mugs of ale.

"Food'll be right out," the girl said and returned to the kitchen.

"This friend of yours," Ellie said, pausing as she thought. "How many know of his child?"

He raised a brow and opened his hands. "Nobody, I should think. Or rather, again I wouldn't know, but it was my impression he had kept the child a secret from everyone."

"Perhaps the mother had family, enemies. But why would they know who you are?"

He took a sip of his ale and set it back down slowly. "I have been asking about her in all corners of the city. Word does tend to travel quickly." He knit his brow. "There is the matter of Bertie's distant cousin, who is the next male relative in line to inherit."

She removed her gloves and held her hands closer to the fire. "As a baron, the title would not pass down."

"No." Mr. Lucas lowered his voice. "His money would, however. He does have piles of it."

Ellie looked at him and folded her hands in her lap. She didn't wish to be rude, so she softened her next comment with a smile. "One might assume *you* to be envious of any potential heir; you were raised practically as family, no?"

The shock in his eyes was instantaneous, followed quickly by an expression of quiet outrage. "I am most certainly not envious of the baron's heir, nor do I need any of his money. I have plenty of my own from my father's wise investments and my own hard work."

Ellie leaned forward and touched his hand. "I meant no offense, however you must see the situation through my eyes. What would you think, if you were me and learning all of these things about a stranger?"

His face relaxed into a rueful smile, and he turned his hand, holding her fingers. "I would think exactly what you are thinking," he admitted. "In light of this conversation, I am surprised you allowed me anywhere near the children today."

Now her smile was wry. "I confess, I'd not considered it until now. You carry yourself as would a gentleman, and your clothing and appearance speak of one to whom funds are no issue. Only at this moment did I wonder if you have a darker purpose here." Her fingers on one hand were finally warming. The others sat lonely in her lap.

He pressed her hand between his before smiling and releasing it. "I readily admit I have no experience dealing with children; they are as mysterious to me as is Egypt. I certainly bear them no ill will, however, and am loyal to the baron; he is most anxious to meet his grandchild."

The barmaid returned with a tray carrying two large bowls of mutton and vegetables. The food was still steaming and smelled delicious. As she set them on the table, Mr. Lucas looked up at her with a smile of thanks, which the girl readily returned. She flicked the barest of glances at Ellie before smiling again at Mr. Lucas as she sauntered off.

To his credit, he seemed not to notice the attention. Handsome as he was, she might rightly assume him to be a heartbreaker of epic proportions. Rather than preen, however, he merely dove into his meal with gusto. The bread on the side of the bowl was thick and hearty, and he tore it in half as she picked up her utensils with a smile.

"Tea and luncheon at the school are light fare for adults," she said.

"Probably plenty for most people," he said with a chuckle, "but I fear my appetite is large." He paused and then frowned. "Do the children not have enough to eat at the orphanages? I know many are seeing strides of reform, but some of the children today seemed truly famished."

She sighed. "I fear they are. Some have heartier appetites than the rest, but as a whole, they always seem hungry. The city leaders are preparing to vote on legislation that would provide excess funds to orphanages and workhouses, but such prospects do meet with opposition."

He didn't respond, but the frown on his face spoke to his feelings on the matter.

They ate for a time in silence, when he spoke again. "What of you, Miss Perkins? How does a woman come to attend college and establish a school that bears her name?"

She dabbed at her mouth with the square of linen the maid had just delivered—apparently as an afterthought or perhaps a reason to again smile at Mr. Lucas. "My mother is a Frenchwoman who inherited an amount of money, and my father was an Englishman who also inherited an amount of money." She paused, smiling. "My maternal grandfather was Swiss, and a colleague of Friedrich Froebel, who established the concept of kindergarten—a way to educate society's poor as a means of bettering the whole. My father died when I was young, so my mother took us to the continent where we divided our time between France and Switzerland. With such academic origins, it followed naturally that we would attend as much schooling as was available to us." She lifted her brows with another smile. "I am the second of five daughters."

He nodded, eyes widening. "My respect to your grandfather for fostering a love for learning in a home full of granddaughters."

"Oh, and my mother, also." She pointed her fork toward the west and added, "She resides in France with the youngest two girls, but believes in allowing us to choose our course of action. By that, I mean she allows us to determine which university we will attend."

He chuckled again. "She sounds very wise, and I commend *her* for encouraging education. England has only seen colleges for women in the last decade—did you attend here or abroad?"

"Here. I chose Almhurst because my father loved Liverpool and it is a connection to him, I suppose. My younger sister is nearly finished at Almhurst, as well; we reside in a home my mother procured here in town near the college."

He finished his meal and sat back in his chair with a sigh. "And your kindergarten? I imagine you took on your share of opponents in establishing it."

She sighed and nodded. "It has not been easy. The boys' schools here and in London see donations of thousands of pounds per annum, and I must beg and scrape for every shilling." She looked at his warm, brown eyes, again remembering the difference she'd felt that morning after escorting Mr. Twizzle from the school and then meeting Mr. Lucas. He regarded her with interest, his handsome face serious as she spoke.

"I have written a grant and will deliver it tomorrow to Mr. Crowden, who maintains an office at the museum. He enjoys that benefit as a generous patron of the organization, and fancies himself an amateur paleontologist. He and his wife, my college mentor, have been my school's biggest support, its sole support in the beginning." She lifted a shoulder. "He is a good friend to my father's family and well-connected. If not for him, Perkins Kindergarten would still be a dream."

"They sound like very good and decent people," Mr. Lucas said softly, and she wondered what he was seeing in her face. Vulnerability, probably. Frustration.

She nodded, her eyes suddenly stinging. "She is brilliant and was instrumental to my success in college. He is the very best sort of man. He does not find my endeavors inappropriate or frivolous." She lightly cleared her throat, feeling self-conscious and exposed. A few kind words from a handsome man and she was blurting out things she rarely discussed.

"What of you?" she now said. "What sort of man cares not one iota that a woman is at the helm of her own school? Or perhaps you do, only are too clever to show it."

He smiled. "The baroness took a hand to raising me alongside Bertie as my own mother died in childbirth. Baroness Francis was a devotee of Mrs. Wollstonecraft."

Ellie laughed. "Say no more. She made a bluestocking of you, then."

His grin was open and easy. Honest. "Indeed. She brooked no foolishness and was perhaps the smartest person I have ever known."

"She sounds wonderful. She is gone? You've spoken only of the baron wishing for his grandchild."

He nodded. "We lost her five years ago to consumption. She did not go peacefully, fought it to her last labored breath." His gaze now was reflective and a bit sad.

"Well," Ellie said, "it requires an amazing woman to raise a boy who is unthreatened by his female counterparts." He leaned closer as she spoke, as the volume of hungry pub-goers increased, bringing with them added noise.

"The baroness always maintained that one secure in his own masculinity had nothing to fear from a smart woman." His warm eyes held hers for a moment, and then he winked at her. He pushed up from his chair and added, "If you'll allow me a moment to settle the bill, I would like to see you safely home."

"Oh," she said, her cheeks warming, "I had not intended for you to buy my meal."

He put a hand on his chest. "Please, you must. I'll never maintain my masculine pride otherwise."

"I very much doubt that." She side-eyed him as she reached for her portmanteau.

He leaned down closer and placed his hand on hers. "Please. It shall be my opportunity to thank you for allowing me to disrupt your school."

He was close enough that she smelled the light remnants of the day's cologne. She finally nodded, not trusting herself to speak, not wanting him to ever step away.

He straightened and made his way through the crowded room to settle the bill. She gathered her things, and his, feeling a thrill at picking up his great coat and hat, as though they were familiar enough with each other for it to be perfectly natural. It was a domestic scene she allowed herself to enjoy for a moment, hugging his coat close to her and again catching his pleasant scent.

What sort of woman would he marry? She considered it as he made his way back to her. She hoped he would marry a woman of substance, someone with sound judgment and a curious mind. She hoped he would find someone like his baroness who had championed the rights of women.

"Your thoughts are a million miles away," he said, placing his leather wallet into his inner suit coat pocket.

She blinked, looking up at him, and telling herself that he was only standing so close to her because it was crowded and there was little room. He put his hand on his great coat and she released it in surprise, not aware she had been clutching it so tightly.

"Are you well?" His brow creased in concern as he took her coat as well and guided her toward the door with a hand on her back. He held her coat up so she could thread her arms through the sleeves and settled it on her shoulders. His knuckles brushed the sensitive skin on her neck as he straightened it and she pulled out a trapped lock of hair.

"I am fine," she said brightly, bracing against the cold wind as the door opened. They waited in the doorway as three people entered, laughing and shaking umbrellas. "Oh dear." She looked outside at the steadily falling rain. "We were fortunate to enjoy the walk from the school without the weather becoming a nuisance."

"I do not suppose you will want to walk home now," Mr. Lucas said, standing close enough behind her that her shoulder brushed against his chest.

She sighed. "I'll take a cab. The night grows dark anyhow." She peered up through the glass on the door. "There's an awning next door, we can stand there."

He put his hat on his head and grinned at her, his arm curving around her to open the door. "Are you ready?"

Her breath caught in her throat as she met his eyes, which seemed to smile every bit as much as his lips. *Eyes that smile,* her mother often said. *A man with eyes that smile is a man worth your time.*

Oh, maman, she thought as she braced herself and dashed out into the rain, *I do hope you are right. But what shall I do if you are?*

Chapter Seven

Graham stood beneath the bright green awning in the pouring rain with the most incredible woman he'd ever met. She grew more beautiful to him with every word she spoke, even when she'd almost accused him of seeking out the baron's heir for nefarious purposes. She was strong and intelligent, and he had a feeling the baroness would have approved of her. If he wasn't much mistaken, he believed she was affected by his nearness, which was only fair, because he wanted very much to pull her close and kiss her right there in the presence of strangers who dashed to and fro in the rain.

He hailed an approaching hansom cab and held her hand while she climbed up. Rain spattered against the brim of his hat and bounced off, dripping into his eyes as she settled into place and he watched like a lovelorn puppy.

She let out a quick puff of breath and shivered, smiling at him. "Thank you for the meal," she said. "Until tomorrow, then?"

He nodded. "Until tomorrow. I shall be a much-improved teacher, I assure you." He held up the packet of information she'd given him when they left the school.

She laughed and he wished he could climb up next to her in the cab. "I look forward to seeing it," she told him and waved as the driver pulled away from the curb.

He stepped back, watching the cab until it was out of

sight. He felt like a fool, but realized that somehow, after a handful of hours, he was falling very much in love with Miss Perkins. He didn't fall in love so quickly. In fact, he'd never fallen in love before. It was not as though he'd never spent time with a beautiful woman, but this was different and completely beyond his sphere of comprehension. He had no business falling in love with a woman whose life was dedicated to her work, and justly so. The children needed her.

He finally turned and entered the inn, wet and chilled, and climbed the stairs to the second floor. The inn was respectable and well-kept, recently remodeled and comfortable. His room was spacious and well appointed, and he looked forward to relaxing after what had proven, surprisingly, to be a strange and tiring day.

He disrobed and changed into comfortable clothing, draping his wet clothes on racks in the dressing area. Once settled in a comfortable chair by the fire, he jotted a letter to the baron, detailing his progress and telling him he was hopeful he'd soon be sending news about the little heir. *To that end, I am teaching a class of fifteen tiny people, if you can believe it. I hope this finds you well, and I shall send continued messages detailing my progress.*

He hoped that would bring a smile to the baron's face. He'd smiled less and less after the death of the baroness, and all hopes he'd had for a meaningful future with Bertie had died with the young man. He was not hoping to replace Bertie in the baron's eyes. There had never been any envy on Graham's part; his relationship with his own father had been warm and fulfilling. But he cared deeply for the man he'd come to regard as an uncle, and hoped desperately to be able to fulfil his wishes soon.

Graham arrived at Perkins Kindergarten early the following morning, firmly determined to control the sheep today rather than be trampled by them. Wielding his curriculum folio like a weapon, he bid good morning to Miss Jeffries and Miss Perkins; the latter flushed and smiled when she greeted him, and he felt his morning was off to a glorious start.

Before the children arrived, he made himself familiar with the teaching tools and manipulatives in the supply cupboard. He counted five sets of Froebel Gifts, the toys Mr. Froebel had designed for teaching young children to create and problem solve and familiarize themselves with the world around them.

The concepts were revolutionary compared to traditional education. Education of children was not a new concept to England, but these methods and the population they served certainly were. While the ideas may have spread in other parts of Europe, he wasn't surprised in the least that Miss Perkins had faced opposition to her efforts.

He frowned as he again counted the five sets of Froebel Gifts. Ideally, the curriculum required one set per child. He set the folio on the large teacher's desk near the supply cupboard and withdrew a few introductory lessons. Retrieving one of the gifts sets, he sat at the desk and began reviewing the lessons with the manipulative toys.

He was engrossed in the process so thoroughly that when Miss Perkins called to him from the doorway, he looked up in surprise.

"I beg your pardon?"

She smiled. "The children are arriving; I am here to give warning."

"Oh. Yes, very good." He cleared his throat. Nearly an hour had passed, and he still had numerous lessons to review.

He had enough grasp of the initial concepts to begin, he decided, and would do his best.

"I shall return as quickly as possible so that you'll have an opportunity to determine which boy is the one you seek." She nodded toward the materials on his desk and added, "I see you're making a genuine go of it today."

He nodded. "I may as well do the job correctly, wouldn't you say? The curriculum is quite interesting." He smiled. "Children here probably enjoy their public schooling education a sight more than I did."

She laughed. "They are fortunate, without a doubt."

"I notice there are only five sets of gifts here—are there more elsewhere? I have fifteen students, after all."

She shook her head, her lips tightening. "We have funds enough for only five sets per class. The grant application I am submitting today on our field trip to the museum would go toward the purchase of additional sets."

He frowned. What was it she had said yesterday? Boys' schools were flush with funding, but she was obliged to scrape for every shilling. The sound of little feet in the hallway pulled his attention from the thought. Graham had money—his own and the inheritance from his father's investments—and he would gladly purchase some Froebel Gifts for the school.

Miss Perkins turned and stood sentry at the door while a hush fell over the hallway. Graham rose and joined her, looking at the orderly queue of little faces awaiting his attention. A glance down the hall showed three other lines of students awaiting their teachers' attention and when each little body was as still as possible, the teachers stood aside and allowed them entrance.

Miss Perkins smiled at him and stepped back, and he looked at his little group of temporary charges. "Good morning, students," he said with a nod and polite smile. He must remember to keep the reins firm to avoid another fiasco like the one yesterday.

"G'morning," came the reply, some mumbled from probable fatigue, others fresh-faced and bright.

"Please enter the room quietly, hang your outer wear on the hooks Miss Perkins assigned yesterday, and take your seats at the story time circle." There. He'd mastered the first task of the day. He stood aside and allowed the children to file in, gesturing toward the hooks along the wall.

He helped a few whose cold fingers fumbled with coat fastenings, and called for a couple energetic friends to walk, not run. When all the children were seated in their semi-circle, he joined them again sitting on the floor, but decided today he would take the role of instructor and make a serious attempt at it.

They responded well, and with a better grasp of the day's structure, he was more in command of the class movements and activity. They read stories, they sang nursery rhymes, and he taught them the basic fundamentals of a country dance, which they embraced with gusto. When they grew rowdy, he clapped his hands twice as he'd seen Miss Brophy do the day before at outside play—like magic, each of her students stopped where they were and echoed her claps, all eyes on her. He taught them the routine, practiced it with them as Miss Perkins had done yesterday when marching them up and down the hallway without making noise, and was delighted when it actually seemed to work.

Morning tea arrived before he was aware so much time had passed. He frowned at the soft bell he heard Miss Jeffries ringing in the hallway indicating they were to go to the great room in ten minutes. There were a few things he'd not yet addressed on the lesson schedule, and he mentally rearranged the next morning's lessons to cover the concepts for which they'd not had time.

As the children sat at their table, partaking of their tea and sandwiches as would small ladies and gentlemen, he felt inordinately pleased. He caught Miss Perkins and the other teachers—even the cooking staff—watching him in wide-eyed surprise. His sense of accomplishment raised another notch in the glow of that surprise. The morning had not been without its issues, but it was a far cry from the day before.

Miss Perkins approached him as they neared the end of teatime, a soft smile playing at the corners of her mouth. "Mr. Lucas, I am suitably impressed."

"Thank you, Miss Perkins. I am gratified." His smile was wry. "Amazing the things one can accomplish with a set of lesson plans rather than simply assuming they will behave with little specific guidance."

"Are you prepared to walk to the library? I thought we might go now rather than after luncheon. They're apt to be less tired. Besides, the rain has stopped and if our luck holds, we'll enjoy clear skies."

He nodded. He would shift the lessons with Froebel's basic block set until after their return. She left to speak with the other teachers, and Graham walked around the children's table, stopping one boy as he drew back an arm to throw a punch at the boy sitting beside him and instructing him to change seats with Stevie Smith. Stevie looked disappointed, as he seemed to be the best of friends with Edward Crispin, and Graham thought back to his own school days when such situations had happened to him. These should consider themselves fortunate; any time a squabble erupted when Graham was young, the headmaster settled it with a paddle.

As the aggressor settled into the new place and Graham moved his plate and teacup over, he caught the child's eye. "Shall we discuss this in private, Mr. Dawson, or are you in possession of yourself?"

John Dawson didn't smile, but he mumbled an apology and nodded. Graham turned to Mark Phillips, the child with whom John had been arguing, to be sure he hadn't been the instigator, and satisfied all was fair and equitable, instructed the children to finish their tea.

It was one of several altercations he'd resolved, and the day had not yet reached noon. How on earth did these women do it, day in and day out?

Across the table, Alexandra Featherstone spilled some tea on the front of her smock and gasped. She looked up, eyes huge, and with one hand hurriedly wiped at the stain. Graham approached and reached down to take the teacup from her, and she flinched.

"There now," he soothed the little girl, with an uncomfortable and unfamiliar lump forming in his throat. "No harm done, just a bit of spilled tea." He placed the cup on its saucer and squatted down next to her. He picked up the serviette from her lap and made a show of dabbing gently on the smock. "It will wash out."

Her eyes were bright with unshed tears. "Washing day's not 'til Friday, and Mrs. Gilly gets awful cross when we get dirty."

To his way of thinking, Mrs. Gilly ought to realize that small children were bound to spill on themselves, probably several times in one day. He was a grown man and spilled his tea three times a week.

He smiled at the little girl. "There, now. We shall see if Miss Perkins knows of a way to fix the stain before you go home this afternoon. In fact, where the fabric is so dark, I'd wager that in an hour we'll not even see the tea."

She nodded and sniffed. He gave her a little wink and managed a wobbly smile from her. As he straightened and looked over the room full of some of the world's most vulnerable, he amended his questions concerning the teachers' stamina day after day, and wondered now how they resisted the foolhardy urge to rescue them all.

Perhaps he could convince the baron to take in fifteen children instead of one. Shaking his head at the thought, he helped the students wipe their mouths and tidy their plates and utensils before leaving the table and forming their queue to return to the classroom. He came to realize one thing for certain; if he hadn't been sent to retrieve a specific child for Baron Francis, he would never have been able to choose one at random.

Chapter Eight

Ellie hoped the weather would remain clear as she and Mr. Lucas walked with the children the short distance to the William Brown Library and Museum. It was a relatively new addition to the city, incorporating the Earl of Derby's natural history collection, which had served as the city's museum to that point.

Ellie loved the new building, which was expansive and contained more wonders than a person could explore in an hour or a day, even. William Brown's generosity to the city was a welcome boon, and the Crowdens, Ellie's best supports, were equally as generous.

Mr. Crowden was often found in the museum offices, and in her arms Ellie carried the portfolio containing the papers she'd written to apply for a grant from the charitable foundation. She was hopeful of receiving the money, but also realistic; she was not the only person in need of funding.

Had someone told her a week ago that she'd be distracted while on her way to deliver the papers, she'd never have believed it would be because of a man. The school occupied her thoughts day and night, and in addition to worrying about day-to-day operations, the faces of the children haunted her. The orphanages were well kept and adhering to new guidelines provided by social pressure from the ladies' societies, but the little ones' eyes bore a sadness and longing that tore at her heart.

The fact that Graham Lucas had crept into her thoughts and kept pulling her focus away from her concerns was in itself, concerning. She walked beside him at the head of the line of children, her lips twitching in pleased amusement at his handling of the little class. He was an intelligent one, that much had been clear from the outset, but his patience was impressive. His dedication to a temporary job was commendable and spoke to the determination of his character. He was not there to teach, however, and she told herself sternly that she would do well to remember it. He would determine which child was the baron's grandson and then would leave.

That would be for the best, because she could not afford to lose her focus. She worked so diligently to make a difference, to provide something life changing to people who would otherwise experience a different path, one with fewer opportunities for health and fortune. She had never once been deterred in her studies, her long hours at college, her frustrating efforts to convince various boards of illustrious individuals of the value of her ideas. Nothing, certainly not a man, had ever come close to pulling her attention from her goals. Most other women found her odd, at best, and incomprehensively ridiculous at worst. The only avenue of success in the world available to a woman was through the success of a talented man of resources. She had known this fact from her early years, and had decided she would make her own way.

"A penny for your thoughts," Mr. Lucas said.

She looked at him and forced herself to smile when her honest reaction was to simply stare. Intense, warm eyes, full lips, defined jawline, neatly trimmed blonde hair—he truly was devastatingly handsome. He was professional and well established, possessed of exceptionally good humor, and if she examined the situation honestly, he was sliding into her heart with his obvious affection and concern for the children. Most men had little time for children, especially those belonging to others.

"A penny for my thoughts," she echoed. "My thoughts are befuddled by you, sir. I've not decided where you fit in society's overall scheme."

He chuckled. "I am not as conveniently tucked into place as a Froebel Gift?"

She laughed. "Those do fit together nicely, do they not? Each has its place in the box."

He tipped his head. "I might say the same of you, madam. What is the quote? Perhaps we are both square pegs not quite fitting into round holes."

"Have you never thought to marry?" Her curiosity prevented circumspection and reserve.

"I am not opposed to the notion." A smile played on his lips. "Truthfully, I have not met a woman with whom I can envision spending inordinate amounts of time."

She laughed again. "Ah, how very bucolic you are. Have you not heard it is entirely acceptable in some circles to spend very little time with one's spouse? Only that which is necessary to present a pretty picture to society."

"I have indeed heard of such unions, been witness to more than a few, in fact." His tone remained light, but there was an undercurrent of intensity to it. He murmured, "That is not the sort of union I want for myself. I hope to find a friend as well as a lover with whom to spend my life. Someone whose interests match my own, who would not be averse to long discussions before the fire, or time spent together at the end of the day in comfortable silence. Where it is enough simply to be together. Truly companions."

She stared at him, mouth slack, before gathering her scattered wits and clearing her throat. She looked straight ahead, relieved to see the museum steps in sight. The silence stretched, not at all the "comfortable" sort he mentioned, and she began to feel the weight of her non-response.

She glanced at him and noted the tight set to his jaw as he also set his sights on the museum.

"Apologies if I've made you uncomfortable," he said.

"No, not at all! I suppose I...I am surprised to find a truly thoughtful man with such refreshing insight. I've not met many." She frowned. "I've met one. Well, two, now. Honestly," she said, lowering her voice, "I doubt I would find a gentleman liberal enough to be comfortable married to a headmistress of a school bearing her name."

He raised a brow as they stopped at the stairs. "Any man who would take issue with it would be an utter fool."

Her mouth went slack again, and as he turned to quiet the children before entering, she drew in a shaky breath. She was completely at sea, wondering if he were a figment of her overworked imagination. She would very much love a family of her own; she'd never thought, however, that it would be a possibility.

"Mr. John Dawson and Mr. Stephen Smith, front of the line, if you please." Mr. Lucas beckoned toward the two boys, who moved forward and fell into place at the head of the queue. "Gentlemen," he said quietly, "I trust we will use respectful voices and keep our hands to ourselves when we enter the museum."

Ellie smiled and covered it with her fingers. He was clearly remembering his own scholastic experiences; to say that he was a natural with the students was an understatement. She allowed herself the tiniest fraction of a moment to imagine he was staying, that he was truly an instructor at Perkins Kindergarten.

"I beg your pardon?" Mr. Lucas was saying to Stephen.

"Ye remind me of a constable what walked the beat on the dockside when I was a young tike." The boy scrunched up his nose, shifting from one foot to the other.

Mr. Lucas' lips twitched. "That must have been some time ago."

"Are ye a constable, then?" Edward Crispin asked. "Me da was a constable."

Mr. Lucas shook his head. "I am not a constable, but as it happens, I have an uncle in the London Metropolitan Police."

"Peter says constables is no good rot," John Dawson now piped in. "Collar kids what done nuffin wrong, day an' night."

The rest of the children nodded solemnly in agreement, and Ellie inwardly sighed. She knew how frequently the children and their siblings had run afoul of the law, often with severe consequences.

"I happen to know many good constables," Mr. Lucas said firmly. "I am a solicitor, and I work with the police on occasion."

"Yer one o' them?" Stephen Smith now asked. "Are ye set to haul us in?"

Mr. Lucas rubbed his forehead.

"Children," Ellie interrupted, "Mr. Lucas is not here to haul you in, or question you, or anything of the like."

"He asked us where we lived before the orphanage," a young girl suddenly interjected. "Yesterday. All sorts of questions." She nodded, and the others soon joined. "I think he is a constable."

Ellie glanced at Mr. Lucas, who shrugged as if to protest his innocence. He said quietly to her, "I was attempting to—"

"I know." She sighed. "Students, Mr. Lucas is temporarily your teacher, and he is not a constable. Am I clear?"

Most of the heads nodded in unison. A few small faces

examined him with open suspicion, but the majority seemed content enough.

Ellie caught a quick movement in her periphery and turned her head just as a man ducked behind a parked carriage. She frowned, squinting at the carriage and thinking she would see the man emerge from the other side. He did not, and she told herself she must have imagined it.

"What is it?" Mr. Lucas asked her.

She slowly shook her head, still looking at the carriage. It began pulling away, and there was nobody standing on the other side. "I thought I saw the man you alerted me to yesterday."

Mr. Lucas stiffened. "Where?"

She gestured to the carriage, which now disappeared around the corner. "Perhaps it was someone else. He really was quite ordinary in appearance and manner."

Mr. Lucas kept watching the disappearing carriage as he placed his hand on the small of her back and nudged her closer. "Come along then, children, and remember our instructions. You will stay with me at all times, like ducklings following their mother."

A few of the students laughed, and the humor quickly spread through the little group until they all laughed as only children can.

"A mother duck!" Stevie Smith chortled. "Ye're a mighty silly mother duck!"

Mr. Lucas put his hand on his chest and tipped his head toward them. "Be that as it may, my instructions remain. You are to follow me, and remain with me at all times." He smiled, but then added, "That is enough. We will enter when you're quiet."

A few lingering giggles eventually faded away as the children sobered. Ellie looked at Mr. Lucas, raised a brow, and held a hand out to the entrance. "Well done, sir," she said. "Do lead on, I shall bring up the rear. Please turn to your left once inside."

She followed the line of children as Mr. Lucas led them inside, and spoke with the docent, whom she had contacted the day before. She then took the reins, leading them through the museum of natural history, pausing at prehistoric exhibits to give the children the opportunity to stare at the ancient animals unearthed in the archaeological society's most recent excavation.

To her surprise, Mr. Lucas was knowledgeable about the recent finds, and quite conversant concerning them. She whispered to him that she would deliver her papers to the office just down the hallway and left the children in his capable hands. What a pity it was that he couldn't stay, that he wasn't interested in teaching as a career. His talents were wasted on the staid work of a solicitor.

She reached Mr. Crowden's office door and knocked, gratified at the answering voice just before the door opened to reveal the distinguished gentleman with salt-and-pepper hair. His face split into a wide smile and he grasped her hand.

"Eloise! I have been awaiting your grant application, is this it?"

She smiled and extended the portfolio. "Indeed it is." She took a breath and added, "Mr. Crowden, I understand your professionalism and your responsibility to the museum board of directors, and I would hope you know I do not expect favors of any sort. You are supportive and more than kind, and I am so grateful."

"My dear, I do not imagine for a moment you would expect any such thing. You needn't even mention it."

"I know." She lifted a shoulder, reflecting on the first time she'd met him when she was a brand-new college student. He had been kind, and was the "other one" she'd mentioned to Mr. Lucas, the only other man she knew aside from her own dear grandfather who did not think she was encroaching on territory that was beyond her rights.

"You'll join us for supper soon, and share first-week-of-school adventures?" He smiled and again squeezed her hand.

"I would love nothing more."

He must have seen something in her face, something not customarily there. "Would you care to visit here for a spell?" His brow creased in concern. "Is something amiss?"

"No, but thank you. I am here with one of my classes today, and a temporary teacher. It has been a most adventuresome week—I shall have plenty to share. I must also retrieve periodicals from the second floor for use in my lecture this evening at Almhurt's education symposium."

He hesitated as though considering whether to pry, but patted her hand again. "Very well, my dear. Good luck this evening, although you'll hardly need it. You've presented so often as to be a university regular. Should you grow weary of your littles, you'd find a place on a larger campus." He smiled. "I can hardly imagine you growing weary of your charges, however. Go now, and I shall deliver your grant application personally to the board of directors."

Ellie thanked him and after a quick embrace, hurried back to Mr. Lucas and the children, whom she found in the room dedicated to medieval tapestry. She watched the temporary teacher as he enchanted the children with his stories, and they gathered close about him as if they would each gladly climb up into his arms.

Her eyes stung, and she blinked back the emotion. The children's craving for warmth and tender affection was easily noted, and she appreciated the sincerity in his approach. He embraced the duty, no matter how temporarily, despite the fact that his initial mission had brought him to her school on an entirely different matter. She now worried that the children would miss him when he was replaced. Perhaps a bigger issue, however, was that she would miss him, too.

Chapter Nine

The next week, and then two, passed quickly, so much so that Graham lost track of time as one day transitioned into the next. He and Miss Perkins dined together each evening, frequenting different pubs and restaurants, and ending the evening in the inn's library, where they shared tea and conversation late into the evening. He then would accompany her in a cab safely to the little townhouse she shared with her sister, Miss Fiona Perkins, whom he had met at Almhurst during Miss Perkins' academic lecture the evening of their visit to the museum.

By now, he had determined that little Stevie Smith was Bertie's biological son. He was as certain as he could be, even after further conversation with the orphanage staff yielded no useful information about his mother. Miss Perkins—Ellie, as he'd come to think of her—had accompanied him as he'd hoped a female presence might elicit more of a helpful response, but none of the current orphanage employees knew anything about the boys' mothers.

He'd determined Stevie to be the one he sought when, upon playing outside following luncheon one afternoon, the child had turned to kick a ball in movement so characteristic of Bertie as to be his late friend's small shadow. The resemblance in that moment had been so striking, his breath had caught in his throat. Ellie, standing beside him, had witnessed the moment, and astutely, quietly observed, "He is the one, is he not?"

Graham had contacted Baron Francis, who was to arrive in town soon. The baron asked him to secure lodging in a townhome so that they might have a warm environment in which the boy could become accustomed to his new family. Graham planned to remain with them, along with the usual retinue of servants.

As luck would have it, a stately house near the Perkins home was on the market, and Graham signed the paperwork with satisfaction. He did not attempt to pretend—even to himself—that his reasoning for snapping it up so quickly had nothing to do with the proximity to Ellie. He'd been gratified at the light in her eyes when she'd learned of it, as he'd become so enamored of her he could hardly hold a thought in his head that didn't involve her.

She interviewed candidates for the teaching position, but thus far, none had seemed what she termed, "a good fit." For his part, Graham was in no hurry to leave. He had established a pleasant and dependable routine with the children, and found to his utter bafflement that he enjoyed it. He looked forward to each day, studied the curriculum and lessons carefully, and tailored each to address specific needs. He knew the children's personalities, strengths and weaknesses by now and was gratified with each bit of progress, no matter how small.

Following dinner the day Graham finalized the lease on the baron's home, he and Ellie walked through it with the seller's solicitor for a final inspection. Much of the furniture was to remain, and Graham made arrangements with the solicitor to finalize the details after the baron's arrival and approval.

After the tour, Ellie entered the library, just off the front hall, while Graham saw the solicitor to the door. When he returned to the library, he stood at the entrance and watched as Ellie trailed her fingers along the spines of several old books lining one of the shelves. Her head tilted slightly to better read the titles, and she absently tucked behind her ear the perpetually escaping silky dark curl of hair.

He leaned a shoulder against the doorway and took advantage of the quiet moment to simply watch her explore, sometimes stopping to examine a title for a protracted moment before slowly moving on to the next. She must have sensed him, because he'd not made a sound, but she turned. In the warm, low light of the wall sconces, he noted the deep, deep blue of her eyes. She paused, silent, and simply met his gaze. Awareness flickered in her eyes, and her chest rose subtly with an indrawn breath.

He thought he should lighten the mood with a witty comment, or apologize for intruding on a private moment, but in the end he slowly crossed the room until he stood before her. Still, neither uttered a word, and he framed her face in his hands. Her eyes remained locked on his until they finally dropped to his mouth, and then fluttered closed. She leaned infinitesimally closer, quietly sighing as though accepting the inevitable, and he lowered his lips to hers.

He was careful, soft, but needn't have worried about shocking her. She wound her arms around his waist and he pulled her closer as the kiss deepened, his lips exploring hers as he had wanted to do from the moment he first laid eyes on her. She was exquisite, a perfect counterpart, and the late night conversations and shared confidences flashed through his head as his lips explored hers. There would never be another like her, not if he traveled the world over.

He splayed his hands wide across her back, finally

returning them again to her face and reluctantly, gently breaking the contact. He was surprised to find himself a bit winded, but gratified that she was equally so. He smiled, still softly holding her face, and traced his thumbs along her cheek and jaw.

"Ellie," he whispered. "I am quite besotted."

She smiled, her arms still encircling his waist, and he realized she'd wound them under his jacket, against his waistcoat. "I am relieved to have company in such a sorry state."

His smile widened, and he kissed her again. She pulled her arms free and encircled his shoulders, threading her fingers in his hair. His heart pounded, and holding her tightly, he pressed her up against the bookcase.

Her breath came out in a gasp as he kissed the side of her neck, nuzzling the sensitive skin behind her ear with the tip of his nose. She sighed his name—the first time he'd heard it on her lips—and he exhaled in satisfaction as he gently nipped her earlobe.

She laughed breathlessly and he brought his lips back to hers, prolonging the contact until reluctantly loosening his grip and allowing them both to breathe. She clutched his shoulders, her lips quirked in a half smile, and ducked her head.

"Are you well?" he whispered.

She nodded and looked at him, her eyes deep blue and her lips delightfully kiss-swollen.

"I am afraid I've mussed your coiffure," he said, catching a hair pin that dropped to her collar.

She stayed within the circle of his embrace, and he was not about to move away as long as she desired the closeness. One arm still wound around her waist, he handed her the hairpin which she took with a smile. She ruffled the hair at his neck with her other hand and looked at him again, slowly shaking her head.

"What is it?" he murmured.

"This is a complication I never imagined."

He raised one brow. "Complication, mmm? I feel quite sophisticated; I've never been a complication before."

Her smile broadened, but a wistful, almost worried wince belied a hint of distress. He thought he might know the source of it.

"I'll not ask anything of you, Ellie, that you are unable to give. We've only just met, and I have no intention of pulling you away from your school, your life."

She flushed and bit her lip. "I do not. . .that is, I am not in the habit of. . ." She waved her hand, fingers still holding the hairpin.

He shook his head. "Nor am I. I would not have you believe I see you as a dalliance, or come to you thusly without thought." His smile was wry. "I've thought of little else for days, in truth. I do not intend to pressure you, but you mustn't think I am not sincere in my attentions." He tucked her hair again behind her ear. "I'll not propose marriage to you tonight, but I also am not going anywhere. I've found I quite enjoy Liverpool and her school system."

She laughed softly and traced his cheekbone with her thumb. She followed the line of his ear with her fingertip and he closed his eyes in pleasure. "I find *I'm* enjoying the company of the charming, temporary employee."

He opened his eyes, determined that she understand his intentions. "I will not ever take you away from the school, or stand in the path of your progress. If you believe nothing else, know that."

Her eyes filled, the unshed tears amplifying the arresting color. "It means more to me than you can imagine. Graham, I do not know. . ." She frowned, her brow knit in worry that threatened to break his heart. "I do not know what will happen, what the future holds, and I have come to cherish you deeply in a short amount of time. I also would not hold you back, or tie you to unconventional circumstances that, in the future, may chafe as the novelty grows dim."

He grinned and again wrapped both arms around her as she encircled hers around his neck. "Unconventional circumstances that involve a unique role-reversal I find more enticing by the day?"

She smiled, but still shook her head. "I am not normal, Graham. That is, I will never be what most people expect. I simply. . .I cannot."

He sighed. "I am a man in my thirties, Ellie. I ought to have married by now, could have married by now. I simply have never found someone I could not only love, but also genuinely like. I wasn't certain you existed."

"Mercy. You oughtn't say such things, you're bound to work your way into my heart."

"Excellent. My plan is progressing beautifully."

She laughed. "Your plan was to teach fifteen orphans and be temporarily employed by a woman?"

"To my eternal surprise, that has become my plan. Miss Perkins, I wonder if you would consider allowing me to evolve from temporary to permanent teacher?"

She blinked. Also to his eternal surprise, he meant every word. His few clients—the baron included—occupied a small part of his professional time. He could easily manage his responsibilities there and teach the little children.

"You're. . .you are serious? Truly?"

"I am. Perhaps we might consider this year a trial period and then reassess at its conclusion." He paused. "My qualifications, however, could present a problem."

She shook her head. "Your education is more than sufficient, and I've observed you with the children—you're a very natural teacher. I train my teachers with my curriculum, at any rate, so you're not necessarily at a disadvantage another candidate would enjoy." She rubbed her forehead and shifted a bit, so he released her and immediately felt a chill.

She rubbed her arms, similarly affected, it seemed. "I would hate for you to have regrets, Graham."

"Madam," he said, exasperated but amused, "I believe you are attempting to talk me out of your life. I would not do any of this if I did not sincerely desire it. I am aware of the unconventionality, Ellie. I am also aware of this: I watched my friend die a few short months ago, and have come to appreciate how fleeting life can be. If I were to leave something that feels to have slipped so naturally into my life, I would be wrong in doing so, and would regret it forever."

He rubbed his knuckles gently on her cheek. "I believe I've laid bare my soul. The decisions, now, are yours."

Chapter Ten

Ellie tossed and turned much of the night, reliving the kiss with Graham—and the subsequent conversation—until she thought she'd go mad. She had fallen for a man who actually tempted her to believe she could balance her school and a family. Other women, pioneers in the field of advancing women's rights and opportunities, managed to do their work and maintain a home, and most of them had supportive husbands. There were others, however, who remained single and Ellie had presumed that would be the course her life took.

She didn't understand why she was so torn—perhaps because she'd known him for such a ridiculously small amount of time—but she felt in her heart he was genuine. Was she truly going to allow fear, for the first time in her life, to determine the course of her decisions?

She finally fell into a fitful sleep but was awakened a short time later by a loud banging on the front door. She looked at her clock and noted the time—4:00 in the morning. As she stumbled from bed and grabbed her robe, her heart beat hard in her chest. Good tidings never came in the nighttime hours.

She ran from her room and reached the landing at the top of the stairs, struggling to put on her robe, and across the hall, her sister Fiona opened her door, blinking in confusion. Someone outside was shouting, and the banging continued, and as Ellie made her way down the stairs, their housekeeper fumbled with the door locks.

She opened the door as Ellie reached the front hall, and Ellie saw a young constable on the other side. A million thoughts chased through her head, each worse than the last. "What is it?" she demanded, clutching the front of her robe so tightly her fingers hurt.

"Miss Perkins? I've been sent to find you. Benchley Orphanage is on fire."

Ellie stared at the flames that shot high into the sky as the carriage took her closer to it. Fiona sat by her side, her deep auburn curls reflecting the flames as the carriage navigated traffic amidst shouts and the loud clanging of fire alarms. Fiona grasped her fingers and held tightly, and while Ellie wished her sister would tell her all would be fine, she knew she couldn't.

The vehicle finally came to a stop and the driver climbed down from his seat. "Tell me if you see Mr. Lucas," Ellie said. "I sent the constable to his address, but I do not know—"

"He will be here as soon as he can," Fiona promised. "I have a good feeling about that one."

The driver opened the door, and as Ellie stepped down, the heat from the flames hit her like a wave. A flurry of activity off to the side drew her attention, and she ran to a group of adults and children with Fiona on her heels.

She reached the orphanage director, who was speaking with two detectives. Other employees were trying to manage groups of crying children. Many of them stood outside without shoes or coats.

"Miss Perkins!" One of the children recognized her, and several flocked to her side, huddling and crying. She put her arms around as many as she could and pulled them close, and Fiona took one of three young toddlers a harried employee was trying to juggle.

"Alice!" Ellie called to a woman with whom she often worked when arranging for the children's school attendance. "Do you know what happened?"

Alice made her way over, her eyes red rimmed and bleary. "One of the older children heard a crash through the kitchen window, and by the time we realized what was happening, the fire was already spreading."

Ellie swallowed. "Are there children still inside?"

Alice shook her head and a tear slipped down her cheek. "I do not know. There are seven older children missing."

Ellie spied several children who had attended Perkins Kindergarten the year before, and many more who were current students. The group tightly huddled around her now mostly consisted of the children in Graham's class.

"Ellie!"

She turned at the shout and saw Graham running toward them in shirtsleeves, trousers, and an overcoat. He'd clearly dressed as hastily as she had, and his hair was mussed as though he'd run his hands through it.

He reached her side and put one arm about her shoulders and the other around Stevie, Stephen, John, and Edward, who lunged at him and clung like vines. "What in the name of God?" He stared at the flames and then turned his attention back to Ellie.

She shrugged. "I do not know, but we must get the children out of the cold."

"Miss Perkins," Alice said, "the detectives have sent for omnibuses to take us to the meeting hall nearby. The Ladies' Aid Society are gathering supplies as we speak."

Ellie nodded and picked up little Alexandra, who shivered so uncontrollably she trembled. Fiona and Graham both removed their coats, as did many constables and other adults, and wrapped them around the cold, thin children.

The orphanage director, Mrs. Warner, finished speaking with the detectives, and as fire wagons tried desperately to contain the flames, she made her way over to Ellie and the others. "The buses will arrive shortly," she said wearily.

"Have you any notion of the cause?" Graham asked her.

"Not yet, but as several of the children, apparently, heard a crash in the kitchen, it may prove to be more than an accident." Her voice was hoarse, and she coughed. She frowned and continued. "I walked around the outside and examined the kitchen window. It was clearly broken, and while the fire officer said windows are often blown out, I argued with him because there is very little glass outside the kitchen window. It's as though something was thrown *in*."

The omnibuses finally arrived, and Ellie, Graham, and Fiona rode with the others to the meeting hall, where Mrs. Warner began the task of organizing the chaos. Itching to do the work herself but not wanting to overstep her bounds, Ellie asked the woman where she would best appreciate the help.

"Talk with the Ladies' Aid Society people, if you will. See what they've collected, and we'll do that much first," Mrs. Warner told her. "I should think first order of business would be blankets and tea."

Ellie agreed, and set about acting as liaison between the groups. Graham assisted with the heavier work of hauling in sleeping mats and setting up the temporary shelter. Fiona followed several women into the meeting hall's kitchen, where preparations for tea and sandwiches began.

While hustling to and fro, Ellie noticed her other teachers' arrival. She gave each a quick embrace, even Miss Drake, whose distress was evident. The women quickly found their students and did their best to help and distract them.

During the first lull in activity when the room warmed and tea was served, Ellie found Mrs. Warner, who stood in a small hallway off the kitchen. She was wiping her face with a sooty handkerchief, and Ellie fished a fresh one from her pocket and handed it to the woman. She then touched her shoulder, searching for words but not finding any.

"The seven are still missing," Mrs. Warner said quietly. "People think we don't care for them, but we do. And we do the best we can with limited resources."

Ellie nodded. "I can certainly relate to those circumstances. I am so sorry this has happened. Have the detectives brought any news?"

"The fire is contained, but the building is a total loss. They can't say for certain, but believe the fire was deliberately set." She looked at Ellie. "Who would do such a thing?" Her eyes filmed over. "To orphans?"

The hours that followed were a blur, and having cancelled school for the day, she and the others remained at the meeting hall with the children, assessing needs. City officials arrived intermittently, as did Mr. and Mrs. Crowden, who donated personal funds and resources. Before leaving, Mr. Crowden took Ellie's hand and said, "Perhaps a bright spot for your day, you'll be happy to know the board has approved your grant application. Once this business is sorted here, arrangements can be made."

"Thank you!" She smiled at the couple who had offered such support from the beginning of her endeavors. "That is indeed wonderful news."

Ellie saw Graham and Fiona as they each kept busy, and nearing the noon hour, she spied Graham speaking with the lead detective. When he turned toward her, she saw that his expression was grimmer than ever. She met him near the front door and put her hand on his arm.

"What is it?"

He shook his head. "Witnesses reported seeing a man in the area, slight of build, plain brown hair, brown hat, brown coat, easily forgettable face except that he stood for a very long time watching the building burn but doing nothing to help."

Her jaw dropped. "Who *is* that man?"

"I do not know. Weeks ago, when I finally decided to confront him, he disappeared. I didn't see him anywhere after that day at the museum." He lifted his hands and dropped them back to his sides. "And now this."

She sighed. "At least we now know to watch for him, and so do authorities." She looked at him again, disheveled, shirtsleeves rolled up, and thought wistfully for a moment about the night before, when everything had seemed complicated but was really quite simple.

He met her eyes, and then gently pulled her into an embrace. "Are you all right?" he whispered.

Her eyes, which had already been sore from fatigue, now burned with tears she'd held back. She nodded, even as they escaped and ran down her face. He held her for a moment, before releasing her as volunteers passed by, looking on with curiosity. She wiped her cheeks and sniffed, feeling very, very tired.

"I will do all I can to make this right," Graham said in a low voice. He leaned a shoulder against the wall and cupped her face in one hand, tracing his thumb along her cheek. "I feel as though I've brought this evil upon you and the children."

She shook her head. "Truly, Graham, you cannot be held responsible for the actions of others. You have been doing your job, searching for the baron's heir, and that someone appears to be standing in the path of it is not your fault." She paused. "You did say a distant nephew stands to inherit?"

He nodded. "It must be he who has done this. The baron

arrives in a few hours, and I'll ask him what he knows of the chap. His name is Milton Knowles, but he may be using an alias." He straightened and nodded toward the door. "I'll give his name to the detectives—it may lead to nothing, but it's a start."

She nodded. "I'm going to check again on the children."

"I'll join you in a moment." He reached for her hand and kissed her fingers, managing a tired smile for the first time since he'd arrived at the scene of the fire. "My intentions will become apparent to all and sundry before long."

She laughed softly. "If they haven't already."

"I did not sleep well last night, even before the constable came knocking at my door." He looked at her as though they stood alone again in the library.

"Nor did I."

"I do hope I've not given you cause for regret."

She shook her head. "Trepidation, possibly, but no regret."

He kissed her hand again and smiled against her fingers, lingering there. "Trepidation is preferable. That is something with which I can work."

"Is that so?" She lifted her mouth in a half-smile. "You seem quite sure of yourself, Mr. Lucas."

"One must be, when teaching a herd of four- and five-year-old people." He nodded toward the main room where little voices echoed into the rafters. "Go. I'll join you momentarily."

He winked at her, which quite made her knees feel weak. She turned back to the children, heart still heavy, but now holding a glimmer of hope.

Chapter Eleven

Graham spied Ellie across the room, sitting with his kindergarten class. She had them gathered in a half circle and was speaking to them animatedly, holding their attention like a master. He took in the scene for a moment, selfishly reveling in the fact that the members of his class were all well and alive.

He barely remembered the events occurring before he arrived at the scene of the fire. When he realized his littles were all safe, the relief had been nearly overwhelming. There were still seven children missing, however, and presumed dead. A pit formed in his stomach at the thought.

Miss Rose, Miss Drake, and Miss Brophy all sat with their charges, a reassuring constant in a storm. As he approached Ellie and his class, he performed the same absent count he'd been doing all day. All fifteen present. The children had each been given fresh sets of clothing, some ill-fitting but all warm, and some wore sweaters that were made of wool that "scratched somethin' fierce."

Stevie was one who wore the sweater because it was a far cry from being chilled, but had mumbled and grumbled throughout the day, pulling at it. He was sitting with his back to Graham and now tugged at the sweater, pulling it partially off and tugging askew the collar of his shirt with it.

Stevie's right shoulder bore a mark that was now visible to Graham as he drew closer, and he dropped to one knee behind him, more in shock than intentionally. Ellie glanced over in surprise, and he sat flat on the floor as though merely joining the circle. He managed a tight smile but then stared again at Stevie's shoulder before the boy righted the shirt and sweater with an impatient scratch.

Bertie had had a birthmark in the same spot as Stevie, and in the exact same shape and shade. It was a nearly perfect five-pointed star, an inch in diameter. If he had needed further identification, that much proved it. He felt a sense of relief, validation that he'd informed the baron he'd found Bertie's son. He took a moment to simply stare at the boy, fully amazed that Bertie's flesh and blood sat there before him.

The day wore on, night fell, and the main room was transformed into a giant dormitory. Ellie's friends, Mr. and Mrs. Crowden, had spent the day making plans for converting a vacant building near the school into the new Benchley Orphanage.

As the children settled down and the exhausted adults tried to convince them to rest, the lead detective investigating the fire returned to the meeting hall and sought out Graham. "It appears Baron Francis' nephew is indeed visiting Liverpool." The detective consulted his notes. "Milton Knowles has been staying near the docks at Williams Tavern for over two weeks."

Graham nodded. "I believe he followed me here. If his aim is as I suspect, he is looking for one of the children, and has clearly grown desperate. He's resorted to burning down the entire orphanage." He shook his head, anger mounting. "How might I assist your efforts to find him?"

"As it happens, we've already brought him in for questioning. Once pressed for answers, he admitted to setting the fire. I do believe your theory about his motive is correct. He mentioned something about being the true heir. At any rate, I would appreciate a word with the baron tomorrow, provided he's arrived in town." The detective scribbled on a piece of paper from his notebook and tore it off, handing it to Graham.

Graham nodded. "Thank you, Detective Ashe. I shall stop in tomorrow for any updates. Oh, also, I have moved from the prior address at the inn to the home where Baron Francis will reside, at least for the season."

Detective Ashe took the information from Graham and nodded, then moved on to speak with Mrs. Warner.

Graham observed the large group of children, housed in their temporary haven that would, God willing, remain just that. He wondered if he ought to take Stevie with him that very evening to ensure his safety. He was weighing the options when Ellie approached, rolling down her sleeves and fastening her cuffs.

"Do you suppose I should take Stevie with me this evening?" he asked her without preamble.

"Oh, well. . ." She paused, looking over her shoulder at the children. "I suppose the only negative aspect of it might be the trauma of separation from the other children after such an event."

He nodded, not wanting to add to the boy's distress by removing him too quickly. He told Ellie what he'd learned from Detective Ashe about Knowles' presence in town.

"Ah." She pursed her lips in thought. "They will hold him overnight in the cells, I hope?"

"I should think so."

"One might presume Mr. Knowles doesn't yet know which child is the baron's grandson, and for that reason, decided to rid himself of the entire orphanage."

"Yes, or he has observed me closely enough to know I've sent for the baron, presumably having ascertained the child's identity. Rather than cast undue suspicion on himself and do harm to one child, perhaps he decided it would be better to stage the entirety of it as a tragic accident."

Her brow knit. "Many others would be lost, but of necessity. One willing to set fire to an entire building full of people—children—likely did so without the trouble of a conscience." She looked again at the children. "Perhaps it would be best to remove him this evening. If Mr. Knowles realizes you've done so, he might at least leave the rest of them alone. We can assume they're all safe as he is in custody, but suppose he's been desperate enough to secure an accomplice, or have elicited help from another source."

Graham nodded. "I can ask the detective if he might spare a pair of officers to patrol the grounds at the house until Mr. Knowles is fully questioned and charged with the crime." He paused. "Perhaps I am only trying to convince myself that it is in Stevie's best interest to take him to safety tonight. I hate the thought of leaving any of them here, truly."

She smiled at him, her eyes tired. "Let's speak with Mrs. Warner."

Mrs. Warner knew of his purpose, as he'd spoken with her multiple times, so she was not surprised when he told her he'd discovered the baron's heir.

"That's a fortunate child," the woman said. "Can't think of a time I've seen an orphan claimed by wealthy relations. Stuff of fairy tales, that."

Rather than disturb the children more than necessary, he waited while Ellie found Stevie and pulled him aside. She knelt down next to him and spoke, holding his little hand between hers. He nodded, and although Graham couldn't see the boy's expression, he did not seem distressed.

Graham gathered his coat and awaited Ellie and Stevie by the front entrance. He had procured the use of a carriage to aid in the baron's arrangements once he reached town, and it now awaited them outside. Ellie and Stevie joined him at the door, and he bent down next to the boy. "Miss Perkins explained what is happening?"

The poor lad seemed bewildered. "I think so."

"Come along, and I shall explain everything in the carriage." He took Stevie's hand, Ellie held the other, and they made their way out into the rain.

Chapter Twelve

Ellie sat beside Stevie in the carriage and held his little hand as they rode through the crowded streets. Rain thrummed steadily on the carriage roof, but the interior was warm and dry. The soft glow of a lantern gave her a clear view of his face as Graham explained who the baron was, and who Stevie's father had been.

"An' he's dead now, too?" Stevie asked, in reference to his father.

Graham winced. He sat across from them, and he now leaned forward and braced his arms on his knees. "I am afraid so, my boy. However, I must tell you that your grandfather is the kindest, most generous man I have ever known. He wants very much to meet you, and he sent me to find you."

"Shall I stay in his house by myself?"

"I will also live there, and you will continue to attend Miss Perkins' school. In fact, we can travel to school each morning together. Your friends will still be there, and Miss Perkins and I will help you so that you do not feel afraid or worried."

He nodded and was so solemn that Ellie's heart ached. "I imagine your grandfather would allow outings together with some of your friends on occasion." She glanced at Graham, who lifted his brows and smiled.

"Yes, most certainly. Your new circumstances may seem strange, but we will be with you, never fear."

"I mostly will miss Edward," he said.

"Edward Crispin is your very good friend, is he not?" Ellie asked. She sandwiched his little hand between her own, warming it.

Stevie nodded. "Like brothers."

Graham nodded. "I shall see to it that Edward is one of our most frequent guests."

He continued speaking in gentle tones, and the carriage made its way across town to the baron's new home.

As they left heavier traffic behind, the large ruts in the streets lessened, and the conveyance's movement gentled. Stevie yawned broadly and swayed toward Ellie. She put her arm around him and he leaned against her side, exhausted and nearly asleep where he sat.

The carriage came to a stop, and Graham looked out of the carriage window with a smile. "They've arrived, and if I'm not mistaken, have been here for a few hours. I suspect a warm bedtime meal will be available if we are hungry." He winked at Stevie.

Graham disembarked and lifted the sleepy boy into his arms. He held out a hand for Ellie, and they walked together into the large home.

The interior was ablaze with light and warmth, no longer a home on the market for sale. Soft music drifted from the parlor, and one maid and footman were in the process of rearranging a wardrobe in the front hall. An older woman appeared from the library, and Graham smiled broadly.

"Mrs. Henacker, you're a sight for sore eyes. Miss Ellie Perkins, this is Baron Francis' housekeeper and one of my favorite people."

The woman beamed, her face awash in smiles. "Master

Graham, a charmer you are." Her face softened as she joined them and looked at Stevie, who had his head tucked against Graham's shoulder. "And who is this gentleman?"

"This gentleman," Graham said as he gently set Stevie on the ground, "is Master Stephen Smith. He is the baron's grandson, and I am proud to say, my pupil!"

Mrs. Henacker's eyes widened. "You don't say!" She smiled and her eyes were bright. "Mercy, it is lovely to meet you, young Master Stephen."

The boy nodded and spoke, but his throat was scratchy and he cleared it. "Lovely to make yer 'quaintance, madam." He looked up at Graham and tugged on his hand. Graham lowered his ear, and Ellie heard the boy say, "I am still Stevie, though?"

"Of course," Graham said, and added, "'Stevie' is our young friend's preferred name."

Mrs. Henacker smiled. "Master Stevie you shall be. Are you hungry? We've only just cleared supper dishes." She looked at Graham, who nodded and then stilled, looking at the library door.

"Sir," he said to the man who stood there, looking at them as though stunned.

Ellie wondered if the baron saw his late son in the boy. His eyes were full of unshed tears, and he slowly made his way into the hall. Baron Francis looked from Stevie to Graham, and back again.

"Sir, may I present your grandson." Graham's voice cracked and he covered it with a smile, his own eyes bright.

Ellie realized how difficult it must have been for Graham to find and identify the boy, knowing he would mean so much to the baron. Graham had also held his own emotions at bay; he also had a past with the boy's father, and as such had also suffered a loss. She reached in her pocket for a handkerchief and wiped her eyes.

The baron knelt down in front of the child and smiled. He was a pleasant looking man, with kind eyes, and Ellie felt a surge of relief. He held out his hand to the boy and said, "Stevie, is it? I am so glad to make your acquaintance. I am Baron Francis, and I am your grandfather."

Stevie shook the elderly man's hand, solemn, and nodded.

Graham rubbed Stevie's shoulder. "We have much to discuss, and many hours in which to do it. I propose a meal and a hot bath and then a good sleep. I believe we may prevail upon the headmistress for one more day away from school."

Ellie laughed. "I believe we *all* require another day away from school." As the baron stood, Graham introduced her and she extended her hand to the gentleman.

Baron Francis smiled and glanced at Graham, who took Ellie's arm as they walked to the dining room. The baron walked a distance ahead, holding Stevie's hand, and asked the boy what kind of hobbies he enjoyed. Stevie looked up at his grandfather and shyly conversed, and Ellie felt a lump form in her throat.

"We'll join you in just a moment," Graham called ahead to the others, and waited until he and Ellie were relatively alone. "I can never. . .I'll never be able to express my gratitude. . ."

She smiled. "Thank you for inviting me to be part of this. It's so lovely, and these children rarely see such good luck."

"Please say you'll stay. Join us for a late supper. Join me for every supper." He cupped her cheek and stood close. She was grimy and exhausted and should probably have been mortified that she'd just met a very kind and distinguished gentleman in such a state, but all she could think of was how much she adored the man who looked as though he wanted very much to kiss her.

"You needn't answer, we needn't be formal," Graham said, and frowned as though searching for the correct words.

"Yes." She put her finger to his lips. "Yes, I will join you for every supper. I quite love you, Mr. Lucas."

He kissed her then, and she did not care one whit that servants might come upon them, standing as they were in the front hall. He pulled back, but touched his forehead to hers. "I love you, Ellie." He smiled. "And am grateful you maneuvered me into a new career. I only hope I remain in my employer's good graces."

She reached up and touched her lips to his before pulling back and grasping his hand. "I believe I might know how you could accomplish that."

He chuckled as they walked to the dining room, where a young Master Stevie was deep in conversation with his grandfather, who smiled at him in wonder. It was the happiest ending Ellie could ever have imagined for a child, and all the better because it was only the beginning. As for herself, she looked at Graham and smiled. She'd found the one man who could support her without doing so grudgingly, and as he seated her at the table, she felt a surge of contentment and satisfaction she hadn't known she'd been missing.

Baron Francis raised his cup of tea and waited for the others to follow suit, even small Stevie, who smiled and lifted his cup carefully. "To family," the baron said, and Ellie's heart was full as they all echoed the sentiment.

Graham had settled next to her, and now reached for her hand beneath the table. With a wink, he raised it and kissed her knuckles. "To love," he said. "And gentlewomen scholars."

She laughed. "And to solicitors and kindergarten teachers and barons and grandsons." She winked at Stevie, who winked back, his little face flushed and happy.

NANCY CAMPBELL ALLEN is the author of 15 published novels and several novellas, which encompass a variety of genres from contemporary romantic suspense to historical fiction. Her Civil War series, Faith of our Fathers, won the Utah Best of State award in 2005 and two of her historicals featuring Isabelle Webb, Pinkerton spy, were finalists for the Whitney Award. Her steampunk novel, *Beauty and the Clockwork Beast,* was released August 2016, through Shadow Mountain. She served on the 2015 LDStorymakers Conference Committee and currently serves as the contest coordinator for The Teen Writers Conference. She has presented at numerous conferences and events since her initial publication in 1999.

Her formal schooling includes a B.S. in Elementary Education from Weber State University and she has worked as a ghost writer and freelance editor, contributing to the releases, *We Knew Howard Hughes*, by Jim Whetton, and *My Life Encapsulated,* by Kenneth Brailsford.

Her agent is Pamela Howell of D4EO Literary Agency.

Nancy loves to read, write, travel and research, and enjoys spending time laughing with family and friends. She and her husband have three children, and she lives in Ogden, Utah with her family and one very large Siberian Husky named Thor.

Visit Nancy's blog: http://NCAllen.blogspot.com
Facebook: Nancy C Allen
Twitter: @necallen

www.ingramcontent.com/pod-product-compliance
Lightning Source LLC
LaVergne TN
LVHW021801060526
838201LV00058B/3187